ORACLE

SUNKEN EARTH

C.W. Trisef

Trisef Book LLC

How to contact the author
Website – OracleSeries.com
Email – trisefbook@gmail.com

Oracle – Sunken Earth
C.W. Trisef

Other titles by C.W. Trisef
Oracle – Fire Island (Book 2 in the Oracle Series)
Oracle – River of Ore (Book 3 in the Oracle Series)
Oracle – Solar Wind (Book 4 in the Oracle Series)
Oracle – Mutant Wood (Book 5 in the Oracle Series)

This book is a work of fiction. Any references to historical events, real people, or real locales are used fictitiously. Other names, characters, places, and incidents are the product of the author's imagination.

Written by – C.W. Trisef
Cover designed by – Giuseppe Lipari
Text designed by – Sheryl Mehary

Book 1 – Edition 1

ISBN-13: 978-1463559212
ISBN-10: 1463559216
Library of Congress Control Number: 2012933718

CHAPTER 0

TEN MONTHS EARLIER

"It's too dangerous, Captain," warned Jaret's Coast Guard crew as he leapt from the safety of the cutter. "You'll never make it!"

"Not with *that* attitude, I won't," he replied bravely, shoving off in his inflatable raft. "If the hurricane gets too close and I haven't returned, promise you'll turn back without me." Despite their protests, he knew his loyal crew would obey.

Leaving the cutter on the edge of safety, Jaret plowed into the boiling sea. The several square miles of Atlantic waters before him were bubbling violently, displacing the oxygen in the air with their gaseous contents, making it hard to breathe. The approaching hurricane was transforming the waves into towering swells and the wind into mighty gales. With considerable difficulty, Jaret navigated his tiny raft among circumstances that he had never encountered in all his many years at sea.

At length, he arrived at his destination: a burning ship, ablaze and sinking fast. With no distress signal or solicitation for assistance, Jaret didn't know what to expect as he moored his raft to the ship and climbed aboard. Walls of smoke combined with rain of ash to render sight useless. He groped his way over broken beams and severed cords, then stopped when he heard voices.

"Give me the Oracle, boy!"

"Never!"

Jaret turned to face the fighting. When the smoke had cleared momentarily, he could see an old man, with a long beard and white staff, contending against a young man whose complexion was fair and radiant. Each of them had one hand on a small sphere, which they were desperately clinging to and striving to pull away from the other.

"It's useless to resist!" shouted the white-haired senior.

"That's what *you* think," the young boy countered, maintaining his firm grasp on the sphere.

"Then you leave me no choice," said the elder.

"Only *you* would say such a thing, Lye," but the boy's words ended abruptly when he was struck by the old man's staff. Amid a flash of brilliant light, the young man fell backwards lifelessly, his head smacking the deck and the sphere falling from his possession.

Another curtain of thick, black smoke fell on the scene, preventing Jaret from observing what happened next. Still, he could hear something rolling across the main deck towards him, like an oversized marble. In shock, he watched as the sphere, which had been the dueling duo's envy, came to a stop at his feet. Bending over to pick it up, he had scarcely touched the sphere when the bottom of a white staff appeared next to it.

"Who are you?" the old man growled.

"Captain Jaret Cooper, sir, of the U.S. Coast Guard," came the reply. "I've come to rescue you and your crew."

"We don't need your rescue," Lye barked condescendingly.

"But, sir, your ship is on fire and sinking fast," Jaret informed him, "not to mention the approaching… "

"Everything is exactly the way I want it," Lye asserted, though Jaret wondered how anyone could desire such dire circumstances. "Now give me that ball and leave!" he insisted, lunging for the sphere.

"Okay," Jaret obliged, "but I'm taking the boy with me." He pointed to the boy, still lying lifelessly on the floor. "He needs medical attention immediately."

"You will do nothing of the sort!" Lye snarled defensively. "He stays with me, as does that ball. Now hand it over and be gone!"

"I'm not leaving without the… "

Lye wielded his staff, striking Jaret, who fell to the deck but quickly rose to his feet to defend himself.

"Leave, you weak mortal!" Lye demanded. "You have no idea what you're meddling in."

Jaret picked up a fallen beam and engaged his opponent in combat. They fought for several moments, Lye's staff clashing frequently with Jaret's wooden sword, shooting a mix of sparks and splinters into the air. Lye moved with impressive and unanticipated swiftness and agility for an old-timer, but when his staff became lodged in Jaret's beam, Jaret swung the opposite end into Lye's abdomen, sending him rolling across the ship.

Jaret rushed to the boy's side. Though he had received a severe blow to the head, the faint rise and fall of the boy's chest manifested that he was still alive. Jaret picked up the injured boy and hauled him to his raft. Since the ship continued to sink, Jaret was able to lower the unconscious body safely into his raft while he himself remained on the ship.

Jaret had cut the moorings, started the engine, and was preparing to board the already-moving raft when he was hurled away by a forceful stream of water. Since the hurricane had long since fallen upon them, Jaret thought he had been struck by its powerful winds. But then, however, he heard Lye's menacing voice.

"I gave you a chance, you stubborn fool," Lye hissed. Using his staff, Lye commanded the water all around them in air and sea to obey his every whim, pummeling Jaret relentlessly with round after round of watery weaponry. "Bet you've never battled anything like this as a measly coast guard!" Lye formed a giant ball of water, like a life-sized raindrop, and enclosed it completely around Jaret. For several seconds, he manipulated it, sending Jaret back and forth and upside down, waiting for him to be out of breath. When Jaret began to squirm for want of air, Lye restated his terms.

"If you want to live," he said, holding out his hand, "give me the Oracle."

Blue in the face, Jaret glanced at his raft, which was already speeding crookedly away from the burning ship. For a split second, he stared at the curious sphere clutched in his hand. It meant nothing to him, but it seemed to mean the world to his sinister antagonist. And so, with what he assumed would be his final breath, Jaret threw the sphere out of Lye's liquid cage. It hit the raft and bounced into the ferocious waves of the ocean, where it bobbed amid charred planks and windswept pieces of the impending shipwreck.

"NO!" Lye screamed. Since Jaret no longer possessed anything of interest, Lye abandoned torturing him and instead bolted after the sphere. Without any reluctance, Lye prepared to dive into the churning sea but was thwarted when Jaret caught him by the train of his robes and yanked him back into the ring.

"Leaving so soon?" Jaret asked before delivering a dizzying punch to Lye's aged face.

With the raft motoring out of sight and the opposing pair busy exchanging jabs, the approaching eye of the hurricane went unnoticed until it had blown directly over them. The wind died, the rain slackened, the ship ceased its swaying. Finding themselves in such instantly calm surroundings, Lye and Jaret paused. A moment of utter terror seized Lye's face.

"Not yet!" he yelled, "Not without…" But it was too late. The boy and sphere were gone. Then, as if placed in a vertical laundry chute, the water surrounding the battered boat disappeared, and what was left of the ship suddenly dropped to the bottom of the sea.

Chapter 1

First Impressions

Like most homes in island communities on early mornings in late summer, the Cooper house was ringing with silence. Every clock agreed it was that most exquisite time of day when the world appeared as still as a photograph. For the first time that day, the temperature had slackened enough to reward the air conditioning a much-needed — albeit short-lived — respite. Too dark to surf and too moonlit to sunbathe, the beach was vacant. A salty sea breeze was accompanied by its sluggish twin, a thin but misty fog, and together they rode the incessant tides into town. Indeed, the only movement stirring the silence was the crashing of the ceaseless waves — too frequent to be forgotten, too alluring to be annoying.

Enter hairdryer.

"Goodbye, serenity," Ret whispered to himself, turning on his side and smothering both ears with his pillow to drown out the airy bellowing of Ana's hairdryer. Entirely by instinct, Ret awoke each day in time to enjoy the predawn stillness. These morning vigils were so involuntary on his part that he assumed himself to share some kind of connection with nature, for he certainly felt a link to the elements around him.

"Why is she up so early this morning?" Ret wondered, his sister's hairdryer drowning out his voice so completely that even *he* could not hear his own words. The clock on Ret's nightstand had its hour hand positioned scarcely past six o'clock, which time, he had come to learn, was far too premature for any of Ana's summertime activities. It was even earlier than when she normally commenced prettifying for one of her normal school days. Then, at the thought of school, Ret realized a grim reality. He buried his face deeper into his pillow.

"Time to get up, Ret," Ana sang from the powder room, switching the hairdryer into low gear to accommodate brief conversation. "We don't want to be late for our first day of high school!" The blowing recommenced in full force immediately after Ana's final word, probably to prevent Ret from expressing his displeasure. Ret rolled out of bed, staggering into the bathroom amid a billowing cloud of hairspray.

"Finished with the hairdryer already?" he asked, nearly choking on the plume's fumes.

"I think it blew a fuse," she explained, moving on to her hair straightener. "It's so hard to find a good hairdryer." Ana spent more and more time in front of the mirror these days but seemed cautiously cognizant not to hide her natural good looks, a respect for beauty taught by her mother. She carefully flattened each strand of her long, brown hair with precision. The heat from her instruments was causing her cheeks to blush slightly, adding color to her fair-skinned and lightly-freckled face. No doubt the additional warmth trapped inside the bathroom felt welcomed against her slim frame.

"You're getting started kind of early today, aren't you?" Ret wondered, squinting into the intrusive mirrors, which reflected the overhead searchlights so well that he felt like a captive insect under a menacing child's magnifying glass. "I mean, school doesn't start for another two hours, right?"

"One hour and fifty-two minutes, to be exact," Ana said, "and you can never look too well-groomed on the first day back to school, you know. This day is always chock-full of first impressions, Ret, and you can never change a first impression. What happens today could set the course for the rest of the year, so you'll want to look your best, act your best, and hope for the best."

"Thanks for the advice," he said, somewhat sarcastically. She had been feeding it to him in regular spoonfuls throughout the last several months.

"I'm just trying to help," was Ana's genuine reply. "It's going to be quite a big transition for me to adjust to high school — new school, new teachers, new friends, new everything! But I can't imagine what a shock it'll be for *you*. I mean, you haven't been to school in who knows how long. We found you what, like ten months ago? And you still can't remember anything before that, can you?"

"No, but it's not the new environment that I'm worried about," Ret confessed.

"Then what is it, Ret?" Ana's sincere interest in Ret's answer was demonstrated by the abrupt pause that she took during her eyelash-curling routine.

"Just look at me," he said, staring at his reflection in the mirror. His now-adjusted eyes afforded him a clear examination of his unique appearance. The abnormality that always clouded his mind first was his pale skin, so white and pure that it seemed to glow like a light bulb. It did not take him long to deduce the difference between his skin and that of his peers. Ana reassured him that his skin would tan over time, but even *she* had been surprised by the absence of color change. Once, Ret exposed his skin to the sun's rays for an entire summer's day — from sunrise to sunset — expecting at least some kind of pigment variation by day's end. But his skin's stubbornness persisted. Not only was there not the slightest trace of sunburn, but his body's outermost layer now seemed to shine even brighter, as if his body behaved exactly contrary to the scarring mechanisms of normal-skinned people.

"At least you'll never have to wear sunscreen," Ana had told him, trying to look on the bright side.

The only characteristic to rival his skin in luster was his eyes, a pair of azure gems that radiated as brilliantly as two transparent sapphires against a backdrop of driven snow. They were so bright, in fact, that they had given Ana's mother quite a scare once: it was Ret's first night with the Coopers since they found him, and when Pauline tiptoed into the spare room where he was sleeping to see how he was faring, she was frightened half to death when she could see Ret's eyes through their closed lids.

And then his hair — its unusualness masked only by his other, more striking features. Ana once informed Ret jokingly that she had found his portrait in the dictionary, next to the word *blonde*. They laughed, but it was true that his hair was unusually fair and, like his skin, practically glowing.

"Just look at me," Ret repeated, still staring at his mimic in the mirror. "I'm a freak! My skin, my eyes, my hair, my hands… "

"So you look different — big deal," Ana sympathized, refocusing her attention on her eyelashes. "There're tons of weird-looking people in high school; you'll fit right in."

"I don't care if I fit in," Ret said. "I'm just tired of being so different — of being treated like I'm an alien from outer space or something."

"Well, for all we know," Ana said, "you could be." As usual, Ana was right: she was as clueless as Ret when it came to the facts about his own personal history. He found it remarkably frustrating to be such an intelligent person and, yet, to be so in the dark about his own past.

"Is it worth it?" Ret asked, changing the subject.

"Is what worth it?" Ana tried to clarify.

"You know, all this high school stuff; is it really worth it?"

"Well, of *course* it's worth it, my ridiculous Ret!" Ana replied. "Just think of all the friends you'll make, all the things you'll learn, all the cute guys — well, in your case, cute *girls* — you'll meet, not to mention all the sports games and themed dances and oh — " Her voice quieted as if in solemn worship. "Oh, I can't wait to go someday: prom." Ret was amazed how, despite her obvious ecstasy, her hand remained so steady while gripping her mascara wand.

"I'm sure all of that is fun and useful and all," Ret continued, "but I doubt I'll find it very, well, fulfilling."

"Suit yourself," she said matter-of-factly. "Which reminds me, we are *not* going to be late today, so you'd better get dressed — unless, of course, you plan to make your maiden voyage into the public school system wearing your pajamas."

"That's not a bad idea," Ret mumbled on his way out of the bathroom.

"It's all in your attitude, my boy," Ana's counsel resumed, though her voice faded as Ret returned to his room. He was hoping that she would have requested him to expound upon what he meant by his assumption that school would not feel very fulfilling to him, for he had been wanting to share his sentiments with at least one person. Even though he had not been enrolled in any formal schooling since being taken in by the Coopers, his education had not been stagnating, and his mind had encountered no atrophy. Quite the opposite was true. Instead of boarding the bus and crowding to class, Ret sought out his own laboratories of learning: curious coves to study rock formations and mineral deposits; tiny tide pools to probe crawling crustaceans and thriving plant life; offshore eddies to examine the tendencies of tides and the cause of currents; the surrounding marshes to mull over the extensities of water and the expanse of the heavens; the sandy beach to admire men's expert navigability on the sea's surface, reflective of the shallow depth of their understanding of the mostly-untouched world beneath that surface. Yes, Ret doubted that any high school classroom could provide the kind of knowledge that he had acquired through repeated observation in a certain setting or by means of a book read in the shade of his favorite tree.

Ret was pained by the prospect of school, as it would most certainly mean the end of his independent studies. There was no denying the connectedness — the attachment — which he felt to the natural world. Indeed, he sensed a certain duty — an acute obligation — to enlighten his mind through the environment which encompasses all mankind. And, like most things, the enlightenment came naturally to him — nearly as naturally as night chases day. Nature's rudiments seemed to be keenly aware of him — his past, his present, and his potential. His past was not his only mystery.

"Ret, Ana; breakfast's ready," a voice called from the kitchen. Ret haphazardly donned pants and a long-sleeved shirt as the outfit for his grand debut, capping his chosen garb with a wide-brimmed hat. Before leaving his room, he added sunglasses and a scarf to his getup. With skin, eyes, and hair now hidden from view, Ret had all but one of his bases covered.

"Pauline, do you have any gloves I can borrow?" Ret asked innocently, sliding into his seat at the kitchen table while her back was turned.

"Of course, dear," she said, flipping the griddle's final buttermilk flapjack atop the teetering stack on the plate in her hand. "They're on the top shelf in that closet by the front door." Her other hand forsook its steadying of the stack just long enough for her to point to the correct closet, her gaze never leaving her morning's culinary masterpiece. "But you shouldn't need to wear gloves today; the paper tells me the heat wave's just getting started." She abandoned her post at the stove to grace the table with her work. She had scarcely set down the dish and taken her first look at Ret when she let out a spooked gasp. "My *word*, Ret, what *are* you wearing?" Pauline asked indignantly. "You look like a — like a convict!"

"Or someone who's about to become one," Ana added, waltzing into the room. A nauseating stream of perfume and other gaseous hair care products was not far behind, following her scent like bloodhounds.

"What is the meaning of this?" Pauline inquired, removing the scarf and sunglasses gently.

"He thinks he looks like a freak," Ana answered for him.

"That's not true," Ret countered calmly.

"Ana, just eat your flapjacks," Pauline instructed.

"Sorry, Mom; only liquids for me," Ana explained, daintily sipping her orange juice. "I've brushed and flossed these pearls twice already this morning. I just can't afford the risk of getting something stuck in my teeth — no, ma'am; not today." Pauline's spirits seemed to sink a bit at this pronouncement. She returned her attention to Ret, still awaiting his answer.

"I just don't want to make a scene, is all," Ret said in hushed tones. "You know I don't like the attention, what with my being, you know, so different and all."

"Oh, Ret," Pauline responded tenderly, kneeling near his side and looking fearlessly into the pair of bright blue eyes that had once frightened her so many months ago. "You needn't worry so much about what other people think of you." She smoothed her hand over his cheek. "And this hat," she said, removing it from Ret's brow. "I love your hair," she told him, curling a lock around her finger. "It reminds me of — "

Her voice vanished. Her gaze fell. Her hand released Ret's hair and sought refuge in the cradle that was the other hand in her lap. Both Ret and Ana glanced at each other soberly, then looked away. They both knew whose name was on her lips — the name she would have spoken had her voice not fled to the shards of her aching heart. Both teenagers were astonished when she continued.

"I named you after him, you know," she told Ret for the first time as he watched tears spread from her eyes to the ridges of premature wrinkles, which caused her tears to linger and to paint her aging skin in a design that was as intricate as her grief. Never knowing how to ease her mother's pain, Ana dragged a few flapjacks onto her plate, momentarily forgetting her dental delicateness. "You remind me so much of him," Pauline whispered, "not so much by how you look, but by who you are." She returned to her seat, and Ret and Ana tried to chew quietly as they finished the flapjack platter. When they heard the school bus barrel around the corner, the family embraced, and Ret closed the door behind them, leaving his ornamental apparel on the table.

To say that the Coopers lived on an island would contradict even the most lenient of dictionaries, as Tybee Island was surrounded by the Atlantic Ocean on all sides except for the narrow strait where it moored to the mainland. Regardless of the terminology, however, Ret certainly considered it to be an isolated place, with the nearest city more than a dozen miles to the west and with the apparent edge of the world less than a dozen yards to the east. Once, after reading a biography of Christopher Columbus, Ret thought that he himself had contracted exploration fever, so itchy was he to imitate the European sailor who launched from the edge of his own world to discover what lay beyond the horizon.

Ret was grateful that he lived on the southern end of the island, making his bus stop the first on the route that snaked northward until it finished near the north coast at Tybee High School. Upon boarding, Ret and Ana were greeted by a gruff and altogether miserable-looking bus driver.

"Morning, chillens," he sneered like a villain in disguise, bits of his breakfast still clinging to his decayed teeth. With a black patch covering one of his eyes, the driver affixed his penetrating glare on Ret, never noticing Ana. Through the wide, smudgy mirror hanging above his head, the bus driver maintained his glare on Ret as they retreated to the backmost bench of the empty bus. Hoping not to draw any more attention to himself, Ret slouched between the high-rising seats, relieved to be out of sight of the bus driver, whose piercing gaze caused Ret's innards to quiver with uneasiness.

Each time the bus halted, Ret would peek over the top of his barricade to steal a glance at the new riders. Much to Ret's surprise, some of his classmates seemed to want to draw nothing *but* attention to themselves. The clothes and hairdos were so outlandish, the most intriguing to Ret being the young man who had dyed his hair green and then molded it into half a dozen foot-long spikes.

"You were right," Ret whispered to Ana, still captivated by the pointy hairstyle. "There really *are* some strange people who go to high school. Maybe I won't stick out as much as I thought."

"And you're *much* more handsome than that slime ball," Ana said reassuringly.

They waited for everyone to pile out of the bus before doing the same. Tybee High struck Ret as an attractive and inviting place to spend the day, its pleasantly painted façades and well-groomed grounds appearing much less torturous and incarcerating than he had imagined. Rows of mature palmettos flanked both sides of the main entrance, their fan-shaped fronds waving to the students in the morning breeze and bidding them inside. Borders of monkey grass thrived at the feet of hedged azaleas, the occasional, residual flower of pink and red hues blooming as evidence of both a prolific spring and the imminence of winter. It was not a large campus, indicative of the modest island's small populace, but upon entering the edifice, Ret reasoned that every teenager in town must have been confined in the commons, so raucous was the rumpus raging within.

"Stay close to me," Ana roared above the clamor, grabbing his hand and yanking him behind her as she drove into the melee. Ret felt like toothpaste as they squeezed through the crowd, somehow arriving at a row of bombarded tables manned by a team of bewildered teachers.

"Cooper, Ana," Ret overheard from his guide's mouth. "Cooper, Ret." Ana returned to Ret's side clutching two slips of paper.

"Oh, good," she sighed, "it looks like we have a few classes together this semester, Ret. Now, here's your class schedule," she explained, handing him the appropriate piece of paper. "It lists the name of the course in this column, followed by the teacher's name, the room number, and the title of the textbook," she said, wildly pointing every whichway on the spreadsheet like an astrologer tracing hidden constellations. "Oh, and your locker number's down here." She noticed Ret's puzzled look. "Trees get stumped, Ret; not brainiacs like you. Now, I've got to find Paige in this mess and see what she thinks of these pants before class." Ana released herself into the fray before yelling back to Ret, "I'll see you in World Geography. Remember: first impressions!"

On the edge of the multitude, shifting in the shadows under a leafy ficus, stood two suit-clad men, one as still as a statue, his partner as jittery as a jackhammer. With eyes like eagles, they surveyed the first-day goings-on with great interest, standing on the periphery like two sharks among a school of fish. Sporting feigned smiles, they spoke to each other through their teeth.

"Do you see him? Do you *see* him?" the jitterbug asked, his hushed voice growing more earnest with every word.

"Patience, my fidgety friend," the motionless man admonished. "We've waited ten months; I'm sure you can manage a few more minutes."

"Do you think it wise to merely stand on the sidelines and wait for him to, what, *appear* before our very eyes?" the impatient man asked. "Should we not, instead, mingle amongst the students and, as they say, divide and conquer? After all, you *are* the principal of this school, are you not?"

"I can see everything just fine from here," the principal informed, his calm tone gradually becoming sterner. "And besides, I hate children."

"Ah, yes, neither am I particularly fond of the little brats," the quick-talking jabber resumed, "their grimy hands that reek of sweaty copper. But he is not exactly a child anymore, now is he, sir? I mean, by now he ought to be… "

"Sixteen years old," the principal coolly interrupted the fumbling fool, his own patience wearing thin.

"Great Scott! Is the boy sixteen already?" the accomplice asked rhetorically. "Where *does* the time go? He most likely looks nothing like we remember him, what with adolescents his age shooting up like weeds and growing their hair long."

"And I thought you were my geography teacher this year," the principal said sarcastically, "not a professor of physiology."

"Well, actually, I'm neither, but you already knew that, now didn't you, old man?" the pretend educator chortled, sending the principal a conspicuous wink as a reminder of their secret.

"I doubt he's changed much at all," the principal admitted. "The extraordinary characteristics of his kind never diminish." He continued to speak as he scanned the student body. "Pale skin — "

"White as snow," the teacher added dreamily.

"Bright eyes — "

"As blue as crystals."

"Golden hair — "

"I see it!" the teacher yelped. "I see the golden hair!"

"Where? *Where*?"

"Over there, near the middle, by the tables; don't you see him?" gasped the teacher, the principal catching him by the arm as a master would restrain his rabid dog.

"Let me go! Let me *go!*"

"Patience, Ronald!" the principal demanded. "We mustn't make a scene." He pulled him closer to his face. "Now, let's review our plan, shall we? We stroll tranquilly toward the boy, greeting students along the way."

"So *now* you want to mingle, eh?" the teacher mocked sardonically. The principal tightened his grip, shooting his captive a threatening glare.

"We walk to the boy," he started again, emphasizing the verbs in each step. "We greet the boy — totally without suspicion. We shake hands with the boy, like this." The principal then used both of his hands to demonstrate the prescribed double-handed shake, abandoning his grip on the teacher.

"RET COOPER!" the teacher hollered, fleeing from the principal's clutches. The escapee entered the swarm of students like a bullet, knocking bodies down like dominoes in all directions. The miffed administrator marched after his disobedient sidekick, stepping over fallen children without proffering any apologies.

"Ret Cooper! Ret Cooper!" the teacher called after the boy, now just a few feet from where he stood. Hearing his name, Ret looked up from studying his class schedule just in time to witness an emotionally-unstable man grab his hand and shake it violently.

"Ret Cooper," he said, out of breath, "it is such a pleasure to meet you." Just then, an austere hand appeared on the troubled teacher's shoulder. Upon contact, the teacher's countenance clouded over with fear.

"Principal Lester W. Stone," he introduced himself, extending his right hand toward Ret.

"Ret Cooper," came the timid reply, Ret cautiously shaking the principal's hand.

"Obviously," Principal Stone remarked. "I see you've met our World Geography teacher, Mr. Ronald Quirk." The principal removed his hand from Mr. Quirk's shoulder in disgust. "Never mind Mr. Quirk's indecent behavior. First-day jitters, I'm afraid; I'm sure you can relate." Principal Stone placed his now-free hand on the back of Ret's, executing the recently-rehearsed double-handed shake. "Welcome to Tybee High School, son," he said, not alarmed by Ret's eccentric eyes. The principal used his left hand to peel Ret's hand apart from their original handshake, turning it cup-shaped and exposing Ret's palm. The principal's eyes plunged toward the handshake, prompting Ret to yank his hand from the sandwich and find his pockets. Principal Stone smiled satisfactorily and hissed, in an eerie voice, "We're glad you're here." The duo turned and strode away from Ret, the principal nearly dragging his teacher.

Ret had heard of principals, but he questioned if this was the normal protocol of first-day festivities. His wonderment was put to rest when he heard the overwhelming silence and realized that everyone in the square was staring at him. The multitude dispersed at the sound of the first bell, which echoed in the noiseless corridors and sealed Ret's first impression.

Principal Stone locked his office door behind him.

"Did you see it?" Mr. Quirk asked urgently.

"Of course I saw it," the principal growled, "no thanks to you."

"What do we do now?"

"We report."

Chapter 2

Truth Uncovered

Ret's gaze rolled back and forth with the flow of the waves, the reach of their shoreward oscillations gradually receding with the ebbing tide. The rising sun blazed a shimmering path across the surface of the sea. A pack of seagulls alighted upon the shore, squawking and squealing as they prepared to feed. Ret watched as the birds buried their beaks in the ground, searching for tasty sand crabs who revealed their whereabouts by the fatal air bubbles they released when the waves withdrew. Witnessing the feast, Ret would have mourned the loss of so many of the crustaceans had he not known them to be so plentiful. With particular interest, he watched one poor fowl that was unable to join the meal because his comrades, though birds of the same feather, continually crowded him out of the festivities. The gull appeared to lack the gall to forsake decorum and embrace rudeness by forcing his way into the clique. Instead, he abandoned the group and hopped hungrily to another locale.

"Is this your favorite spot, too?" Pauline asked as she approached, calling out to Ret over the roar of the nearby waves. She was referring to his secluded nook, situated just out of plain sight where the island's miles-long beach wrapped around its southern tip. "Mind telling me why you love this part of the shore so much?" she said, sitting down next to Ret, slightly sinking in the sand that was still damp from the most recent tide.

"Because no one ever comes down here," answered Ret, happy to share his feelings with someone he trusted completely. "Because I can be alone to think. Because the sun's never in my eyes."

"Could it also be because this is the place of your first memory?" she suggested unobtrusively. He responded with a confused look, which was proof to Pauline that her listener was completely in the dark.

"Ana tells me you're not very fond of school," she said, changing the subject without permission from Ret, who was painfully curious to learn about memories from his past.

"I'd rather not go back," he explained.

"Oh, Ret," Pauline interjected softly, making certain not to sound upset or abrasive. "It's only been the first week."

"I have no friends; everybody stares at me; and even my teachers can't look me in the eye," Ret began to list his reasons.

"I'm sure things will change soon."

"Change? *Change?*" Ret asked quietly, sounding a tad defeated. "I've tried that, and I don't look any different."

"I wasn't implying that you would change soon, silly," Pauline clarified, her continued patience evident in her playful voice and caring smile. "I don't want *you* to change. I like you just the way you are." His spirits seemed to perk up a bit. "Truth has a way of changing things, Ret, especially when it's the whole truth." The conversation ceased for a few moments, as if Pauline intended for her verbal cliffhanger to spur deep reflection.

Ret's attention returned to the hungry seagull who had been shunned by his feathery friends. He wondered how this creature managed to survive, being subject to such foul treatment. He assumed that the bird would succumb to desperation and seek a scanty meal from the litter strewn a little further away, lowering his standards from meat to rubbish. Instead, the seagull remained at the water's edge, bracing itself against the next surge of salt water. When the outstretched wave recoiled and the froth dissipated, the gull stood motionless for a moment before taking one quick snap at the sand. Ret had seen no burbling of bubbles, neither scurrying of critters; yet the bird munched victoriously on the first of many sand crabs, each procured in like manner. Ret marveled; the seagull knew something that he did not.

"It was cloudy — that day, ten months ago," Pauline resumed the conversation, as if her fixed stare into the hazy sky reminded her of some story. She was totally unaware of the scene that Ret had been observing so intently — a scene whose analysis had to be put on hold as Ret's flustered mind prepared to focus on yet another new subject. "It had been a restless night for me, as most were when Jaret was away on duty. He was an officer in the Coast Guard and had been sent on an urgent assignment to some of the islands in the Bahamas. A hurricane was approaching — a severe one, predicted to tear through the Caribbean islands before regaining strength and making landfall somewhere on the Florida panhandle. Jaret and his crew were needed to help with the evacuations, the rescue effort, the cleanup — "

Ret interrupted: "The other day, you told me that I was named after him..."

"That's right. He always wanted a son." Pauline patted Ret's leg tenderly to reassure him that she did not mind him asking questions. In fact, she welcomed them the more she tasted of the vindicating power of confession. Her eyes glistened with pure love as she spoke of her departed spouse. In the past two minutes, Ret had learned more about his namesake than he had gathered in the last ten months. Pauline hitherto possessed neither the power nor the desire to resurrect the tragic tale of her spouse, and Ana remained mum to spare her mom the grief. As a result, Ret often questioned the character of the man who was pictured in the family portraits.

"It was about midday when the telephone rang to tell me the news: Jaret had been involved in a 'freak accident,' they called it. While on patrol, he and his crew received reports of a ship that caught fire several leagues east of Miami. The craft had sent out no distress signal, but even landlubbers like you and me know that a burning ship isn't a good thing. Through radio, Jaret conferred with the other vessels in the area to see what should be done to help the ship in danger. The hurricane was getting too close for ships to be in the area anymore, and everyone agreed that it was an unidentified boat that hadn't responded to any of their attempted communications."

"So they just left it?" Ret's conscience asked.

"No, no, Ret," Pauline intervened. "They didn't just leave it to burn. Jaret was much too noble to do a thing like that."

"So what did he do?"

"Well, he realized that there was really only one ship in that sea that he could control: his own. His crew had their doubts, but they were easily persuaded. Jaret had such a way with people. He wasn't manipulative or anything like that. He was confident, and fearless; bold, but rational." Pauline paused briefly before uttering each adjective. "Stern, but loving; if you knew him, you loved him; and if you didn't know him, there was something about him that made you trust him — that made you *want* to trust him." Her diaphragm seemed to lift her as she slowly and bravely spoke each word of her tribute, gazing into the air's nothingness as if entranced in some daydream. "He was tall, and handsome — very handsome; strong, and thoughtful; and he had the cutest little dimple on his face, just below his — "

"The ship, Pauline," Ret said, rescuing his storyteller from the past. "What happened to the ship?" She sighed but continued.

"It didn't take long for the cutter to reach the site."

"*Cutter?*" Ret inquired. "What's a cutter?"

"A small boat used by the Coast Guard; usually with a single mast," was her reply.

"Oh."

"They used coordinates until they could see the smoke. Afterwards, the crew told me that when they were yet a ways off, they could see that the ship was totally ablaze and sinking fast. They also said that several square miles of the sea's surface, especially around the ship, were bubbling violently — like a pot of boiling water or a glass of freshly-poured soda. None of them had ever seen anything like it before."

"Did they turn back?" Ret was curious.

"Whether they wanted to or not, Jaret insisted that he go it alone. He told them it was too dangerous to get the whole crew involved."

"So what did he do?"

"He steered the ship to safety and then moved forward without them. He left his crew and cutter at the edge of the bubbling waters and continued onward alone in the RIB."

"RIB?"

"Sorry. Rigid-inflatable boat," Pauline spelled out the acronym. "It's basically a lightweight raft blown up with air. Most cutters come equipped with one."

"You mean he got into an inflatable raft in the middle of the ocean? And took it into a boiling sea towards a burning ship with a hurricane fast approaching?" Ret summarized the situation with great intrigue, impressed by the brave actions of his newfound hero. Pauline nodded proudly, to which Ret replied, "Cool."

"His crew warned him that the abnormal water probably contained too much air to keep his RIB afloat, but he never entertained the idea. Jaret had clocked more time in a RIB than all of his crew combined. He knew that the RIB displaced very little water and that its inflatable collar would keep it buoyant even if water ever came aboard the raft. He launched from the cutter, stayed afloat across the bubbling sea, and disappeared into the billowing smoke." Pauline stopped her narrative. When she spoke again, her voice, raspy and quivering, was hardly louder than a whisper. "That was the last time anyone ever saw Jaret Cooper. The Coast Guard conducted a full-scale search: cutters and boats; planes and helicopters; even sonar and deep-sea divers. But they found nothing."

"Nothing?" Ret was astounded. "Not even from the shipwreck?"

"Not even from the shipwreck," Pauline repeated to emphasize the impossibility. "They couldn't even begin the search until the hurricane had passed a few days later. Turns out the hurricane shifted its course, striking further up the panhandle, and when you factor in the Gulf Stream and the trade winds, well, it's no surprise that most of the wreckage caused by the hurricane washed up along the shores of Georgia and South Carolina. Some of the debris, including what was presumed to be the shipwreck, even washed ashore right here on Tybee Island!"

"That must have been quite an unpleasant coincidence for you," Ret said, thinking of the taunting injustice Pauline must have felt as everything — save the man who was her everything — returned to land.

"It was pretty unexpected, I can tell you that much," she admitted, "but I don't believe in coincidences, Ret, no matter how unpleasant they might seem." Silence prevailed again. Ret hoped that Pauline would not suddenly cork her reminiscing, as it was finally answering some of the questions that he had been gnawing at for months.

"So, Ret," she said with a bit less ache in her heart. "Do you want to know why you love this part of the shore so much?" She didn't give him much time to think. "Because this is where *you* washed up on shore."

"In this very spot?"

"And do you want to know what you were in?" Pauline asked the flabbergasted boy.

"Clothes, I hope."

"Yes, you were in clothes, my little comedian. But you were also in — *Jaret's RIB*." Ret's jaw dropped. Pauline purposely let the next few moments elapse in silence so as to allow Ret ample time to contemplate the anomaly. At last, he spoke.

"How in the world did I end up in — "

"I'd give my right arm to know," Pauline said, employing exaggeration to make a point.

"But how'd they know it was the same raft?" Ret wondered.

"Its identification number matched the one in the Coast Guard's records," Pauline answered, obviously having explored every jot and tittle in this case. "Not to mention the official Coast Guard seals that were emblazoned on the sides. Surely you remember the day we found you?"

Ret reached into the recesses of his mind. "I vaguely remember a girl's face and a high-pitched scream."

"Perfect: your first memory," Pauline said, referring to her earlier statement. "That was when Ana peeked over the side of the raft, poked you in the arm until you regained consciousness, and then screamed when you opened your eyes." She waited for Ret to say something, but his mind was too swamped with so much new information to think of anything to say. So she continued. "Ana was combing through the wreckage like a scavenger, amassing great collections of odd treasures like most thirteen-year-olds would do. I was also on the shore...," her voice trailed off. "I was preparing Jaret's gravesite. Even though his body was never found, the Coast Guard told me to arrange a funeral or write a eulogy or hold a burial — anything to provide the public with some closure. They said it was a 'necessary procedure.' So we held a private burial service, just Ana and me."

"Where?" Ret wondered.

She scanned the sea. "You'll find out in a few minutes." Ret did not understand but felt it best not to probe.

"So what did you do with me after you found me?"

"The government took over from there, seeing as you technically were property from an incident involving the armed forces. They conducted a variety of tests and an array of experiments, hoping to figure out who you were, where you came from, what happened to Jaret, and why you looked so — so…" She searched for the right word and then, smiling, said, "So beautiful."

"Beautiful?"

"I added that part. But instead of clues, all they uncovered were more questions. The X-rays and CAT-scans came back blank. It was puzzling, as if you absorbed the very energy that the doctors attempted to pass through your body. They tried to do an MRI, but something about you interfered with the machine's magnetic field — and quite violently, I might add. I'm sure you remember that."

"Yeah," Ret vaguely recalled. "I remember over-hearing them saying something about how I broke their equipment."

"Let's just say I'm glad I wasn't footing the bill," Pauline said, rolling her eyes in relief. "Most curious of all, however, were the biopsies and blood work. The scientists' microscopes found unknown structures in your cells and strange particles in your blood. They couldn't explain it. Some thought you had been electro-cuted — struck by lightning or something. Others hypothesized that you were once exposed to radiation or some kind of nuclear radioactivity. But in the end, they concluded nothing, except that you were filled with a few more elements than the rest of us, whatever that means."

"So why didn't they keep me as one of their guinea pigs?" Ret wanted to know, remembering how the tests abruptly ended.

"There was nothing more to test. Their resources had been exhausted and sharpest minds stumped by an innocent thirteen-year-old boy, which is how old they presumed you to be. Personally, I believed you were a few years older, on account of your, shall I say, robust stature." She squeezed one of Ret's brawny forearms, which made both of them chuckle. "You were one of the healthiest specimens that anyone had ever seen: not so much as a single blemish on your body — except for the scars on your hands, of course. And since you had suffered complete memory loss, the government thought it no crime to let me adopt you, provided they could keep a close eye on you."

Ret was taken aback. "But why did you want to adopt *me?*" Pauline thought for a moment before speaking, choosing her words very carefully.

"Because there was something about you that helped me to feel closer to Jaret — some sort of connection that linked us together again. Forgive me if that sounds selfish. Jaret's RIB came back, Ret, bringing you instead of him. You — a living gift from a fading memory. It's what Jaret would have done." She paused. "Or, perhaps, it's what he did."

Ret didn't know what to think anymore, his mind overheating. He blinked several times and shifted his eyes out to sea, hoping to glean some composure from the collectedness of the ocean. The tide had reached the lowest point at which it dared to retreat. The shore along the island's southern tip was unique in that it sloped less steeply, causing the low tides to expose an unusually long swath of the flatter beach.

"Sometimes," Ret said, assuming that it was his turn to share some of his feelings, "sometimes I feel a lot like that lone rock out there." He pointed to a dark lump, quite a ways down shore, that had only recently been unveiled by the waning tide. "It's the only rock I've ever seen on this beach. There're lots of shells and seaweed and stuff, but only one rock. And look at it: it's shaped so differently — so tall and thin. And it never receives any visitors, at least that I've noticed. But I can see why: it's so far out there and almost always buried in deep water that you'd have to go out of your way to see it."

"I wanted it that way," Pauline said, almost under her breath. Ret shot her the same, perplexed look that his face had been sporting for most of the morning. "That's no rock," she explained. "It's a tombstone." Pauline rose to her feet and started walking toward the object of their conversation. Ret's astonishment provided her with a few seconds' headstart before he, too, stood to follow after her. Her shoulder-length hair seemed to become more voluminous the more it was exposed to the growing humidity in the air. As she walked, the sand sank under her weight. It was a long, pensive trudge to the corpse-less cemetery. They stood together in silence for a few moments, the waves repeatedly stretching to tickle their toes.

"He always wanted to be buried at sea," Pauline broke the silence, "but I knew, should his passing precede mine, that I could never live without at least some place to visit him." She smiled as her gaze focused on the marker. "So we compromised."

"At low tide, Jaret Cooper is deceased, at least in the world's view. But when the tide returns and washes 'necessary procedures' from sight, he comes back to life, if only in my view." Then Ret's much-anticipated answer came: "That's why this is my favorite spot, too, Ret. It's the place where nature's ingredients combine to deliver the hope to which I so desperately cling. Wind, water, earth — it's as if the elements want me to hold out a little longer."

"I don't know why you've come to us, Ret," said Pauline, "but perhaps, with a little more time, the truth — the whole truth — about our pasts will be uncovered." She put her arm around him briefly, then turned and followed her previous footprints as she paced back up shore. Still standing next to the gravestone, Ret bowed his head, partly out of reverence but mostly because his brain felt heavy from all of the fresh material given him to ponder.

Still staring downward, Ret noticed a cluster of V-shaped markings on the rippled sand surrounding the headstone. Intrigued, he studied the etchings more carefully, which he assumed were small scars in the earth's skin. He was about to leave the phenomenon for the geologists to explain when, suddenly, a few of the symbols disappeared as sand crabs emerged from underneath them. It was at that moment when Ret realized what the snapping seagull already knew: the secret lay in the scars.

Chapter 3

Evening of Nosebleeds

In less than a month's time, Ret had quickly developed an acute distaste for Shakespearean sonnets. He marveled how so few words could be interpreted to describe virtually anything while meaning nothing at all to him. He honestly tried to appreciate *Romeo and Juliet,* but, as much as his teacher may have fawned over it, by play's end, he considered it nothing more than a tragic tale about poor communication skills. The end of his English class's scrutiny of Shakespearean literature could not have been more welcomed.

In contrast, Ret found his brief hour of studying the sciences to be something akin to pure bliss. Every lecture answered a question; every experiment questioned an answer; and every minute he became more aware of the world around him. He was particularly fond of the Periodic Table of Elements, never forgetting the memorable day when his teacher first presented it to the class. For whatever reason, Ret reveled in the revelations of modern science.

"Why are your fingers purple?" Ana asked Ret when they met in the hall on their way to World Geography.

"In science lab today, we were experimenting with different foods to find out their starch content," he eagerly explained, examining the splotches on his hands, "and I sort of spilled the iodine."

"Well, butterfingers," she joked endearingly as they neared their next class, "you'd better watch out for the Purple People Eater." Suddenly, Mr. Quirk appeared in the doorway to greet his next batch of students. "Because here he comes now," Ana added, rolling her eyes.

"Welcome, children!" Mr. Quirk squealed, dancing a jig across the threshold as he reentered his classroom at the sound of the bell. Ret and Ana hurried to the pair of seats being saved for them across the room.

"Thanks, Paige," Ana whispered, sliding into one of the chairs that had been reserved by her best friend.

"Hi, Ret," Paige waved, fluttering her petite fingers at him.

"Hey," Ret replied. As he strode to the vacant desk behind her, Paige's face blushed, as it usually did when

Ret was near. She was much less flamboyant than Ana, though equally as fair, and she always wore her blonde hair in soft curls.

"Welcome to another exciting afternoon of studying the extraordinary subject of World Geography!" Mr. Quirk announced with great enthusiasm. A large boy sitting in the back row breathed a deep moan of dissatisfaction.

"Why, Mr. Ledbetter," the instructor said, waltzing toward the student's desk. "Something to say, have we?" With his plump elbow positioned on his desktop so as to allow his hand to cradle his large head, the porky lad gave his teacher a blank stare and then belched.

"Charming," Mr. Quirk said amid the giggling of his students.

"More like Harvey *Bedwetter*," Ana jabbed, though only loud enough for Ret and Paige to hear. Mr. Quirk tried to quiet his class before leaning over to address his disruptive student face to face.

"Shall I summon the nurse, Mr. Ledbetter?" he scowled. "Perhaps she can detect the cause of your…irritation, hmm?" The unimpressed stare persisted. Mr. Quirk resumed his erect posture, turning from the boy to readdress the rest of the class. "At any rate," he said raising his arms, one of which knocked Harvey's supporting arm out from underneath his head, which crashed into his desktop with a loud thud, "today we continue our study of the Caribbean Islands." The entire class murmured.

"But that's what we've been studying since the first day of school," a discontented student whined.

"Yeah," a different voice agreed, "I thought this was *World* Geography."

"Kids today," Mr. Quirk muttered, facing the board to conceal his own displeasure. "It's as if they want a quality education or something. Pity."

"When can we move on to something else?" the complaints carried on. Mr. Quirk executed an abrupt about-face.

"We will *move on,"* Mr. Quirk answered, reusing the words of the question in a tone that made them seem beneath his superior vocabulary, "as soon as you can demonstrate that the material has become — " He paused to focus his attention on Ret before concluding, " — a part of you." Ana observed the subtle stare with a curious eye. After a few moments, Mr. Quirk wiggled his head as if to shake off some trance, as a wet dog would shiver to free his coat of bathwater. "Now," he said, regaining his composure, "for the remainder of the period, each of you will read the eighth chapter in the textbook in its entirety." The whole class vocalized their disfavor, which seemed to provide Mr. Quirk with some sort of sick satisfaction. "And I have yet to even mention the quiz," he snickered, retreating to his desk.

Ret was convinced that Ronald Quirk was not the real name of the man who claimed to be their teacher, for his surname too perfectly described him. He was one of the oddest-looking creatures that Ret — and most of the other students — had ever laid eyes on, which held a great deal of meaning coming from Ret. Every few seconds, one of Mr. Quirk's eyes would twitch violently, sending a wave of disruption through his entire face. There seemed to be no method to the madness of his ocular spasms. The rumor quickly spread amongst the student body that if Mr. Quirk's left eye squirmed while he was speaking to you, it meant he disliked you, while if the twinges came from the right eye, he did not think you were so revolting. But no one claimed to know for certain, as there was always something else to gawk at when conversing with Mr. Quirk. His frequent twitching proved to be quite the optical nightmare for his eyeglasses, which he patiently readjusted after each tremor. His hair was a ghastly mix of black and gray and every shade in between, and some students believed it to be a toupee, seeing as it always looked so disheveled. Others, however, preferred to call it a wig, stating that the curls were a bit too long and stiff for a toupee. In fact, Mr. Quirk's locks were so loopy that they resembled something of a cross between seasoned curly fries and a Slinky that had been stretched too far. And he had the most difficult time getting people to listen to him because his forceful twitching caused his curls to bounce atop his brow.

What's more, his nose was crooked, which made everything else on his face look uneven. He was an exceptionally scrawny man, especially in the legs, with a waist that seemed to come up higher than normal. While most of his fellow educators sported a business-casual sort of style, Mr. Quirk preferred his own unique manner of dress, which the students called business-ridiculous. On this particular day, for instance, his outfit consisted of an ivory-colored t-shirt and a pair of light blue jeans that must have been sewn out of scraps of Saran wrap, so tightly they adhered to his bony legs. The getup would have scored as one of his more modest costumes had it not been for the green cardigan. It was the kind with oval patches on the elbows and a single row of fringe that dangled along the span of each forearm, although the multicolored frills hung in such irregular intervals that they looked more like the accumulation of a lifelong collection of streamers from the handlebars of little children's tricycles. Rather than read the assigned chapter, Ret found it more interesting to see if the fringe on Mr. Quirk's coat contained every color of visible light on the electromagnetic spectrum, about which he had recently learned in science class. When the beloved dismissal bell rang, Mr. Quirk remained at his desk, saying not a word of farewell, too engrossed in his own thoughts, whatever they may be.

"See you at your house before the game, Ana," Paige said as she went her separate way through the crowd of students, spilling out of their classes like a colony of disturbed ants.

"Game?" Ret asked.

"The football game," Ana said as if he should have known. "You know, the rivalry football game that everyone's been talking about for, like, a month now? It's only the biggest game of the season. Don't worry; I already bought tickets for us."

"Us?" Ret cringed.

"Us; it means you and me," she said in jest. "And Paige is coming, too."

"But, Ana," Ret fussed, "you know I'm not really into sports."

"Just because you can beat just about anyone in just about anything doesn't mean you can't have a good time at a high school football game," Ana told him. "And besides, everyone knows you don't go to a football game for the sport of it."

"Then why do you go?" Ret wondered.

"To scope out the guys, of course." Ret should have known. "At least, that's why Paige and I go. And that's why *you* need to come." Ana noticed that Ret did not understand; she made it more obvious. "So Paige will come, too." Ana smiled as she pulled away from Ret, leaving him to contemplate what she had insinuated.

Later that afternoon, Ret sat outside on the porch and patiently waited for Ana and Paige to at last be ready to go to the football game. He passed the time by watching nature as it changed its scenery. Nature's cyclical behavior was astonishing to Ret, as he contemplated the four seasons. He particularly enjoyed the times of year when his hemisphere would bounce into spring or fall into autumn. He thought of the seasons as nature's very own changing of the guard, each with its own unique style of guardianship. Nature's autumnal sentinel had already begun to wield its sword on Tybee Island, the shards of its seasonal swinging appearing everywhere: in cooler air that nipped summer garb back into storage; in clusters of brittle leaves and strands of Spanish moss, blown from the limbs of trees by the more prevalent winds; in acorns that rattled rooftops as they fell like hailstones from ancient oaks.

Ret could almost feel the elements rotating shifts as the curtain closed on their respective acts in earth's year-long play. Spring's delicacies buckle under summer's heat; summer's vibrancies fade into fall's bareness; autumn's fatigue crawls into winter's hibernation; winter's chill melts into spring's warm colors — all coexisting in perfect harmony and not a single thing trying to dominate a scene, disrupt an act, or steal the show. Ret could feel it; he sensed it all.

❍ ❍ ❍

The roar of the crowd could be heard from the street as Pauline dropped the trio off at the football game.

"Have a good time," she yelled to them from the car.

"Oh, Mrs. Cooper," Paige said, suddenly remembering something. "My dad told me he'd like to pick us up after the game, if that's okay with you." Pauline looked a bit surprised, but it was nothing compared to the shocked faces of Ret and Ana.

"Well…" Pauline replied slowly, as if at a loss for words. "Well, that's fine with me, but may I ask as to the occasion? I don't think I've ever seen Mr. Coy in public — "

"I know," Paige interrupted, slightly embarrassed. "I asked him to."

"Very well," Pauline said. "Now, go have fun, you three."

"Got it, Mom," Ana said.

"See you, Mrs. Cooper," Paige said.

"Thanks, Pauline," Ret said to their chauffeur, whose encouraging smile was enough to prevent him from crawling back into the car.

Ret so thoroughly detested attending tonight's

football game — no matter how eternally significant everyone made it seem — that he almost wished to instead be sitting in English class, enduring a monotonous lecture on yet another Shakespearean soliloquy. This was not because he was shy or timid or because he feared hard seats or loud noises; neither was it due to any personal bias toward jocks or cheerleaders or imposing crowds. In fact, he relished athletic activities and any form of physical recreation, they being his sole source of social interaction prior to his enrollment in school this year. The neighborhood youth once welcomed Ret in their pick-up games and unorganized sports, mostly on account of his large stature, but he needed only one match to prove his invaluableness. He immediately became the first-pick at team-making time, and every boy and girl wished to be on his side, as it most certainly meant victory.

But soon, Ret frowned at an unexpected turn of events. He fell from his top-pick status to not being picked at all. Word on the street placed an unofficial ban on Ret from all after-school pastimes and spontaneous athletics. Even Ana managed to excuse herself increasingly more often from Ret's sporty petitions, whether involving game boards or sport courts. She told him that no one likes to play against someone who always wins — that everyone needs to lose once in a while. But Ret did not understand, for he played to make friends and have fun, never to win or to lose. He struggled to comprehend his peers' competitiveness. From the sidelines, he was troubled to watch such an intangible force pit allies against each other and turn friend into foe. Wondering where such a demon could have originated, Ret ruled out nature as a possible birthplace, for, as he had noticed, all things work together in perfect union in the natural world. It was true, he knew, that some elements and compounds were superior to others, but Ret was also aware that their individual constitutions and inborn functions were far too different and much too varied to warrant any comparability.

Hence the lens through which Ret viewed the world: every person as a unique element in a globalized mixture, each performing an essential function — a function that no other element could adequately perform.

"We're winning! We're winning!" Ana announced as they neared the entrance to the stadium, the scoreboard now within sight. She handed three tickets to the young woman who stood at the turnstile to collect them.

"Hi, Ret," the ticket taker charmed. "How's Tybee High treating you so far?"

"Uh, good," Ret replied, though confused why she was speaking to him.

"Better than your first day, I reckon," she joked, laughing daintily.

"Yeah."

"Save me a seat?" she asked as she slipped his torn ticket stub into his shirt pocket.

"Umm, sure," Ret promised, assuming it to be the gentlemanly thing to do.

"Come on, Ret," Ana said loudly, pulling him along. "We'd better hurry if we're going to find THREE empty seats in this sellout crowd." She yanked Ret into her private huddle. "Who do you think you are, Mr. Suave?"

"What do you mean?" he wondered.

"I mean, what are you doing, flirting with a girl like her?"

"Flirting?" Ret tried to clarify.

"She's trouble," Ana informed. "You don't want to get mixed up with the wrong crowd, Ret. Now promise me you'll try harder to stay out of trouble?"

"I promise," Ret agreed. "But Ana," he continued, smiling, "everyone knows you don't go to a football game for the sport of it."

"Oh, brother," she said, rolling her eyes and poorly suppressing a smile of her own.

Like a fearless war general, Ana led her few but mighty troops into the stands. Ret left it to Ana to find space for three on the congested bleachers, especially since it was her idea to arrive fashionably late. He regretted his lack of input, however, when Ana pointed to a small sliver of bench on the topmost row near the middle of the grandstand, a spot that appeared to have room enough for maybe one.

"Come on," she motioned, starting up the stairs. As the trio made their ascent, the surrounding crowd couldn't help but notice Ret instead of the game.

"Hey, look! It's Ret Cooper," said one hushed voice.

"You mean that guy from the first day of school?" said another.

"He's in my English class."

"What's up with his skin?"

"I think he's cute."

Then a familiar voice was heard nearby: "You should see his eyes," said Harvey Ledbetter. "They're so weird!"

"Not as weird as you, Bedwetter," Ana rebuked as she strode past Harvey.

By the time they arrived in the nosebleed section and wiggled into their chosen gap, the players of the game had been supplanted by dancers of some halftime show, in which Ret quickly lost interest. Instead, he surveyed his surroundings: the setting sun that found reflection in the sea of sunglasses that was the other half of the stadium; the balding patches on the grassy field where play most commonly took place; the feigned friendship between rivals' fans, forced to intermingle in order to procure their midgame treats at the snack bar.

At the base of his section of bleachers, Ret spotted the face of his ticket-taker. Scanning the stands, Ret assumed she was searching for him. Rubbing her bare arms in futile defiance of the chilly breeze, her fairness was now muffled by the twilight. Despite Ana's warning, she scarcely seemed like a trouble-maker. Ret shifted his gaze toward Ana; she and Paige were still captivated by the halftime presentation. Just as Ret was about to reveal his whereabouts, the ticket collector was wooed by a group of young men seated in front of her. Ret recognized them as the same rough crowd who tried to entreat Ana and Paige when they purposely hurried past them just moments earlier. Like so many others, their patronage obviously stemmed from an ulterior motive, and Ret was beginning to wonder if anyone attended sporting events for the sake of the actual game.

"Told you so," Ana said soberly to Ret, who had long since been convinced that Ana possessed additional sets of eyes, so miraculously was she able to observe multiple scenes simultaneously.

Ret spent the better part of the third quarter deep in thought. Over the last ten months, he had quickly mastered anything and everything that he had ever attempted, and still, despite his dexterous hands and agile mind, there was yet one mystery that he could not quite put his finger on — there was still one puzzle that he had yet to conquer: people.

Too fickle to figure out and too mercurial to demystify, Ret had always assumed people to be good by nature. He did more than merely look for the best — he found it; and rather than bestow the benefit of the doubt, he chose not to doubt at all. Perhaps it was a flaw of his naivety. Maybe it was the overriding quality of his utopian universe. Or, most probable, it was the aura of innocence radiating from his own good-naturedness. He saw in others what he himself was.

But, with eyes opened wider by public school and heart now burdened by his associations with the ticket-taker, Ret decided that it was high time to realign his people paradigm. For the first time, he entertained the idea that not all people were as pure and unadulterated as he was — that some elements in this globalized mixture called the world could be manipulated for dark purposes.

"Hey, isn't that what's his bucket?" Ana pointed to a squirming referee on the opposite sideline who was clutching one of the bright orange end poles of the first down measuring chain.

"It's Mr. Quirk!" a surprised student yelled from a few rows below, several others vocalizing their amazement in like manner.

"What's Quirk doing on the field?" Ana wanted to know. At the end of the play, Mr. Quirk scurried onto the field with his chain gang, resembling a spunky ball boy shagging tennis balls at a Wimbledon match. Thanks to Ana's eagle eyes, the audience now had something to entertain them, as the victor of the game had now become certain.

"Who thinks I should call the police and tell them that one of their prisoners escaped?" Harvey Ledbetter proclaimed, raising his cell phone in the air. His wisecrack in reference to the referee's traditional black- and white-striped uniform earned him a few cheers.

"Well that's not very nice," Paige said quietly, though loudly enough for Ret to overhear. Ret slowly turned his head to face her. Not only were these the first words he heard from her since bidding farewell to Pauline, but Ret was also relieved and impressed to discover Paige to be of his increasingly rare breed of compassionate peacemakers. Feeling Ret's gaze, Paige's cheeks blushed as her head sunk between her shoulders.

"Hey, Bedwetter," Ana called out, "prisoners wear horizontal stripes, not vertical." Her correction was greeted by a heartier round of applause than the original jab. Harvey lowered his phone in embarrassed defeat.

When the clock finally expired, a flood of fans fled the stands and rushed the field. Ana seized the opportunity to grab her companions, slip down the bleachers, and beat the crowd to the parking lot where Paige's father was likely awaiting them. During their descent, Ret's curiosity was sparked when he saw Mr. Quirk conversing in a most suspicious manner with the ticket-taker and her clique of hoodlums. He wondered why they, of all people, were taking Mr. Quirk so seriously and why he, of all adults, would have anything to do with such a group. Ret watched the post-game huddle disperse before it escaped from view when he set foot on ground level.

En route to the parking lot, the trio took the path behind the bleachers, finding it to be much less grid-locked than any alternate way through the field, now sardined with celebratory fans. They dodged debris and other fallen litter as they shuffled along the earthen trail. Emerging from the shadows at the approaching end of the grandstand were the silhouettes of two hooded figures. Realizing them to be part of the same meddle-some gang that had tried to get their attention earlier, Ana and Paige instinctively wrapped themselves more securely in their jackets and lengthened their strides, making certain to avoid eye contact. The two suspicious individuals positioned themselves, shoulder to shoulder, in the middle of the walkway, blocking the narrow exit into the parking lot. Ana and Paige slowed to a snail's pace, unsure of what to do and unwilling to inch any nearer. With faces hidden and voices mute, the two dark figures began to advance toward the frightened females.

Ret knew that it was up to him and him alone to protect his sister and her friend from whatever might happen next. With no time to lose, Ret jumped in front of Ana and Paige and faced the approaching villains.

"Stop right there!" he ordered, extending both arms. With the palms of his hands turned toward the intruders, Ret was clueless as to his next move, and the unabated march of the antagonists sent his heart racing. Then, in the blink of an eye, Ret felt a wave of energy enter his frame from the ground. Like lightning, the pulse jolted up his body, darted down his arms, and surged into his hands. From the ground near his feet, two parallel streams of dirt raced up to his hands, then straight towards the two attackers, pummeling them like a gush from a fire hydrant. The brief but geyser-like spouts buried their immobilized victims in earth. Amazed, Ret slowly turned his palms toward his wide-eyed face. One of the scars on his right hand was glowing.

"Caught red-*handed,*" a jittery voice hissed from the shadows. A referee stepped into the afterglow of dusk. It was Ronald Quirk.

"You know, I really got to *hand* it to you…" he said, his continued pun giving him the giggles. He slithered over to the scene of the commotion, planting one foot on the buried torso of one of the attackers. "Never, in a million years, would I have guessed that your gifts would have surfaced to you so quickly."

"Quirk!" Principal Stone appeared on the scene. "What goes on here?"

"Ah, Lester!" Mr. Quirk saluted. "Always a man of dramatic entrances, and oh, what splendid timing, yes, quite apropos…"

"Ronald, we must be going," Principal Stone advised.

"But, sir — "

"Now, Quirk! We *must* be going."

"But what about — "

"Cooper? Yes, Mr. Cooper, I will see you in my office, first thing Monday morning." Mr. Quirk continued to complain as Principal Stone carried him away into the night. After a motionless moment of silent confusion, Ana and Paige sped toward the parking lot. Ret bent down to aid in unearthing the two bodies, fully conscious but dazed. He used his shirt to wipe a trickle of blood that was dribbling from the nose of the first man. When Ret turned to help the other person, he was stunned to find the female ticket-taker buried under the dirt. Speechless, he staggered to his feet and hurried after Ana and Paige.

"How vath ze game?" asked Ivan, the Coys' Russian butler, as the trio piled into the limousine waiting for them in the parking lot.

"Inconceivable!" Ana blurted out, her thoughts of what she had just witnessed exploding from her mouth without fully contemplating her words. Realizing her blunder, she quickly tried to play it off, saying, "Inconceivable…that…that we would win by so much."

Sitting together on the back row of the limo, Ana leaned across Paige and quietly, though earnestly, asked Ret, "What was *that* all about?" Her dumbfounded face demanded an explanation, but all Ret could provide was a pair of raised shoulders and a vacant expression. He relaxed his clenched fist to allow a moment's glance: the scar was still illuminated, clearly visible despite the unusual darkness inside the car.

Immediately upon entering the limo, Paige's spirits seemed to sink when her father was nowhere to be seen. "Looks like Dad just sent Ivan again," she mumbled almost inaudibly. Though dejected, she wasn't too surprised.

Silence prevailed for the remainder of the short ride home. The sun had long since slipped behind the horizon when they arrived at the Cooper home. The porch light bathed the front yard in a triangular glow, evidence that Pauline was expecting her children.

"Thanks for the ride, Ivan," Ana said as she hurried toward the house. "See you on Monday, Paige."

"Yes, thank you, sir," Ret agreed. Arriving at the front door and finding it to be unlocked, they turned to wave goodbye to Paige, with Ivan politely idling in the driveway, waiting for the Coopers to safely enter their home.

"Bye," the Coopers waved.

As Ivan pulled out of the driveway, the voice of Mr. Coy was suddenly heard from the other seat bench in the limo.

"On the boy's hand…" he whispered to himself from the shadows.

"Oh, Dad!" Paige said, a bit startled. "You *are* here."

"…Where have I seen that before?" Mr. Coy continued, his mind still fixed on the scene of Ret and Ana waving goodbye to them.

"Oh, you mean the purple spots on Ret's hands?" Paige groped for an answer.

Mr. Coy broke his trance and then slowly lowered his gaze until it focused on his daughter. With great concern, almost alarm, in his eyes, he asked, "What spots?"

CHAPTER 4

TRIANGLES, TRUNKS, AND TUXES

"What the blazes was that?" Ana barked at Ret, following him into his room and carefully shutting the door behind them so as to not alarm Pauline.

"Of all the crazy stunts…

"Granted, we *are* in high school now, where it seems like everyone's got a whoopee-cushion or a rubber chicken or some kind of gag stuffed in their locker…. And it *was* the biggest game of the season, which always seems to bring out the beach balls and crowd-pleasing, game-stopping nonsense…"

She was pacing around the room now, her gaze fixed on the circular trail that she was wearing into the floor.

"Of course, there *are* loads of people who know kung fu or karate or jujitsu or tae-kwon-do. I mean, don't get me wrong, you're buff and brawny and good at just about everything, but — "

For the first time, her rambling tongue and swirling mind stopped to give her a chance to look at Ret. He was sitting on the edge of his bed, slowly and methodically taking off his shoes, looking as though he didn't have a care in the world.

"Ret!" Ana yelled, trying to break him out of his apparent apathy. Still ignoring her, she walked across the room and sat next to him on the bed, leaning forward so that she could look Ret directly in the eye. In a more subdued tone, she said, "What *was* that tonight?"

"Pretty cool, huh?" he answered, rocking his head back and forth with a smile like a motorcycle-lover who had just been given a Harley.

"Cool?" Ana repeated indignantly. "Cool? So you planned this whole thing?"

"Of course not, Ana," Ret explained. "Don't get so worked up."

"Worked up?" One thing that Ret had learned about Ana was that when she was upset, she began all of her responses by repeating the word or two that she most disagreed with. "I'm not worked up."

Ret shot her a look that said, "You're kidding, right?"

"Okay, so I'm a little worked up." Ana couldn't hide from her flushed face, glistening forehead, and frazzled bangs. "But I just can't believe what I saw tonight. You hurled dirt at those guys like how Spiderman shoots web! What, is this a normal occurrence for you or something because I only ever see this kind of crazy stuff on TV and in the movies?"

"Want to see something else that's crazy?" Ret teased. Ana's eyes widened.

"Promise you won't scream?" Ret asked. Ana nodded.

"Take a look at this." Ret slowly unclenched his fist, revealing his glowing scar.

Ana inhaled a lungful of air and then quickly clamped her mouth with her hand. When the shock and awe had passed, she removed her hand and poked the illuminated scar.

"What do you think it means?" she asked him, full of curiosity.

"Your guess is as good as mine," he said. "It's obviously in the shape of a triangle, so that could mean a lot of different things. And then there's this small mark inside the left angle." He pointed to it on his palm.

"Maybe it's a booger," Ana suggested. Ret wasn't amused.

"It's never glowed before," he added, "so something must have happened tonight that set it off."

"Hmm…I wonder what *that* could have been," Ana said sarcastically. "Well, don't look at me for an interpretation. I guess we could always take you to a palm reader."

"Clever," Ret smirked.

"You're right; it'd be a lot easier to just take you to good old Captain Quirk. He seemed to know a thing or two about what was going on."

"Yeah," Ret remembered. "What exactly did he say to me?"

"Something about your gifts, I think."

"That's it — my gifts!" Ret said, as if he had deciphered the next part of some ancient riddle. "What's that supposed to mean?"

"It means you're gifted," Ana explained, making quotation marks out of her fingers to signify some special status.

"Gifted at what?"

"Hurling dirt at people, of course," she said. "By the way, what was it like?"

"Well," Ret thought back to the event, "it felt really good, actually. Not because I hurt those people or taught them a lesson or anything like that. I just knew that they were going to hurt you and Paige, so it felt good to prevent that, I guess." Ana listened intently as Ret tried to describe something so surreal. "And then I felt strong, I felt powerful — like everything was in a vacuum, weightless, and I could somehow control it. And then it just kind of stopped."

"Weird," Ana remarked, dumbfounded. "And did you feel tired or drained afterwards?"

"It actually left me feeling happier — and lighter. And then I felt awful for hurting those two goons. And, Ana, you'll never believe this: One of the goons was that girl who said 'hi' to me when she took our tickets; you know, the one you told me to stay away from?"

"No way! Who was the other one?" Ana asked.

"Not sure," Ret said. "Some guy."

"Well, I guess they got what was coming to them, Ret," Ana said, trying to make him feel better. "And besides, you stopped them from hurting us, and we were innocent." She smiled at him. "Thanks, by the way."

"Sure," Ret replied. "Anytime, I guess." They laughed.

Just then, Ana received a text message. It was from Paige. Ret didn't have to try very hard to look over Ana's shoulder to read the text. "Is Ret OK?" it read. Ana didn't reply and tried to shove her phone back into her pocket before Ret could notice.

Ret raised his eyebrows and said "Sure am" as Ana stood up, smiled, and left the room.

❍ ❍ ❍

The next day, Ret breezed through his homework so that he could devote the rest of the weekend to studying a subject that was much more intriguing: his gifts, as Mr. Quirk had called them. With the warm sun shining in the sky and shimmering in the sea, Ret slipped away to his favorite nook, where he knew he could be alone to concentrate and to experiment.

He spent several minutes just analyzing his hands. His magnifying glass afforded him a closer look at the triangular-shaped scar on the palm of his right hand; at least, Ret had always *thought* that the marks on his hands were scars. Purple in color and slightly raised, each looked like some sort of cauterized branding. The designs had meant nothing to him until now. Ret even zoomed in on the small speck inside the left angle of the triangle, just to make sure that it really wasn't a booger. Also illuminated, it looked like a single-pointed hook. The light brown glow, though now much dimmer than it had been the previous night, shone through the tissue and clearly distinguished the hook and triangle from the other two, unlit scars on that same palm.

Still clueless, Ret set aside the magnifying glass and tried a more hands-on approach. He did everything that came to mind. He picked up fistfuls of sand and clenched them as tightly and as long as he could, hoping for something to happen. He gathered handfuls of sand and let the small granules sift through his fingertips. He let his hands hover above the sand; he sent his fingers crawling underground. He even formed two crude statues out of wetter sand and held up his hands to stop them, attempting to recreate the previous night's more threatening scene.

Hours passed. Ret was out of ideas. He felt no powers take control; he saw no flurries of dirt lunge from the ground. He was beginning to think that this was all some masterfully-planned practical joke, though he realized that was impossible. He was glad to see Ana approaching him from across the beach.

"What're you doing?" she asked brightly.

"Nothing," was Ret's honest reply. He had his chin resting in his hand, so the few words that he spoke were slurred.

"Any luck with the dirt moving?"

"None," he said, sounding very disappointed.

"Maybe it only works with a certain kind of soil?" Ana suggested hopefully.

"I've tried a dozen different combinations."

"Did you try getting it wet?"

"Tried it."

"Keeping it dry?"

"Tried that, too."

"Well gosh," Ana said, "maybe it only works when you don't want it to."

Ret had never considered such a condition. "What'd you find at the library?" he asked.

"Loads!" Ana admitted, whipping out her phone to revisit the list that she had made. "After sifting through the 150 thousand results that came up when I Googled the word *triangle,"* she rolled her eyes at the exaggeration, "I found a few leads that might interest you."

"Let's hear it."

"Okay," she cleared her throat, ready to show off her hard work. "Have you ever heard of…," she said, pausing for dramatic effect, "…the Pythagorean Theorem?"

A few crickets chirped from the nearby brush.

"That only works with *right* triangles," Ret informed her.

"Right," she said, undefeated. "Next: Pascal's triangle?" Ret scoured his memory. After a long, silent pause, Ana resumed. "Zero for two."

"Okay, how about this one," she pressed on, scrolling down the list on her phone. "Penrose triangle?"

"Sounds impossible," Ret said, recalling the unfeasible shape.

"Equilateral triangle?"

"Definitely not true of this triangle," Ret concluded.

"Didn't think so," Ana agreed. "Besides, I think that's some place in Guinea. How about the Pyramids of Giza?"

"Triangular sides, yes, but square base."

"Close enough," Ana moved on, losing patience. "Sierpinski triangle?" Ret gave her a confused look, having never heard of such a thing. "Yeah, got nothing on that one," she said. "Alright, this one sounds promising: isosceles."

"Ana," Ret called her by name, emphasizing the ridiculousness of such a simple idea that wasn't even true of the image on Ret's hand.

"Alright, alright," she consented. "I just remembered him from Greek mythology, that's all." Ret shook his head but let it go. Ana fed him another possibility: "Sydney Opera House?"

"What does that have to do with…"

"It *looks* like triangles, okay? I'm trying here; come on, Ret." Ana shut her phone in failure.

"Looks like we're both at dead ends," Ret said.

❍ ❍ ❍

At school on Monday, Ret was captivated by yet another fascinating lecture in science class. As part of their unit on rocks and minerals, the teacher had invited a guest speaker to educate the class on his field of work as a glass blower. Somewhere in the speaker's explanation of the process of melting sand into glass, Ret heard the word *stone*. Ret's heart stopped.

"Principal Stone," he mouthed. Ret had completely forgotten about the brief moment the other night when Principal Stone had asked to see him first thing this morning. Ret hoped that the Principal had forgotten, too.

But Ret couldn't quite push his belated appointment fully out of his mind. He respected authority, no matter how questionable that authority seemed. Besides, he had committed no crime, and he hoped that maybe Principal Stone knew a thing or two surrounding the strange events of that night. And so, as much as he did not want to leave such a riveting lecture, Ret embarked for the principal's office.

Ret was about to knock on Principal Stone's oak door when he thought he heard someone say his name. Intrigued, Ret put his ear up to the door and breathed more softly.

"Yes, my lord," Ret heard Principal Stone say. "Everything went as planned at the game: Cooper took the bait, and, according to Quirk, the symbol has been illuminated." Hearing no reply, Ret figured that the Principal was speaking to someone on the phone.

"We have not been so fortunate with that part of the plan, sir: Quirk tells me that Cooper has failed to demonstrate any recollection of the event. Shall I advise Ronald to instruct his students in a more comprehensive study of the Caribbean Islands?" Stone paused again and then said, "It shall be done, my lord." He went quiet again.

"There is still no sign of it, my liege," the Principal responded to what must have been another question from his superior. "My men have searched every museum in the area and combed the shores dozens of times looking for it. It *has* been almost a year since the incident…" Ret could hear the static of a raised voice coming through the phone from the other end of the conversation. Whoever it was, he did not sound very pleased.

"Yes, yes, my lord," Stone's quivering voice promised obedience. "We will widen our search." There was silence in the office for several moments. Then Principal Stone spoke up again.

"Actually, sir, there is one other thing I've been meaning to ask. I was wondering if there might be any way to, well, sort of speed up the plan?" He sounded nervous. "What I mean is I believe it's only a matter of time before Quirk jumps the gun and foils the entire plot. Such a fidgety man, that Quirk, and even the other night, had I not intervened…" The raised voice was heard again.

"My apologies, my lord," a reprimanded Stone said a few moments later. "I will remind Ronald that the plan must proceed at its current pace so as to allow you sufficient time to recuperate." The conversation abruptly ended in the sound of a dial tone. After breathing a sigh of relief, Principal Stone emerged from his chair, which creaked loudly under his weight, and advanced toward the door. Ret scarcely had time to retreat a few steps when the door flew open. Principal Stone froze in the doorway, sporting a facial expression as cold as his name.

"Mr. Cooper," he said, "come to drop eaves, have we?"

"You wanted to see me, sir?" Ret reminded him, ignoring the accusation.

"Yes, yes; come in, come in."

The office of Principal Lester W. Stone was suspicious, to say the least. It didn't have any of the normal things one would expect to find in a principal's office. There were no collections of encyclopedias or reference manuals, which was befitting since there wasn't a bookcase on which to place them. There was no school flag hanging in the corner or any knickknacks that bore the school colors or mascot. The windows were shut and locked, and any light that wanted to pour in was snuffed out by the tightly-drawn curtains. Besides a small desk and its black leather chair, there was no furniture in the room, not even a chair for Ret to sit on. Two odd-shaped trunks caught Ret's eye. Old and mysterious objects, they looked like treasure chests from a pirate ship, and they made Ret very curious. The trunks would have appeared shinier except for the dirt and moss stuck in the elaborate crevices of the intricate outer designs.

Noticing Ret's distraction, Principal Stone said, "Pull up a few of those boxes, why don't you?" He pointed to a few unopened boxes accumulating dust against one of the walls.

Ret found it odd for someone who was in his second year of serving as principal to still have unpacking to do.

"So, Ret, my boy," he said, leaning back in his reclining chair, "how's school going for you so far?"

"Fine." Had he not been privy to Principal Stone's most recent phone call, Ret may have confided more in him. These days, however, his childlike naivety was waning.

"Well then, lucky for you last week's hurricane barely missed the island, eh? Had it struck Tybee, we'd likely be sitting in a pile of wet rubble right now," Stone said. Ret glanced down at the boxes of mismatched junk that he was sitting on.

"Have you ever been caught in a hurricane, Ret?" Principal Stone asked while signing some paperwork.

"Yes," Ret replied. Though unsure of what the Principal was trying to get out of him, Ret was no liar.

"Oh, really?" Stone said with great interest. "Which one?"

"Florida. Last year." That was all the information Ret was willing to surrender.

"Ah, yes," Stone recalled. "That was quite the storm, wasn't it? Left a sizeable trail of wreckage strewn up and down the Tybee coast, you know."

"Yeah, I know." Ret's thoughts turned to the tragic tale of Jaret.

"If I remember correctly, that occurred just before Mr. Smith unexpectedly retired. He was the principal of this fine institution then, of course. Would you believe that I convinced him to devote an entire school day to cleaning up the debris?" Principal Stone boasted. "He agreed that such a service project would be an excellent way to end his career in the community. In fact, it was so meaningful that Smith and the school board selected *me* as his successor." Ret sat patiently as Principal Stone indulged in his accomplishments. "Yes, the students loved the project, and they found some pretty incredible artifacts, too." Ret watched the artistic swoops and swirls of Stone's signature as he turned over another document. "Did *you* ever find anything interesting in that wreckage, Ret?"

Ret thought for a moment. He pictured how Pauline described Jaret's RIB washing ashore with himself inside of it. "Yes," he answered truthfully.

Principal Stone dropped his pen on the desktop. Suddenly enthralled by the conversation, he asked, "Was it…round?"

In his mind, Ret imagined what the rounded edges of the inflatable RIB must have looked like. "Yeah," he said.

"Did it have any…any markings on it?"

Again, Ret imagined the Coast Guard seals and identification number that Pauline had told him were imprinted on the small craft. "Yeah, I think it did."

"What did you do with it?" Principal Stone interrogated, now with great concern in his voice.

Ret wondered why his high school principal would be so worried about the RIB. "Pauline put it in the attic, I think," Ret said. "The Coast Guard let her keep it."

Principal Stone's tense face relaxed at this news. He leaned back in his chair again. "Well that was nice of them, now, wasn't it?" He smiled. "I think I've kept you from class long enough, my boy. Have a nice day. Close the door on your way out."

"But don't you want to talk about what happened at the football game?" Ret asked.

"Oh, you mean how Tybee slaughtered that group of ninnies on the football field? Wasn't that game somethin' else?"

"Not about the game," Ret said. "About how my sister and her friend were attacked and how Quirk was there and he — "

"Ah, yes, I remember now. I'll speak to Mr. Quirk about it later today."

"But — "

"Now off you go," Principal Stone shooed him out the door. "So much to learn, and so little time in which to learn it." And he shut the door.

❍ ❍ ❍

On his way home from school, Ret counted thirty-seven jack-o-lanterns from his window seat on the bus, but thoughts of Halloween fled his mind as he spent the rest of the afternoon at the beach, working with all types and forms of dirt in hopes of rediscovering his so-called "gifts." The pair of self-made statues, which he had previously sculpted to recreate the scene at the football game, had now been half-eroded by the waves. Their gradual but steady disintegration, coupled with the waning glow of Ret's triangular scar, caused him to worry that his gifts were fading.

"I've got something that'll cheer you up," Ana sang as she approached Ret, the frown on his face giving away his disappointment after another unsuccessful afternoon of experimenting. "Winter Formal's just around the corner, and I've already found you a date."

"You what? A date? Ana!"

"Now, now; don't get your knickers in a twist."

"First the football game; now this?" Ret expressed his displeasure. "What's Winter Formal anyway?"

"Really, Ret. As smart as you are, I'm amazed how you know so little about the things that are truly important in life," Ana said. "Winter Formal is a dance — a *formal* dance, in the *winter.*"

For the sake of peace, Ret had made it a habit of swallowing his pride whenever she pointed out obvious details like that.

"So that means it's like a quarter of a year away then."

"Eight weeks, to be exact," she corrected him. "Girls need time for these sorts of things, Ret. There's a dress to be found, colors to be coordinated, flowers to be ordered, hair to be done, nails to be painted, groups to be arranged, pictures to be taken — all you have to do is find a tuxedo."

"Well I don't want to go."

"Is that all you ever think about, Ret? Yourself?" Ret's obstinate attitude melted at such a searching question. He looked up at Ana; her face harbored neither anger nor malice. His gaze returned downward. In that moment, he wished that he could manipulate the sand to bury him with his selfishness. Ana finished her thought, though spoken in a gentler tone.

"What I meant was," she said, "didn't you ever think that there might be someone who'd like to go with you?"

"No," he answered, not even having to think about that.

"Oh, please, Ret. You know, there *is* one game that you lose at every single time. Do you want to know what it is?" She had Ret's attention. "The dating game. You're awful at it."

"So who's my date?"

"Paige, of course," the matchmaker informed. The idea of attending a school dance suddenly did not seem so bad to Ret. He knew Paige; Paige knew him; and they felt somewhat comfortable around each other.

"She doesn't like to dance, does she?" Ret asked his burning question.

"Oh, Ret, she'll do anything you say."

"Unlike someone else I know." They exchanged humored looks.

"Now, I told Paige that you'd stop by her house in a week or two to formally ask her to attend the dance with you and to ask her dad for permission."

"Ask her dad for permission?" Ret restated with disgust. "What, are we getting married or something?"

"I wouldn't be opposed to the idea," Ana retorted. "The pleasantries, Ret, the pleasantries."

"But he's Mr. Coy. If he doesn't like me, he'll whip out one of his machetes and cut my legs off."

"I guess we'll save some money on your tux then, won't we?" There was yet another game that Ret could never win, no matter how hard he tried: arguing with Ana. "And besides, if he gets unruly, just bury him in dirt."

"Funny," Ret said straight-faced. "So who's your date?"

"I haven't found one yet," Ana replied, sounding a bit frustrated. "A traditional black tux simply won't go with my dress, so my date must be willing to wear a powder blue tux."

"Terrific," Ret rolled his eyes. "I can't *wait* to go now."

"Well then," she said, standing up to leave, "it's getting dark, and Mom will have supper waiting for us."

"You go on ahead," Ret said.

"Okay, but don't cry when there's no gumbo left," she teased, purposely kicking over one of Ret's eroding statues and walking backwards so she could still face Ret while talking to him. Ret could taste their favorite meal on his tongue when he spotted a pile of broken glass directly in Ana's path. Her next step positioned her foot directly above the sharp pile.

"Ana, watch out for that glass — " Ret yelled, extending his right arm to point at the imminent danger. Just before Ana's foot came crashing down on the pile, every shard of the broken glass shot into Ret's extended hand like a yo-yo recoiling up its string. Ana stumbled, not sure of where to step when she couldn't locate the glass anywhere beneath her.

"Whoa," Ret said with exhilaration. After several hours of failed attempts, the same phenomenon that had occurred the other night had happened once again, except this time in reverse.

"Your hand's not even bleeding," Ana observed with awe, considering how forcefully the pointed pieces had collected themselves in his hand. The scar, whose light had almost completely faded just minutes ago, now shined brightly again, reflecting through the glass kaleidoscope in his grasp and creating shadows that danced on their astonished faces.

"Looks like it only works when someone's in danger," Ret hypothesized.

"Oh, Ret," Ana giggled, "you're like my own little superhero!" She gave him a hearty hug, knocking him over while still clutching the glass. Then she ran off towards home. "Best of all," she stopped midway to yell back to him, "you don't have an arch nemesis like all the other superheroes!"

That's when Ret realized he had forgotten to tell Ana about his visit to Principal Stone's office.

Chapter 5

Coy Manor

The days were getting shorter now. Each morning, the sun seemed to sleep in a little longer than it had the day before, and, after increasingly briefer work days, it seemed to end its shift a bit earlier every evening. Ret observed how this gradual, almost imperceptible change affected everything. Day after day, when boring homework gave way to distraction, Ret would stare out his bedroom window, which he always kept open. Even if it was only slightly cracked ajar, it served as a sort of outlet for him — some way to keep in touch with the outside world.

From up the street, he watched a flock of birds suddenly emerge and take flight over the sea, no doubt chasing summer, which had fled south for the winter. Moments later, Ret learned the cause of their departure as Ana came striding toward the house from that direction. He listened as she shut the front door and came bustling up the stairs. Ret could tell she was headed for his room.

"Paige tells me you haven't asked her to the dance yet," she stated, leaning against the door jamb with her arms crossed. Ret sighed and let his head fall to his desk. Despite his best efforts to postpone the task, he was unwise to think that he could fool the Grim Reaper.

"Come, Ret," she called, as a master would its dog. "Come." He slowly turned his head to shoot her a perplexed look. "We're going to take care of this right now." After another sigh, Ret rose to his feet, well aware that there was no way out of this one.

While Ana waltzed through the backdoor of the house, Ret dragged himself along behind her. They made their way down the family's private boardwalk toward the water's edge. Ana's footsteps sounded like a horse's trot on the wooden planks of the narrow bridge that spanned the marshland from the Cooper's backyard to the placid shores of Tybee Creek. Ret's trudging, on the other hand, resembled the slogging of a sloth.

Tybee Creek was the name given to the small inlet of water that flowed along the south shore of Tybee Island and joined the Atlantic Ocean at the island's southeastern tip. Directly across the creek sat another plot of land called Little Tybee Island, though more than double the size of its namesake. Unlike its sister island, Little Tybee was truly surrounded on all sides by water, making it largely inaccessible, for there didn't exist any sort of bridge to span the creek. As such, and for as long as anyone could remember, Little Tybee had always been a pure, uninhabited nature preserve.

Only in recent years was someone known to be living on Little Tybee. The news started out as a rumor that quickly circulated through town. Most people balked at the idea that someone would be so bold as to intrude on their prized preserve, which was a source of great pride for the locals. But there was no denying the shipments that began to arrive on the island. Dozens of ships brought load after load of tools, building materials, and heavy machinery. Helicopters lowered cargos of boxes, bundles, and crates. In time, a group of concerned Tybee citizens appealed to local law enforcement, only to learn that, while the details could not be disclosed, whatever was happening on Little Tybee had been approved by the federal government. As such, the only thing that the people could do was observe from afar the day-to-day goings-on of their anonymous neighbor. Even from their closest vantage point a few thousand feet away, they could see the walls of an elaborate mansion being erected on the most prominent hillside of Little Tybee Island's north-eastern shore.

And then a new student showed up at school one day. At her teacher's request, the little, blonde girl stood and introduced herself to her middle school class. When asked what part of the island she had moved to, a hush fell over the students at her answer.

"Little Tybee Island," the innocent voice replied. The room became alive with whispered conversations of curious children. Even the teacher was taken aback, for no one had known anything about the mysterious inhabitant of Little Tybee Island, let alone that there were *two* of them. All that was known was rumor. The students kept their distance from their new schoolmate, except for one girl in her class.

"Sometimes the greatest blessings lie behind our fears, Ret," Ana told him as she finished recounting the story of the first day she met Paige, who quickly became her best friend. They had nearly reached the other side of Tybee Creek now. Ana had spent the short trip reminiscing out loud while Ret silently manned the oars of the kayak. He could paddle to Paige's house in his sleep, having rowed there and back countless times as Ana's private gondolier. It was difficult for Ana to navigate the swift currents and avoid the shoals when the tide withdrew, and Ret enjoyed the physical exertion anyway.

When the nose of the kayak ran ashore, Ret jumped out and heaved it on the sand with Ana patiently waiting until the craft came to a complete stop.

"I'll wait here until you get back," she informed him.

"You mean you're not coming with me?" Ret asked.

"Of course not," she said. "I can't do *everything* for you." So Ret turned and started up the hillside, shuffling through sea oats and various other dune plants on his way to Coy Manor.

To classify the Coy residence even as a mansion would be a bit of an understatement, to be sure, for it more accurately could be described as something akin to a palace. It was obviously not the designer's goal to conceal the structure or have it blend in with its surroundings, so boldly did it stand out and tower above even the tallest of oaks and pines on the island. Ret concluded that there seemed to be every style of architecture — ancient or modern — present on the manor: flying buttresses casting their gothic shadows on stained glass windows; medieval turrets with their conical tops pointing heavenward; rows of marble pillars standing with pride in their Greek heritage; painted domes and unsupported arches appearing to defy gravity; a futuristic cable system supporting a large balcony that protruded from the cliffside and hung over the crashing waves below.

The landscape matched the impressive and varied construction of the home. One section boasted enough kinds of fruit, vegetable, and herb to feed a small country.

In a separate part, exotic trees drooped their broad leaves above the still waters of a lagoon. Another corner featured dozens of varieties of palm trees that swayed back and forth in the breeze and scarcely shaded the sun-loving cacti below. A trimmed hedge enclosed a traditional English garden with marigolds bursting at the roots of roses and hibiscus. A series of waterfalls, interspersed throughout the arboretum, fed a large pond, which was replete with reptiles and all manner of animal life.

If observed in pieces, Coy Manor was brilliantly beautiful, but as a whole, it looked very odd. Of a truth, if the entire world were condensed to just a few acres — if all of nature's creations and humanity's inventions were compiled into one place — then the result would be Coy Manor. And if this were true, then Ret was very intrigued to see what lie within its walls.

As soon as Ret approached the front gate, an unhappy voice greeted him.

"Vhat ith yourr name," the repulsed voice snapped. Ret assumed the voice belonged to Ivan, the Coys' butler, but the gate attendant, whoever and wherever he was, had spoken so quickly and with such a thick Russian accent that Ret did not understand what he had said.

"Excuse me?" Ret replied politely to the gate.

"I thaid, vhat ith yourr name!" the voice repeated, this time with even greater impatience and disgust.

"*What* about my name?"

"Yourr name, boy! Yourr *name!"* the Russian voice shouted. "Tell me yourr name!"

"I'm sorry," Ret apologized. "I couldn't understand you."

"Of courth, of courth," the annoyed voice barked. "No one can *ayver* underthand vhat ze *Rruthian* vith ze leethp ith thaying. Eet's alvays ze poorr leetle Rruthian vith ze thpeech prroblem."

"My name is Ret Cooper," Ret answered, interrupting the lamenting voice, which was painful just to listen to.

"I am afraid you are not on ze litht," the Russian informed.

"List?" Ret wondered. "What list?"

"Ze *guetht* litht."

"How many names are on your guest list?" Ret asked, knowing there couldn't be very many.

"Fourr," the Russian said.

"There's only *four* names?"

"Vhat can I thay? Ve do not receive many guethtth."

"I can't imagine why…" Ret muttered under his breath.

"Vell, zith ith unoothooal," the monotone Russian said, thinking to himself. "One of ourr guethtth iz a Cooper ath vell."

"Ana!" Ret said. "Ana; she's my sister."

"Vell don't you feel loocky, eh, boy? But, loocky for *me*, I cannot admit anyone vho ith not accompanied by a guetht vhothe name appearth on ze leetht — in zith cathe, Ana Cooper. Tho I am thorry — not rreally — buth you mutht be going…"

"Ret! Ret!" Paige's voice yelled as she took command of the intercom.

"Mith Paige, my dear," the Russian protested, suddenly sounding very polite. "I mutht inseest…"

"Never mind, Ivan," Paige told him, confirming Ret's assumption as to the identity of the attendant. "Ret is one of my friends." The gate unlocked and slowly started to swing open. "Come in, Ret. Come in!" Ret started up the winding walkway that led to the majestic front entry. Even from far away, he could faintly see Paige standing on the threshold, her silhouette dwarfed by the exceptionally tall double doors.

"Hi, Paige," Ret greeted her as he reached the top of the front steps. "I'm here to ask you to Winter Formal."

"Wonderful!" she said excitedly. "Let me go and get my dad." She turned and skipped away, disappearing through one of the many passageways that led away from the entrance hall. "Make yourself at home."

Ret feebly stepped through the doorway. The sound of his footsteps echoed against silent walls as he tiptoed on the tiles that covered the floor, each one a different size and material than the next. The foyer was semicircular in shape with dozens of doorways along its arc. Surveying his surroundings, Ret's gaze turned upward to examine with awe the dome ceiling. The cylindrical shaft stretched into the heavens before culminating in its glass dome top, which allowed the midday sunlight to pour into the room. Distracted by this architectural feat, Ret's slow advance toward the center of the room was halted when his foot struck something. He didn't see anything in his path, but he could hear something wobbling back and forth as if it was about to fall over. No sooner had he instinctively extended his arms to catch whatever was teetering than a stone bust appeared in front of him and fell into his arms. Ret fumbled with the sculpture, which included the head and shoulders of an old woman.

"Ah, Mr. Cooper, I see you've met Mom." The firm voice of Mr. Coy filled the air as he emerged from the shadows of one of the many doorways. Paige followed close behind her father as they strode toward a nervous Ret, still clutching the bust.

"A fine catch," Mr. Coy continued, adjusting the cuffs of his designer suit.

"I'm sorry, sir," Ret apologized, "but I didn't even see it — "

"I know," Mr. Coy said with seriousness, suddenly looking at Ret. "That's why I put it there." Paige reached to relieve Ret of her grandmother's head. As she returned it to the place where it had previously fallen from, Ret watched in disbelief as the entire bust and Paige's hands disappeared from view. They heard the sculpture come to rest on some surface and then, as Paige stepped back, her hands reappeared.

Speechless, Ret stared at Paige incredulously. Grinning, she turned to her father.

"Father, Ret's come to ask me to the Winter Formal dance next month."

Mr. Coy stared searchingly at Ret, his dark eyes overshadowed by his narrowing brow. "Come with me," he ordered like an executioner. Then, turning on his heels, he marched through one of the doorways where he was swallowed by the shadows. Confused and slightly alarmed, Ret looked at Paige. She gave him a playful nudge, and he darted after her father.

As Ret proceeded down the corridor, he could not see Mr. Coy, but he certainly could hear him, which was fortunate for Ret since he had very little idea where he was going. The hallway seemed to stretch on for miles, and its décor seemed to span the centuries. One portion was draped in as many fabrics as you would see hanging at some international bazaar; another was lit by flaming torches and guarded by armored knights; and yet another was all windows but made dim by dense, jungle-like vegetation through which Mr. Coy had apparently just cut a fresh trail, which helped Ret to know that he wasn't too far behind his guide. After rounding one corner, Ret nearly plunged into a deep pool of clear water, which could only be crossed by use of stepping stones. The staircases proved to be unexpectedly challenging: one stairway's steps each differed in height and width from the next, so much, in fact, that Ret had to jump several feet at times; a separate staircase was, well, quite maddening, for Ret had never known a set of descending stairs to return you halfway up before getting you all the way down. When Ret shouted a time or two to get Mr. Coy's attention, the response was only the authoritative clash of his heels or the grunt of his efforts or the splash of some water or the sound of whatever lay ahead. The corridors snaked every which way, twisting and turning as if they were the veins and arteries of this labyrinth's very own circulatory system. Ret was finding this quest to be quite ridiculous (and Mr. Coy's behavior altogether rude) just to ask his daughter to a dance that he didn't really want to attend.

Reaching the top of another flight of stairs, Ret spotted Mr. Coy for the first time since starting his wild goose chase. Though only slightly out of breath himself, Ret assumed that Mr. Coy was truly as physically fit as the middle-aged man looked, for he hardly seemed winded at all. He was standing perfectly still with his back towards Ret in a large room at the end of another hallway. Ret staggered through the hall until he reached the doorway of the room where Mr. Coy stood staring at a painting on the wall.

Ret leaned against the door frame and said, "I'm here, sir." No sooner had the words escaped his lips than Mr. Coy spun around and hurled a machete in Ret's direction, driving it into the wall just inches from Ret's face. His eyes lunged to the side of their sockets, examining the weapon whose blade still bore bits of shredded vegetation from its recent use in one of the previous corridors.

"I *told* you he'd whip out a machete, Ana," Ret whispered to himself, wishing she were present to observe the sorry state of things. Ret vowed that, in the future, he would play suitor only to daughters of widows or otherwise single mothers.

"I traveled to Naples, once," Mr. Coy stated, not at all interested in Ret's wellbeing, "because I was hungry — hungry for pizza." He slowly paced away from the painting on the wall. "But I was disappointed when I received my order," he continued, "because all of the slices were square." His gaze was fixed on the floor. "And I was hungry for — for a different *shape*." Ret listened politely, though very alert.

"I thought I'd try Paris," he went on, changing the direction of his footsteps, "to satisfy my sweet tooth." Ret doubted that Mr. Coy's perceived austerity permitted such indulgence. "The ice-cream was delicious, yes," he said, "but the cone was quite unsatisfactory. You see, all they had were waffle cones, and I was craving one of a different — of a different *design.*" Ret visually scanned Mr. Coy to see if he had any more surprises in store for him.

"I journeyed all over Eurasia," Mr. Coy continued his travelogue, "visiting this world's most acclaimed libraries and universities." He had slowly gravitated near the window now. "I retraced the steps of Plato, Socrates, Aristotle, Newton — all the greatest minds this planet has ever known." He raised his head to gaze out the window. "I learned many things, to be sure," he admitted, "but not the one, little piece that I was looking for."

"So I changed my approach." He turned and stared into Ret's eyes. Ret braced for flying weapons, but Mr. Coy only spoke to him, though directly for the first time, asking, "How do you catch a Swedish fish?" Ret's poise gave way to bewilderment. "How do you harpoon a baby's wail?" Mr. Coy took a step toward Ret with each question. "How do you hook a loan shark?" Ret felt his back against the wall. "How do you get a handle on an elusive urchin?"

Mr. Coy paused, as if waiting for Ret's solution to his paradoxes. With a hint of fear in his voice, Ret answered, "I don't know, sir."

"He *doesn't* know!" Mr. Coy shouted, turning around and stomping away from Ret. "He doesn't *know*, folks." His showy reaction made it seem like he was on stage in front of a live audience, and Ret glanced around the room to see if any onlookers were peeping through the windows or staring down from the shadows of the ceiling. "You know, Ret," Mr. Coy said, suddenly very casual, "neither do I." He plopped down on a couch on the other side of the room.

Ret glanced at the machete, still wedged in the wall. It was the only thing preventing him from darting down the straight and narrow corridor and out of this madness back into the real world. He studied Mr. Coy as he lounged, feet up, on the sofa, the covering of which had been made from the hides of two spotted leopards whose heads now sat on both ends as armrests. Rumor always spoke of Mr. Coy as an odd duck, and you can imagine the kinds of myths that would circulate about someone who had never before been seen or heard in public. The truth is, no one knew anything about Mr. Coy, except that he had a daughter and lived in "that dreadful mansion across the creek on (what used to be) our beautiful preserve." Ret was now convinced that the rumors were true, and, what with all of the things he had witnessed in the last hour, he knew that he could have the islanders and reporters in an uproar for weeks — that is, if he made it out of Coy Manor alive.

Mr. Coy was humming and mumbling contentedly to himself as he rubbed his hand over the soft leopard skin. His person seemed to have completely changed from just moments ago. He still had the meticulously slicked, black hair and fine-twined apparel of a high-power mogul, but something about his countenance now made him more approachable — more, well, normal.

With Mr. Coy finally distracted and momentarily unthreatening, Ret unclenched his right hand and looked down to inspect his scar, which he had wanted to do ever since his close encounter with the machete. To his utter surprise, the scar was not illuminated, as it had been the other times when he was near danger, and he couldn't entertain the idea that he might possibly be safe.

Ret had scarcely glanced at his scar when, without any warning at all, Mr. Coy lunged to his feet and started pacing toward Ret from across the room. The furrowed brow and intimidating demeanor of Mr. Coy had returned, his face now entirely void of cheer. Ret pulled the machete from its wedge and held it in defense as Mr. Coy drew near.

"I *knew* it!" he said with emotion, still advancing toward Ret. "How *unbelievable* — after traveling the world — to find, residing a hop, skip, and a jump away from me — across the measly creek, no doubt — ," he was now only a few steps away from Ret, "would I be able to find the hook — *and* the triangle — in the palm of *your* hand." Like lightning, Mr. Coy grabbed Ret's wrist. He squeezed it until the scarred hand rolled open and an elated expression grew on his face. Mr. Coy's joy slackened, however, when he felt the cold, wet blade of the machete on his throat.

"Not bad," he told Ret, impressed by the young man's self-defense, though obviously not worried about it.

"What do you want from me?" Ret demanded through his teeth.

Mr. Coy's thrilled smile waned until it turned into a devilish grin, like a crook when everything is going his way. He released Ret's wrist and stared into his eyes.

"My boy," he rasped, his voice low and steady. Mr. Coy slowly reached into his pocket, careful not to make any sudden moves. Ret dug the machete deeper into his skin, fearing what trick his captive had up his sleeve.

"My dear boy," Mr. Coy repeated. Ret would not be fooled by any feigned tenderness. Mr. Coy's hand emerged from his pocket, holding a small, spherical object, no bigger than an orange. Ret stared at it curiously and then with shocked amazement when he saw, etched in the surface of the sphere and identical to the scar on his hand, the design of the hook inside the triangle, as well as five other designs.

"The real question is, Mr. Cooper," said Coy, "what do *you* want from *me?*"

CHAPTER 6

COY MANNER

"Now put the knife down, boy," Mr. Coy said. "I won't hurt you." Ret lowered the machete, dropping it on the floor as his attention turned to his sudden surge of questions.

"What…what is," Ret stammered, " — where did you…" His mouth couldn't keep up with his spinning head. "How come I…"

"…can't speak in complete sentences? I haven't the foggiest, but it's driving me mad," Mr. Coy said, returning the sphere to his pocket and taking a few steps to the center of the room. "Allow me to introduce myself." He turned sharply on his heels to face Ret, cocked his head upward with a very dignified expression like a person of high rank, and cleared his throat. "I am Sir Benjamin Coy I," he said loudly and proudly, "professor of global diversity, doctor of mechanical engineering, former Admiral of the U.S. navy..."

Ret's jaw was beginning to drop in both awe and disbelief. Mr. Coy continued to toot his own horn: "…Master of my soul, captain of my ship, maker of my own destiny…"

Ret was almost certain he was exaggerating. "…Owner of the world's largest collection of oven mitts; fluent in twelve languages and seven dialects, including English; voted by my sophomore class as most likely to circle the globe in a hot air balloon, which I did later that summer, I might add…"

Ret, rolling his eyes, added, "How about father of Paige Coy?"

"Ah, yes," Mr. Coy acknowledged. "I always forget about that one."

"Anything else?" Ret asked, obviously perturbed. Mr. Coy, who would have liked to continue with his resume, noticed his listener's disinterest.

"Why yes, just one more…" he said, reaching back into his pocket. "…Possessor of this curious-looking, round-shaped, hard-as-a-rock ball thingamabob."

Ret stared at the sphere in silence for a few moments. "May I see it?" he asked sheepishly, reaching to take it from Mr. Coy.

"We see with our eyes, not with our hands, Mr. Cooper," Coy replied. "But, seeing as your hands might be the only source for opening our eyes to this mystery, here you go." He pitched it to Ret, who caught it as delicately as he would an egg, not knowing what to expect.

Whatever it was, the sphere was perfectly round, and it fit quite snugly in Ret's cupped hands. At first, Ret thought it was made of glass, and although it was completely transparent, it felt too durable and heavy to be made of something as fragile and light as glass. Still, the substance was so intensely clear that Ret could see perfectly through it, except for six translucent areas where the markings were inscribed on the surface. Ret examined the designs more closely. Though obviously distinct from each other, they were all about the same size, spread out and lined up along the center of the sphere, like how the equator wraps around the earth. Ret could only fully identify one of the sphere's inscriptions: the hook and triangle. The remaining five were too difficult to decipher, as the crystal-clear background did little to outline their unique sort of milky opaqueness. Ret had always encountered a similar problem when trying to examine the scars on his hands: there was not enough variation between the color of the scars and the pigment of his hands to render a detailed description of each scar. Only until recently, when the hook and triangle had become illuminated, could Ret clearly discern the scar's distinguishing features.

The sphere hadn't been in Ret's possession very long at all when it suddenly seemed to come to life. It gently lifted off Ret's palms until it hovered in his bowl-shaped hands, as the like poles of two magnets would repel each other. Still levitating, the sphere rotated until its inscription of the hook and triangle lined up directly across from that same scar on Ret's right hand. Quite involuntarily, Ret's entire being was enveloped in the profound connection between him and the sphere; his ears fell silent, his eyes zoomed in, and his mind became astonishingly clear.

Mr. Coy suddenly chimed in, moving his mouth like a ventriloquist: "Say, Mr. Coy, how did you come to possess a thing like this?" Ret, breaking free from his trance, shot him a confused look, though not entirely surprised to find Mr. Coy talking to himself. "Why, Ret, I thought you'd never ask!"

"I was in Cambodia for the day, on assignment to save an endangered herd of wild water buffalo from that country's peskiest group of poachers. I had nearly nabbed those eggheads when the United States government gave me a ring and proposed a new engagement — a unique mission in which my expertise was desperately needed." Mr. Coy turned his back to Ret and slowly paced aimlessly around the room. Ret's studious gaze remained transfixed on the curious sphere still cradled in his hands.

"They told me, in what turned out to be a rather lengthy briefing," Mr. Coy continued, "that there had been a shipwreck — and an unusual one, at that — in the Western Atlantic. The vessel had gone up in flames and down in waves before being completely dispersed by an oncoming hurricane." Mr. Coy's story grabbed Ret's attention, whose ears perked up like a dog in pursuit. He watched as Mr. Coy strolled from one side of the room to the other, deliberately taking irregular strides near the center of the room as if not to step on something that was lying on the floor.

"There was mention, too," said Coy, "of some sort of widespread bubbling — a kind of wondrous effervescence, if you will — that covered the sea and, regrettably, burst the bubble of a smaller craft that had come to the rescue, taking the life of its captain, if I remember correctly."

"That's correct," Ret interjected, wishing to honor Jaret by removing from the narrative any uncertainty about his brave attempt.

"Ah," said Mr. Coy, "so you have been briefed as well, I see. No doubt the abridged version…"

"So there's more?" Ret eagerly asked.

"Well of *course* there's more, boy," Mr. Coy replied. "Even if no one knows what it is, there's still *more*. Unfortunately, it is highly confidential information, which is why I'm going to tell you all about it." Mr.

Coy began another jaunt across the room, once again intentionally avoiding the same two spots of the floor. Ret, noticing the spots to be slightly indented, assumed the pair of potholes to be nothing more than the squeaky victims of weak floor joists.

"First, the wrecked ship," Mr. Coy proceeded. "In distress — despite never signaling so? Set ablaze — a freak accident or ignited by mutinous freaks? Foolishly afore a hurricane — out of time-strapped desperation or the assurance of untraceably marooned evidence?"

"And what of the fatal rescue mission, eh?" The direction of Mr. Coy's footing changed with the altered path of his train of thought. "The media swarmed the heroic military man's tragedy, finding it to be the bee's knees of the entire ordeal. Jaret's disappearing act took such prominence on stage, in fact, that all the other gigs remained behind curtain. For instance, which section of the international audience had assembled to mourn the casualties aboard the *wrecked* ship?" Ret stood puzzled, the thought having never crossed his mind.

"And why was a missing ship never reported?" Mr. Coy asked. "There isn't a nation or corporation so rich that it doesn't report such a blow to its cash flow without taxpayers up in arms or shareholders down in the mouth. What's more, every single vessel able to float that day was later accounted for, which means that, according to the record books and nautical logs, that ship — "

" — didn't exist," Ret finished the deduction.

"Quite right," Coy agreed. He was walking now along the curved wall located directly across the room from where Ret was standing. A large window, several yards long and without panes, let in the late afternoon sunlight, which cast Mr. Coy's long shadow on the floor.

"As you know," Mr. Coy continued, "while the meat of the subsequent and hardly half-baked investigation was the search for the Coast Guard's most seasoned captain, simmering on the back burner was the government's ulterior motive of puzzling together the unanswered ingredients of the entire tale, which some officials believed to possibly be a threat to national security. Besides the snarls and knots that crews discovered as they combed through the hurricane's aftermath, a few promising artifacts were found among the wreckage, including a brawny orphan in a bloated raft." Ret didn't understand, so Mr. Coy, looking down as if a bit annoyed, clarified: "You." Ret felt slightly flattered that Mr. Coy thought he was promising.

"But when the government's vast treasury of brilliant minds couldn't make sense of any of it, they made their best decision yet by summoning *me* to bring a fresh start to their dead ends." He stopped and raised his hand in the air. "Life lesson number one, Cooper," he said, holding up one finger. "If you've tried *every*thing and still failed at *some*thing, it means you haven't done

one thing: you haven't been coy." He looked at Ret and said, whispering gutturally, "So you'd better get — Ben Coy." He stood motionless for several moments, staring at Ret, as if his counsel should have some profound effect upon Ret. His only movement came from one of his thin, black eyebrows that was dancing up and down above his eye. Then, without warning, he pranced around the room like an elegant deer in a happy meadow. Despite the randomness of his skipping, Ret observed how he still avoided the two divots in the center of the floor. Then he halted as suddenly as he had begun.

"So what *more* can you tell me about me?" Ret asked, silently irritated by Mr. Coy's flippant behavior.

"What, do I look like some crack-pot, soothsaying fortune-teller to you?" Ret held his tongue. "That's what horoscopes are for. But I understand why you might relish this chance to catch up on your past, which you must ardently seek out, so I will tell you this: we were all a bit disappointed when your medical tests merely added more question marks to the situation, though your results were freakish enough to deserve exclamation points, if you ask me."

"*I'm* the freak," Ret muttered under his breath. For the first time in his life, Ret felt like he wasn't the strangest person in the room.

"But, while the detectives called the case closed and the newscasters grew bored from lack of progress,"

Mr. Coy carried on, "I, and I alone, prevented the plug from being pulled on the ailing incident. The government allowed me to relocate to this handsome island where I could continue my research with the full strength of all my instruments as well as keep tabs on you from a close distance."

"So much for privacy," Ret shrugged.

"Don't hold your breath," Mr. Coy advised. "Your medical records ruined that from the get-go."

"I feel so — so exposed, so invaded," Ret admitted, "like some type of experiment — some kind of teenage mutant."

"Well unless you have a black belt around your waist and a hard shell on your back, there's nothing to worry about," Mr. Coy reassured. "No one knows anything about my continuing research except for a few top government officials, and I bet even *they* have forgotten about it, seeing as they still haven't come looking for one of the other few promising items that washed ashore — " Ret anxiously looked at Mr. Coy. " — What you're holding in your hands."

"You mean you stole this from the government?" Ret asked indignantly, holding up the sphere.

"*Stole* is such a coarse, untactful word," Mr. Coy cringed, "certainly a discredit to my name. I would prefer to say that it was artfully and slyly…well, procured. Yes, procured — by someone who they would least expect, and by someone who had to have been — had to have been *coy*." A pleased smile curled his lips. "Besides," he added, "the government just keeps these sorts of dead-end trinkets locked up some place, and their ambivalence to its importance is indicative by their failure to come looking for it."

"So it's important?" Ret probed.

"More so to you than to me," Mr. Coy said, "and that's not only on the one hand." He glared at Ret wide-eyed. "The same can be said on the other hand!" Mr. Coy burst into laughter. Ret wasn't sure whether to laugh *with* him or *at* him. It took him a moment to calm down.

"I've spent too many of my waking hours in the ancient world not to recognize a resurrected relic when I see one. Just look at it: too perfect to be manmade, but too symbolic to have been forged by nature. I've devoted the past year to unraveling its secrets — unearthing its meaning — but to no avail."

"Well, I guess that means you haven't been coy," Ret suggested with a clever smile. Mr. Coy stared at him, disgruntled and speechless, like someone who had just had his thunder stolen — or *procured*, rather.

"As a matter of fact, *boy,*" Mr. Coy snapped, "I have been so *extremely* coy that I didn't even have to travel halfway around the world to investigate my next lead, because *you* came to *me*. I never could quite figure out how you fit into this jigsaw puzzle until the other night when I took you and your sister home after that baseball game."

"You mean the football game?"

"Whatever it was, that's beside the point," a flustered Coy remarked. "When you waved goodbye to us from your porch, I saw the scars on the palm of your hand, and immediately my memory was jogged. It is quite uncommon for something so disfiguring to be in a place as unusual as the palm of the hand, and my mind rolled back to the day when I vocalized this same thought to the team of doctors analyzing your medical records. They thought nothing of it, but *I* should have known! I should have known to trust my own impressions because, ironically, *you* are just what the doctor ordered!"

"So you've figured out what all of this means?" Ret asked, looking at his hands with a hopeful excitement that matched the enthusiasm that was gradually building with Mr. Coy's every word.

"Of course not!" Mr. Coy retorted, though with the kind of jubilance that would be displayed if he had, in fact, cracked the code. "This is merely the tip of the iceberg, my boy! The tip of the iceberg! You see, as soon as I arrived home that night, I retrieved that sphere doohickey, and, by George! — one of the images was glowing. Was glowing! Just as I saw on your hand. Only *then* could I fully decipher the first of the markings, and it was as plain as day: a hook inside the left angle of a triangle. Plain as hook! Triangle as day!" Mr. Coy was drunk with ecstasy. He was shouting now, and his face looked flushed. Like a sports coach who had just won the championship trophy, he had been flailing his arms and kicking his legs so violently that his shirt had come untucked, and the top of his hair had come unslicked.

While Mr. Coy was bouncing off the walls, Ret seized the opportunity to take a load off on his host's fancy leopard couch. He had almost sat down when Mr. Coy flew over the backside of the couch, lounging lengthwise and leaving no room for his guest.

"Don't sit on my couch," he ordered, having suddenly regained his composure. "And I'll be having my whachamacallit back." He extended his hand and impatiently fluttered his fingers back and forth. Ret reluctantly returned it to Mr. Coy.

"It looks like something you'd find in one of Principal Stone's treasure chests," Ret remarked, already missing the trinket that had so quickly come to feel a part of him.

"What'd you say about my chest, boy?" Mr. Coy growled.

"Nothing," Ret reassured. "I just said the sphere looks like something you'd find in Principal Stone's treasure chests. That's all."

"Treasure chests?" Mr. Coy asked incredulously. "Son, have you been playing too many video games lately?"

"No," Ret dismissed the accusation, a little insulted.

"And this *Principal Stone* fellow," he mocked, "is he some villain who haunts you in your dreams?" He let out a hearty chuckle.

"No, he's the principal at school," Ret stated, feeling put upon. "What kind of father doesn't even know who his own daughter's principal is?"

The room fell silent. Ret held his breath and bit his tongue, shocked at the words that came out of his own mouth. He braced for Mr. Coy's reaction, but it took him by surprise. Mr. Coy had swallowed his smile and replaced it with a very sober stare. He was not looking at Ret; instead, it was if he was gazing at the scene of a tragic event. His eyes fell, partially hidden behind their heavy lids. His breathing slowed. He bowed his head.

Ret rushed to repair the damage he had done: "I'm sorry, sir, I didn't mean — "

Ret's apology was interrupted when Mr. Coy silently raised his hand, signaling Ret to stop.

"Please, Ret, sit down" he said in a serious tone of voice. He slid his legs off the couch to make room. Ret cautiously sat on the edge of the cushion, his hands jittering nervously in his lap.

"Tell me what I ought to know about my daughter's principal," he asked politely.

"Well," Ret thought for a moment, trying to think of something unsuspicious that he knew about Principal Stone. "This is his second year at Tybee High," said Ret, "and he, uh, doesn't really have any place to sit in his office…"

"You've been in his office?" Mr. Coy wanted to know.

"Well, yes," Ret admitted. "That's when I saw the chests."

"These chests seem to have made quite an impression on you," Mr. Coy observed. "Did Principal Stone talk to you about them?"

"Actually," Ret thought, "no, now that you mention it, he didn't say anything about them. He basically just talked about himself the whole time — how he moved to the area two summers ago and convinced the retiring principal to let the entire school help with the clean up after the hurricane — " Ret continued to summarize his visit with Principal Stone, hoping that it was helping Mr. Coy to somehow feel better.

"And what were you doing in the principal's office in the first place?"

"Well, that's actually something I should probably tell you about," Ret began. "The night when you saw the scar glowing on my hand was the first time one of my scars had ever glowed like that before. We think it was somehow activated — by us being in danger, triggered by my adrenaline, or something like that. That's the best we could come up with."

"We?" Mr. Coy asked.

"Me and my sister, Ana."

"Right."

"You see, just before you picked us up," Ret continued, "these two people tried to attack us behind the bleachers, and, well, I sort of got in front of them and buried them in dirt."

"And you got in trouble for that?"

"Well, yes, because I didn't even touch the ground. I just put up my hands to stop them, and the dirt sorta flew on top of them. And then Mr. Quirk showed up and said something about my powers returning to me, but Principal Stone carried him off and told me to report to his office the following Monday."

"And who is this Mr. Quirk fellow?" Coy asked.

"He's one of our teachers at school," Ret explained, again a bit shocked by how uninformed he was about his own daughter's life, though he dare not vocalize it.

"Quirk," Mr. Coy mumbled to himself. "A peculiar name, indeed. I'm sure we would get along fine, he and I."

"Probably better than Principal Stone," Ret remarked. "It's like Mr. Quirk is his annoying sidekick or something."

"So you buried these bandits in dirt without ever touching the ground, you say? I see," said Mr. Coy, obviously very deep in thought. "I wonder why my Paige never mentioned any of this to me." Ret worried if Mr. Coy now thought he was some kind of trouble-maker or poor influence and wouldn't let him take his daughter to the winter formal dance. After all, that was the whole reason why he came to Coy Manor in the first place.

"Which reminds me, Mr. Coy," Ret resumed. "The winter formal dance is coming up soon, and I was wondering if…"

"A dance, you say?" Mr. Coy interrupted.

"Yeah," Ret said, "and I was wondering if…"

"Soon, you said?"

"Yes," Ret courteously answered, a little bugged that Mr. Coy was elongating a question that Ret was already finding difficult to ask. "And I…"

"Where will it be?" Mr. Coy asked.

"At the school."

"And when is it, exactly?" He had suddenly turned into a very concerned parent.

"The last Friday before we break for the holidays." Ret decided to just let Mr. Coy ask the questions.

"And will there be any parents or teachers at the dance, you know, as chaperones?" Mr. Coy wanted to know.

"Well, yes…I'm sure there will be," Ret said, slightly confused.

"And you said those chests are inside the principal's office, is that right?"

"Yes, but sir," Ret hurried to say, "I just want to know if I can take Paige to the dance!"

Again: silence. Ret sighed, relieved that the deed was done. Without a word, Mr. Coy slowly turned to face Ret with a look of utter bewilderment. It was the strangest look that anyone had ever given him, which was fitting since Mr. Coy was, without a doubt, the strangest and most bewildering man Ret had ever met. When several moments had passed, Ret timidly asked, "Well?"

"Now *I* have a question for *you*, Mr. Cooper," Coy announced, jumping off the couch and suddenly snapping out of his doldrums. He yanked Ret to his feet and forced him to the center of the room. With one hand, Mr. Coy grabbed Ret's chin and pushed his face upward. "Now don't look down," he instructed. Then, with his other hand, Mr. Coy picked up each of Ret's feet and placed them directly over the two dips in the floor that he had purposely been avoiding all afternoon. Ret was about to lash out in protest when it became clear to him that Mr. Coy was scheming again. Ret played along, a momentary smile forming on his face as he resolved not to be tricked this time by Mr. Coy.

"Keep your chin up," Mr. Coy demanded, releasing Ret and walking backwards. "I'm watching you." Ret maintained eye contact with Mr. Coy, and although he never glanced down, Ret slowly and imperceptibly shuffled both of his feet inwardly until he could feel they were off the dips in the floor, knowing he would outsmart Mr. Coy and not be humiliated again.

"My question is this," Mr. Coy resumed. He rushed to the long, full-length window along the wall and pulled a row of vertical blinds behind him as he dashed the several yards to the other end of the window. The swaying blinds continued to permit the afternoon glow into the room. "Tell me, Mr. Cooper," Coy said, his hand gripping the shutter string. "Have you ever — *Ben Coy?"* Mr. Coy shut the blinds, greatly dimming the light in the room. At the snap of the shutting blinds, Ret felt two strong clasps pin his feet to the floor. Like lightning, his eyes jolted downward, where he saw how two metal hooks had appeared in the shallow dips in the floor and tightly clamped his feet to the ground. Each time Ret had watched Mr. Coy avoid the spots, he had never seen anything lurking within them. Like the invisible bust of Grandmother Coy, the clasps had appeared out of thin air. Ret wondered if the extinguishing of the room's light had anything to do with this phenomenon, but he had only ever known things to hide in the dark — not in the *light*.

"Hold your breath," warned a grinning Mr. Coy. Ret inhaled as he felt the floor immediately around his feet give way, pulling him down through the floorboards and plunging him into water. When the pedestal came to rest on a sandy floor, Ret wondered if he had been ejected from Mr. Coy's cliffside home and onto the bottom of the ocean. When the cloud of displaced sand had settled, Ret's heart stopped to see more than a dozen tiger sharks circling around him menacingly.

When Ret looked down at his feet to see if there was any way of escaping from the metal clasps still holding him captive, he noticed something shimmering in the water: his scar was glowing brightly on his hand! Hope and excitement washed away his fear and panic. With arms at his side and with palms down, Ret stood calmly, believing something would come to his rescue, though not knowing what his lifeline might be.

Seconds passed. The sharks were closing in on him now, but Ret saw no walls of mud or barrage of rocks come to his aid. When he checked on his bonds, he was puzzled to see strands of sand particles swirling around his feet. He watched, curiously and a bit impatiently, as the sand poured into the locks of the metal clamps, when suddenly the locks released their prisoner.

No sooner had Ret's attention returned to his predators than, in an instant, a twelve-foot tiger shark charged, hurtling towards Ret with its massive jaws open wide. With little time to think, Ret braced himself and prepared to strike the beast in the head. He threw his fist at the shark but recoiled in pain when it instead collided with an invisible wall, which the tiger shark also bounced off like a basketball but not without leaving jagged teeth marks along its surface. Immediately, the water drained in Ret's private glass cage. He could hear Mr. Coy cheering and clapping. Catching his breath, Ret followed his ears through a narrow passageway and into an adjacent room where he rejoined Mr. Coy.

"Bravo, bravo!" he congratulated. "Well done, my lad! *Very* well done. Calm under pressure, brave in the face of death, and — " Mr. Coy paused, inspecting Ret's neck, " — underwater so long without any gills. Hip, hip, hooray! I was afraid you might drown, had you not un*locked* the secret of draining the cage! Very coy indeed, Mr. Cooper. I knew I liked you."

"Weird way of showing it," Ret said, wringing water from his shorts. "I could have died, sir."

"Yes, I myself wasn't entirely sure how you would escape," Mr. Coy admitted, "but I certainly knew *this* would come in handy." He grabbed Ret's wrist and revealed his glowing scar.

Ret yanked it back, a bit upset.

"So where are we?" Ret asked.

"Still in the manor, of course, in the east wing's upstairs basement," Mr. Coy explained. "At least, I *think* that's where this is." He scratched his head. "Anywho, this is my personal aquarium, constructed completely of glass." Ret reached down to remove one of his flip-flops and fling it free of water when he saw a squid pass under his feet. "Watch your step!" Mr. Coy cautioned. "Oh, and you'll have to forgive my tiger sharks; apparently they think you're the cat's meow."

"Which is faster, Ret: hot or cold?" Mr. Coy riddled. Ret gave him a blank stare. "Hot," Coy answered. "You can catch a cold." He handed Ret a dry shirt, which he promptly exchanged for his wet one.

Mr. Coy started up a set of glass stairs. Ret followed him, ascending up through the glorified fish tank. Ret thought the sudden lull in conversation was purposely allowed by Mr. Coy so that Ret could take in the impressive beauty of the aquarium, which rivaled a miniature ocean. Schools of swift-moving, shiny-bellied fish parted around the enclosed staircase, which also passed through a huge rock of coral. Rays patrolled the sands below while jelly fish soared like balloons over the carnival of color that was the vibrant reef. The tank seemed to stretch on endlessly, and Ret could identify only a handful of the myriad of specimens: crabs and lobsters, swordfish and tuna, sharks and, "Is that a whale?" Ret asked in amazement, pointing to a slow-moving figure in the darkest recesses.

"Killer, to be exact," came the reply. "Wouldn't hurt a krill," Mr. Coy chuckled.

"Sir, I've been wondering," Ret said, "how do you make things disappear and reappear — you know, like the statue of your mother and that trick you played on me in the other room?"

"*Trick* is such a vulgar, uncouth word," Mr. Coy corrected, "hardly befitting someone as coy as I, so gifted in the clever craft of artifice."

"Okay," Ret conceded, "but how does it work?"

"I call it the Black Mirror," said Mr. Coy. "It's quite simple to understand, really, but you'll forever be in the dark unless you are familiar with the fundamentals of light. Sunlight contains all the colors we can see, yet it has no color at all, which is why it is sometimes called white light. The color of an object, therefore, is the color that it reflects while absorbing the others. For example, a black car parked in summertime heat is considerably warmer than a white car because black absorbs all colors while white reflects just as many."

"Okay," Ret followed.

"Now a mirror is nothing more than a reflective coating applied to a rigid substance, most commonly glass. The reflection comes from the coating, not from the glass, hence the difference between a mirror and a window. I devised a chemically-advanced black coating: it absorbs sunlight, turns black, and then actually reflects its blackness. With a constant supply of white light channeled from the sun as well as an equally constant supply of black light reflected by the mirror, anything caught where they meet has no choice but to disappear. Wouldn't you agree?"

Ret wasn't yet sure what to say.

"The same can be said of life," Mr. Coy related. "Where opposites meet, things become clear." Mr. Coy glanced behind him just long enough to see Ret's puzzled face. "Did that clear things up for you?"

Ret's mind was too enveloped in its own thoughts to notice much of his ever-changing surroundings as he and Mr. Coy snaked up and down and all around the manor. He did, however, wonder if his guide knew where he was going, but the concern soon left Ret when he realized they kept passing through rooms and corridors where he had never set foot before. It was quite a relief when they arrived in the semicircular foyer, where Ana had joined Paige.

"Finally," Ana rejoiced.

"Ret, your shorts are wet," Paige observed, even though they had partially dried during the trek from the aquarium.

"I apologize," Mr. Coy said, "that was my doing. It seems, during our visit together, I made Mr. Cooper feel so fitfully nervous that he couldn't quite control himself." Ana suppressed a laugh while Paige covered her grin with her hand and blushed. Ret glared at Mr. Coy, who gave him a wink and a smile.

"Paige, this is a fine young man," Mr. Coy informed his daughter, putting his arm around Ret. "I'm sure we will all enjoy the dance together."

"*All* of us?" Ret questioned, vocalizing the vexation on the girls' faces.

"Yes, all of us," Mr. Coy reaffirmed. "I'll be attending as a chaperone."

"Oh, Dad!" Paige exploded with joy. She fell on her father and wrapped her arms around his neck. "I'm so happy."

"Yes, well…uh," Mr. Coy mumbled uncomfortably. At a loss of what to do, he gently patted his daughter's back.

"I don't know what you did," Paige confessed emotionally, turning to Ret, "but thank you. Thank you!" She hugged him, kissed him on the cheek, and scurried off through one of the doorways. Mr. Coy and Ret stood motionless for a moment, dazed and confused, their mouths slightly open out of shock, both unsure of what just happened.

"Men," Ana summarized, rolling her eyes. "Thank you, Mr. Coy. See you soon." She grabbed Ret by the arm and pulled him through the front door.

“Goodbye, sir,” Ret said.

Now nearly dusk, they hurried through the gardens of Coy Manor, passed through the front gate, and scampered down the hillside.

“Dating 101, Ret,” Ana said, smiling. “Girls don’t like guys who still wet the bed.” Ret playfully picked up his sister, heaved her giggling over his shoulder, and carried her the rest of the way to the kayak.

Chapter 7

Mediterranean Mayhem

Besides a crisp chill in the air, the onset of winter had also brought a tangible excitement to Tybee Island. Homes were aglitter with holiday décor while shops were abuzz with late-season tourists. High spirits filled the halls of every school as students anxiously awaited their winter break. Even the streets seemed to sing of sleigh bells and snow balls, notwithstanding the absence of both. Despite the high level of festive merriment surging through the island community's power grid, a certain young woman in the Cooper home was inadvertently attempting to trip the breaker.

"Mother, where *is* my necklace?" a flustered Ana demanded more than questioned. Ret knew she was annoyed because she addressed Pauline by her full title and not by the usual *Mom*. For the last several minutes,

Ret had been standing in front of the mirror to see if he looked as ridiculous as he felt in his tuxedo. From his bow tie to his shoe laces, Ret felt like he was in a strait-jacket, and the vibrancy of his skin, hair, and eyes contrasted brilliantly against his black suit.

"You look fine, Ret," Ana said without even glancing in his direction, "now help me find my necklace."

"Alright," Ret conceded peacefully, "what does it look like?"

"It's a string of red corals," she described.

"Red corals?" Ret asked, recalling something he had once read about the prized rock jewels. "You mean, the stuff they harvest from the bottom of the ocean?"

"Probably," Ana ignored. "Aha! Here it is!" She sought help from the mirror as she draped the beaded necklace around her neck. Suddenly, Ret appeared at her side.

"You *do* know those are the exoskeletons of tiny organisms, right?" he teased.

"Why no, Ret, I didn't know that," she replied sarcastically. "Do *you* know what the theme of tonight's dance is?" He gave her a blank stare. *"A Night on the Mediterranean,"* she announced dreamily, taking Ret by the hand and futilely trying to dance with him. "And that's exactly where Dad bought this necklace — from a merchantman on the coast of Libya."

"And *why* did he buy it for you?" Pauline asked, joining them.

"Because it's beautiful," Ana said, matter-of-factly.

"Yes," Pauline agreed, "*and* because red corals are worn as a talisman in some cultures to protect against evil spirits." Ret and Ana looked at each other incredulously, doubting the folklore. "He always worried about his girls when he was away. He loved us." Pauline, her eyes moistening, put her arm around her daughter. "All of us," she added, including Ret in her embrace.

"Now," Pauline said with soberness, "I want you to be extra careful tonight, young lady. Do you understand?"

"Yes, Mother," Ana replied, bored by the repeated reminder.

"You're very beautiful, and you're only a freshman, and — "

"Don't worry, Mom," Ana reassured. "Bubba's a real gentleman."

"And just how much do you know about this *Bubba* fellow, hmm?" Pauline pressed. "You say he's an upperclassman, but which class exactly?" She chased Ana with her questions into the bathroom. "I've spoken with several neighbors, and none of them is familiar with a boy named Bubba." Ana hurried back into her room, trying to escape the interrogation. "And how about a last name — you still haven't given me one."

"Like I told you before, *Mother*," Ana said, obviously perturbed, "our conversation was brief. He asked if he could take me to the dance; I asked if he would wear a powder-blue tux. He said he'd be delighted to and that he'd pick me up at eight. That's it," she stated with closure.

"What do you mean *that's it?*" Pauline protested, launching another barrage of questions. "And how did he know your name? *Does* he know your name? You told me you've never spoken to each other before. And he didn't ask for your address? How does he know where you live?"

"What does it matter, Mother? It's just a school dance. And besides," Ana said romantically, "he's *really* cute."

"That's what I'm afraid of," Pauline confessed.

Just then, the doorbell rang, sending a shockwave of electricity through Ana.

"Oh," she gasped, "that must be Bubba. Hurry, Ret; go downstairs and let him in. I'll be down in a minute." Ret gladly obeyed.

It wasn't until Ret saw Bubba's attire that he started to feel better about his own. Ret had never seen such a ridiculous outfit, finding it to be more appropriate for trick-or-treating. The top hat was one thing, but it was the light blue shoes that put Ret over the top. Maybe it was just his size, but the suit seemed a bit too small for

Bubba, and even though it was laughable, Ret doubted that anyone would dare to make fun of him for fear of being pulverized. Still, perhaps on account of the ruffled shirt, combined with the coattails, Ana's date looked like a blue jay.

"Hey, Bubba," Ret greeted him at the door, "I'm …"

"Ret, it's a pleasure to meet you," Bubba interrupted, giving Ret a hearty handshake and striding by him on his way inside.

"Won't you come in," Ret mumbled to himself, still facing the empty porch.

"This is a fine home you've got here," Bubba observed, strolling through several rooms like an appraiser, "excellent layout, if you ask me."

Ret figured he ought to entertain their guest. "So you're familiar with — "

"Oh, yes," Bubba interjected again. "I just finished a two-week internship for the city's archives department. Of all the models, this one makes the most sense, what with the two-car garage, the guest bathroom downstairs, and the attic above the master bedroom."

"No," Ret corrected, though confused by the subject of their dialogue, "the attic's above the other bedrooms."

"Oh, of course it is," Bubba conceded, making eye contact with Ret for the first time. "That's right." Bubba sat on the couch and began to rapidly type on his cell phone. This afforded Ret a moment to study him unawares. His suit wrapped around his figure snugly enough to reveal the curves of a chiseled physique, but this was not nearly as intriguing to Ret, unlike Ana, as was Bubba's curiously-colored skin. As his hands were gloved, the only skin visible was on his face and neck, which all seemed very normal except for a small area behind each ear, which looked very pale. Then Ret noticed the hair at the back of Bubba's head, which looked bright red — the little of it he could see, that is, since his top hat had been pulled down nearly all the way. It all appeared a bit bizarre, what with such hair color inconsistent with that of his eyebrows, but, then again, it was not all that uncommon for young people to dye their hair.

Ret's gaze shifted when Ana came into view. With angelic serenity, she silently made her descent, the only sound coming from her dress as it dusted the carpeted stairs at her feet. The long sleeves of her faintly pink gown stretched in vain to kiss her long white gloves. Her treasured red coral necklace accented her crimson lips, and her hair had been delicately tied up behind her head.

Before Bubba could rise to his feet at the sight of Ana, something happened so instantaneously that it nearly went unnoticed. Ret first felt his finger twinge and then saw one of Ana's red corals shoot from her necklace and pelt Bubba in the face. It was enough to knock him back in his seat, and though he surprisingly did not rub the injured area, Ret noticed a slight white mark where the contact had been made. Ana daintily raised her hand to her necklace, thinking her jewelry had adjusted during her descent, and Bubba played it cool. Ret tried to secretly inspect his hand, for his scar seemed to faintly glow, although he wondered if that was merely the reflection of Bubba's suit.

"My, you look gorgeous," Bubba admiringly told Ana. He raised her hand to his lips and gently kissed it. Ret rolled his eyes, Ana giving him a look like she had just met her very own knight in shining armor.

"So you must be Bubba," Pauline's voice preceded her as she, too, came downstairs.

"Ah, Mrs. Cooper," Bubba greeted with a smile. "Now I see where Ana gets her good looks." Pauline was obviously very flattered, partly by the compliment but mostly by the realization that Ana wasn't kidding about her date's attractiveness.

"Smooth move, Bubba," Ret muttered inaudibly.

Suddenly charmed, Pauline said, "Well, *Bubba*, tell us a little about yourself."

"Why, Mrs. Cooper," Bubba replied modestly, "I'd much rather learn about your lovely daughter, Ana." As he moved to put his arm around her, Ret sensed another jerk of his finger and watched as a second red coral hurled itself from Ana's necklace, colliding with Bubba's chin.

"Ouch," Bubba winced.

"What?" Ana worried when she didn't feel his embrace. "Is something wrong?"

"Oh, no!" Bubba fibbed. "It's just that you're so — so *hot!*" Pauline and Ana burst into laughter as their enchanting comedian pretended to recoil from touching a hot surface.

"No, really," Pauline politely persisted, "you must tell us more about yourself, Bubba."

"Well," he began, looking a bit nervous. Then the doorbell intervened.

"Saved by the bell," Ret mumbled.

Pauline crossed the room to the entry and opened the door. On the other side stood Paige. Her large blonde curls glided on the slick black shoulders of her silk dress with even the slightest movement. A white sash wrapped around her waist and culminated in a modest-sized bow, matching Ret's white vest and pleated shirt. For a brief moment, everyone in the room fell silent, slightly taken aback by the conspicuous beauty of such an inconspic-uous girl.

Pleasantries were exchanged, pictures were taken, and the couples readied themselves to leave. When Ana and Bubba were safely outside, Ret picked up one of the fallen red corals for further inspection. He noticed a brown smudge on its surface and, wiping it off, found it to be some sort of oily, powdery substance.

"Whatcha got there?" Paige poked.

"Oh, nothing," Ret said hastily.

"It's beautiful," she observed. "Did you get it for me?"

"Uh, yes," pretended Ret. "Here you go."

"I will treasure it always," Paige promised sweetly, slipping it into her pocket.

"Come on," Ret urged, wanting to change the subject. "Let's not keep everyone waiting."

They made their way to the curb in front of the Cooper's home where a black limousine was awaiting them. Inside, they found Mr. Coy in the back seat, with Ivan, the Coys' Russian butler, at the wheel as their chauffeur.

"Good evening, Mr. Coy," Ana said politely.

"So far," Coy replied. All that could be seen of him was his dark silhouette, so dim was the moonlight, so dark were the windows' tint. No one joined him on his side of the cabin, where he had extinguished all of the dome lights. Paige and the Coopers didn't think twice about Mr. Coy's odd and mysterious behavior, but Bubba was brimming with wonder.

"The famous Mr. Coy," Bubba said in awe.

"Are you sure you don't mean *infamous?"* Coy snickered under his breath.

"Are they true?" Bubba wondered earnestly. "You know, the things they say about you?"

"Is it true you're dressed like a blueberry?" Mr. Coy rebutted. Ana blushed while Ret suppressed a laugh.

"Dad!" Paige snapped, expressing her disapproval.

"Well, at least *some* of the things are true," Bubba concluded, rolling his eyes. Feeling a bit disappointed, he leaned back in his seat and put his hand on Ana's knee. Astonished by such forward behavior, Ret kept a careful watch.

"You got a name, bluey?" Mr. Coy asked.

"Bubba," was his answer.

"Suits you well," Coy assessed. "Now I've a question for you." Mr. Coy lunged forward, prompting everyone to shrink unexpectedly with fright. "Have you ever — *Ben Coy?*" The sudden shock caused Bubba to squeeze Ana's leg. Rather impulsively, Ret's hand jolted, sending another red coral as a projectile towards Bubba's wandering hand. Bubba's hand retreated, writhing in pain.

"I've been trying to be coy all night!" Bubba said in consternation.

"Tho thorry to interrupt," Ivan announced from the cockpit, "but ve have arrive-ed."

And they certainly had. Ivan parked in front of Tybee High and opened the passenger door, extending his hand to assist the girls.

When everyone else had exited, Ret, who was feeling somewhat apprehensive about the evening, turned to Mr. Coy and asked, "Any advice, sir?"

"Yes," he said cheerily. "Always tip your hat and shine your shoes." When Ret looked back at Mr. Coy for an explanation, he noticed a curious cap on his head. Its flat top, which extended beyond his head a few inches in all directions and was extraordinarily clear, remained in place thanks to an elastic string pulled under his chin. In many respects, it looked like a cross between an upside-down dinner plate and a party hat. Then Ret glanced at the black shoes of Mr. Coy's tuxedo, which were as shiny as glass. Mr. Coy reached to adjust his hat, which sent bright light shining downward from underneath its overhanging rim.

"Tip your hat," he repeated. Then he rose from his seat and squatted in the middle of the limousine. For a brief moment, the light from his hat shined on his shoes, and then he disappeared from sight. "And shine your shoes," his voice said. He reappeared when he leaned back in his chair, the hat's light shining on his lap.

"The black mirror," Ret deduced with amazement.

"Travel size," Mr. Coy smiled with pride. "All thanks to miniature solar panels. Now, don't you have a dance to attend?"

"We both do," Ret reminded him.

"Yes, well, don't wait for me." And, with that, Mr. Coy stepped out of the car and vanished from sight.

And just in time, too. Ret had scarcely caught up with Ivan, who was following behind Bubba and the girls as they made their way to the school's main doors, when he heard someone yell, "There he is!" Suddenly, an army of reporters and newscasters emerged from the shadows, video rolling and cameras flashing. Ret's heart skipped a beat as he realized his worst nightmare was coming true — that he would be made the center of attention at an event he hardly wanted to attend — when, to his surprise, the crowd surged around Ivan.

"Mr. Coy! Mr. Coy!" they shouted at the bewildered butler. "What made you decide to finally reveal yourself?"

"Mr. Coy! Mr. Coy!" every mouth hollered at Ivan. "What business brought you to Tybee Island?"

"What goes on in your elaborate house?"

"Why did you ruin our nature preserve?"

"Why have you never shown your face before?"

The cameras' flashes blinded Ivan like lightning. The commentators' microphones sprang up in front of him like weeds. Ret and his friends were squeezed to the sidelines.

"He's not my dad! He's not Mr. Coy!" Paige protested till she was red in the face, her voice lost in the uproar. She turned to her party and asked, "Where *is* my dad?"

"Ret was the last one out of the limo," Ana was quick to point out. Paige turned to Ret for an answer.

"He's around here somewhere," was all he could say. They watched as Mr. Kirkpatrick, the assistant principal, pried Ivan away from the mob and rushed him inside the school.

"Zith ith an outrrage!" Ivan declared once they were safely on the other side of the melee.

"I sincerely apologize, Mr. Coy," Mr. Kirkpatrick said, his anxiety apparent. "I am Mr. Kirkpatrick, the assistant principal. Principal Stone wishes he could have been here to meet you, but he had other business to attend to this evening."

"My name ith *not* Mithterr Coy!" Ivan's fury only exacerbated his thick accent and lisp.

"I know you're upset, sir," Mr. Kirkpatrick consoled, talking quickly, "but we're certainly glad to have your help chaperoning tonight. Do you mind taking this station at the beverage counter?"

"And I am *not* a thaperrone!" Ivan stated. "In my countrry, ve doo not haf zethe thaperrone zingth. Do you know vhat we haf in my countrry? A czar! Czarth ith vhat ve haf — or, at leatht ve uthed to. None of zethe thaperrone people."

"Here you go," the assistant principal nudged, shepherding Ivan behind the drink bar. "Enjoy your night on the Mediterranean," he said, happily walking away. "Oh, and have a few drinks on the house!"

Realizing he was stuck at his post, Ivan surveyed his surroundings. "A thaperrone — ha! At leatht ze decorrationth ith love-ely. Rremindth me of beaooteefool Rruthia."

The dance's Mediterranean theme was most befitting for such a formal event. The school's ordinary commons had been transformed into a museum of Old World style and detail. Elaborate tapestries concealed lockers while ornate rugs dampened the mincing of girls' heels. Metal wall grills hung between paintings of manicured vineyards and portraits of fruit and floral displays. Bright-colored table cloths ran along the bases of wrought iron candleholders and dishes of pure olive oil. Unsightly corners had been turned into attractive nooks where friends lounged in orange and golden yellow armchairs under portions of a fabricated tile roof. A few windows had been cracked to allow the salty sea breeze to mingle with the scent of lavender and rosemary shrubs.

"How romantic," Ana sighed as they toured the commons, determined not to let the evening's raucous start lessen her fantasy.

"I can't believe he's not here," Paige said, obviously upset. "I just can't believe it! No, actually, I *can* because this is what always happens. He *always* breaks his promises."

"It's okay, Paige," Ret said, trying to console her. "I'm sure he'll turn up soon. You never know with your dad; he may just appear out of thin air." She gave him a funny look. "I'm sure what he's doing is very important."

"That's what he always says," Paige said, rolling her eyes. "I need a Pepsi." She made a beeline for the drink shack. Ret followed her, relieved that the dance floor wasn't part of her stress relief.

"I'll have the usual, Ivan," she ordered.

"Coming rright up," he obeyed. "I zink I am getting ze hang of zith thaperrone zing, vouldn't you thay? All ov *ze* childeren love me!"

"That's because they all think you're Mr. Coy," Ret pointed out.

"Yeah," Paige said in between sips, "apparently being a deadbeat dad makes you a celebrity."

"Ana, my dear," Ivan said loudly, seeing her coming. "Vhat can I get foorr you and your blue frriend?" Ana skipped from the dance floor to the beverage counter, pulling Bubba behind her. The song had just ended, and they were breathing heavily and happily.

"Oh, just some water, Ivan," she panted, though smiling. "Bubba sure knows how to dance. Nice apron, Ivan."

"Zank you," Ivan replied. "I found it in one of ze drawerrs. Your vaterr, madam."

"Thank you," Ana said, receiving the cup from Ivan. She turned to face Ret and Paige and asked, "Some dance, huh?" With his elbow on the bar, Ret supported his head with his fist while Paige downed the rest of her Pepsi, slammed the cup on the counter, and wiped her upper lip clean with the back of her hand.

"Come on, girl," Ana said, grabbing Paige by the wrist. "Tell me all about it in the ladies' room." They hurried off.

Ret passed the time by keeping a careful eye on Bubba. On account of his outlandish suit, he was not hard to spot as he wandered among the student body. Strangely, he never stopped to talk with anyone, and no one seemed to recognize him, which Ret thought was odd for such an outgoing upperclassman. If anything, he looked suspicious, especially when Ret saw him finally speaking with someone.

"Evening, Quirk."

"Evening, Bubba. Love the suit."

"I feel like a clown," Bubba said. He glanced at Mr. Quirk's garb, a bright yellow, double-breasted suit with green polka dots, and added insultingly, "Now I know how you must feel every day."

"*I* think you look rather dashing," Quirk admitted.

"You would," Bubba said. "Where's Stone?"

"Not here, as planned."

"Did he get my text?" Bubba asked.

"Oh, yes," Quirk answered. "He sends his thanks."

"Cooper took the bait."

"He always does," said Quirk. "And his sister?"

"She's head over heels for me, which is understandable."

"Well you'd better head back to Mr. Cooper's side," Quirk instructed, "because here come those heels now." He discreetly pointed towards Ana and Paige as they reemerged from the restroom. "Come and get me when you're ready," Quirk reminded, "and remember: act natural," and suddenly his body became alive with the music as he galloped onto the dance floor.

The beat and bass of the lively dance sounded more like a faint pulse to Mr. Coy as he undetectably made his way to the administrators' offices. Once safely inside the main wing, he tipped his hat, cutting off the stored solar light and reappearing.

"Waste not," he said to himself. In no time at all, he located Principal Stone's office. He checked the doorknob: locked.

"My specialty," Coy grinned. He retrieved a small item from his pocket and rolled it between his hands until it was long and thin. Then he slowly forced the semi-solid substance into the keyhole and waited for it to harden. After a few seconds, he turned his freshly-formed key and gently pushed open the door.

"If only the creators of Silly Putty knew what they were on to." Coy stepped into the office to let the faint light from the hall penetrate the shadows within.

"There you are," Mr. Coy said, spotting the two trunks just as Ret had described. He knelt in front of them and analyzed his next move. Though they were both closed, only one of the trunks was clasped shut by a large, metal lock.

"I never was the overachieving type," Coy admitted. "I'll get to you next," he said, deciding not to bother with the ominous lock until later. He undid the simple fastener on the unlocked chest and lifted up the lid, sending dirt and dust into the air and onto the floor. He pinched a ring on his finger, which began to glow brightly, aiding him as he started to rummage.

Meanwhile, life on the Mediterranean carried on swimmingly.

"Who's up for a little Turkish delight?" Bubba announced as he served Ana a plate, followed by Ret and Paige. "I'll be right back. Save some for me!" As he paced away, he winked at Ana.

"Isn't he wonderful?" Ana asked, lost in her daydream.

"Yeah," Ret answered sarcastically, his mouth full of dessert, "delightful."

Bubba pushed and shoved his way onto the dance floor until he found Mr. Quirk.

"Quirk," he exclaimed, "it's time!"

"Not now, Bubba," he protested. "Can't you see I'm leading the conga?"

"Your diversion's working, now get going!" Bubba yanked Quirk from his place at the head of the line. Quirk slipped out of the room while Bubba returned to the table.

"Ana, Ana!" he called. "Follow me. I've got a surprise for you." She stood up without delay and giddily went to him. A few seconds later, Ret grabbed Paige's hand.

"Come on," he said. "He's up to something."

Ret's gaze remained fixed on Bubba as he snaked with Ana through the crowd, out of the dance hall, and down one of the long corridors of classrooms. Having escaped the music, Ret was no longer calling after them in vain.

"Where do you think you're going, Bubba?" Bubba turned around sharply to face his questioner. "I've been watching you all night." Ret continued to advance toward them, pulling Paige behind him. "Now it's time for some answers."

Ret had just come to a complete stop when Ana and Paige suddenly became hostages simultaneously. While Bubba pinned his arm against Ana's throat and yanked her up against him, Ret felt Paige's hand slip away and then heard her scream as Mr. Quirk held her in the same position. Ret held his ground in the middle, not sure where to look.

"Surprise," Bubba whispered in Ana's ear.

"Get your hands off me, you creep!" Ana demanded.

"Tsk-tsk, Miss Cooper," Quirk hissed, "that's not how Tybee High treats its guests."

"I knew it," Ret chimed in. "You don't even go to school here, do you, Bubba?"

"Took you long enough," Bubba teased.

"Now, Ret," Quirk asserted, "cooperate with us, or watch your friends suffer."

"Don't give in, Ret," Ana advised, squirming in Bubba's chokehold, "I can take 'em."

"What do you want with *me?*" Ret asked. "I'm of no use to you."

"It's true," Quirk said. "By yourself, you're just a meddlesome twerp. *But*, add a certain spherical artifact to the equation, and you suddenly become the quintessential element — the top dog, the big cheese, the hotshot, the whole enchilada, the ivory dome, the real McCoy, the kit and caboodle, the VIP of this mystery — "

"Quirk!" Bubba interjected.

" — though I still think you're a meddlesome twerp," Quirk finished.

"Did you say spherical artifact?" Ret asked, pretending not to know anything about Mr. Coy's sphere in order to see if Mr. Quirk knew any additional information about it.

"Don't play dumb with me, boy," Quirk snapped. "After countless months of searching, we finally know where it's been all this time — in *your* attic! Principal Stone has likely raided your home by now, which means all we need is *you.*"

"You robbed our house?" Ana said indignantly. "Ret, what is he talking about? I've got to call Mom. Let me go!"

It was after Ana had finished speaking when Ret noticed the white mark on Bubba's face again. He suddenly knew what to do. For several seconds, he stood entirely motionless until he knew everyone was watching him. Then, with both hands at his side, he quickly jerked both of his index fingers. A pair of red corals launched from Ana's necklace, each one pelting one of Bubba's eyes. He released his hold to rub his eyes, by which time Ana had spun around and pulled Bubba's top hat tightly over his face. Ana flew to Ret's side. On their way out, they grabbed Paige, who managed to slip away from Quirk when the red coral, which was still nestled in her pocket from earlier that evening, shot straight up one of Mr. Quirk's nostrils, sending him into violent convulsions of coughing and snorting.

They hadn't fled far when they realized they were being pursued. Bubba, sprinting at full speed, quickly surpassed Mr. Quirk, who was still trying to snot-rocket the red coral out of his nose. Bubba's true colors were fully visible now: the absence of his hat left uncovered his hair, bright red and flaming like fire, and his rubbing had not only knocked the colored contacts out of his eyes, which now were also red, but also removed the makeup around his eyes, revealing pale white skin.

"How's life past midnight, Cinderella?" Ana jabbed, making fun of Bubba's new look as they neared the door to the dance hall. "I'd be mad, too, if *my* head was on fire."

During the faceoff between Ret and his antagonists, an event sparked by Ivan proved to be the killjoy of the entire dance. Word had gotten around that Paige Coy's father was in the building, and as the lure of the dance floor began to wane, most of the students had gathered around the drink bar to gape and gawk at the famous Mr. Coy. Ivan had since ceased trying to set straight his true identity, for no one quite believed him, and he didn't exactly loathe all of the attention. The students were captivated — or, perhaps, entertained — by his accent, and he had no problem answering their questions about his former life in his homeland.

The trouble arose when someone asked Ivan to conjure up a typical Russian soda, which he gladly did. When Ivan handed the fizzing beverage to the requestor, the boy accepted it sheepishly. Soon, the crowd began to chant, "Chug, chug, chug, chug!" That's when Ivan turned to the lad and said, "Vell, boy, good luck. Orr, ath zay thay in ze Maydeeteerranean, mathel tov!"

"Did he just say *Molotov?"* someone in the group asked. In an instant, the chants to chug turned into whispers of worry.

"No, I think he said *mazel tov,"* a girl correctly pointed out, too quietly to be heard above the uneasy crowd's murmuring. "It means 'good luck' in Hebrew." But it was too late.

"It's a Molotov cocktail!" a young man shrieked. "It's a bomb! He's a Russian spy!"

At the word *bomb*, everything about the situation exploded — everything except the drink, of course. The guests scattered every whichway like insects before pesticide. The music stopped, the lights went on, and pure pandemonium reigned.

"Vath it thomething I thaid?" Ivan wondered, standing still behind the counter. "Don't zhey teach Hebrew in thchool zhethe dayth?"

The dance was engulfed in these chaotic circumstances when Ret and the girls returned to the scene. They darted towards the bar, where they found Ivan still in shock.

"I *don't* haf a bomb, I thwayr!" he promised.

"Come on, Ivan," they said, "let's get out of here." They set off for the car.

Quirk and Bubba struggled to pursue their runaways in the teeming crowd.

"A bomb?" Quirk asked, repeating what he was hearing from all around him. "Did you bring the bomb?"

"No," Bubba said, "but I wish I had – they're getting away!"

The transition from music to mayhem did not go unnoticed by Mr. Coy. He knew his time was limited. He abandoned his unsuccessful attempts to unlock the second trunk and grabbed what he had found in the first one: a single sheet of worn parchment paper bearing ancient characters. Then he shut the lid, closed the door, and activated his black mirror. He was calmly sitting in the limousine when his daughter and the Coopers piled in.

"Put the pedal to the metal, Ivan," Ana ordered, "now!"

"I doo not know vhat zhat meanth," he spoke rapidly, "but, judging by zhe tone ov your voice, I veell drrive verry quick-ely."

"Hey, look," Ret pointed out cheerfully, "it's your dad." Paige said nothing, refusing to even look at her father.

"How was the dance?" Mr. Coy thought he should ask.

"A total bomb!" Ana blurted out.

"Where's your Smurf friend?" Coy asked. Ana

made no reply, turning to look out the window. Ret gave Mr. Coy a sign to not press the subject.

"Right," Coy said, agreeing with Ret who was sitting between Ana and Paige, both staring out their windows. "And I thought girls *enjoyed* school dances. *I've* learned something tonight."

"Just hurry up and take us home," Ana implored. "Mom's in danger; she's not answering her phone."

Mr. Coy looked at Ret for clarification.

"Quirk ambushed us again tonight," Ret explained. "He said Principal Stone raided our house in search of your sphere."

"*Your* sphere?" Ana balked. "Just what exactly is going on here?"

"Paper or plastic?" Mr. Coy asked, grimacing playfully. "No matter — cat's out of the bag."

Just then they arrived at the Cooper house, which was blockaded by police vehicles. They all hurried out of the car. Ignoring the caution tape's perimeter, Ana dashed inside the house. Paige stood by Ret.

"I'll handle the boys in blue," Mr. Coy told them, adjusting his belt. He strutted into the group of police officers. Ret couldn't hear what he told them, but in a matter of minutes, they cleaned up and left the scene entirely.

Inside the house, the three of them found Ana sitting on the couch, consoling her mother, who looked terribly shaken up.

"I was in bed, reading," she said, her lips quivering. "I heard voices — men's voices, unfamiliar." She was staring distraughtly into space as she recounted the event. "They thundered upstairs, headed straight for the attic. They were searching, searching for something — and didn't find it — and got angry." Her sniffles interrupted her narrative after every couple of words. "I ran — they caught me — two of them. They yelled at me — where is it, where is it! I told them I didn't know." Her tears were on the verge. "Then they searched the whole house — and did this." She swept the room with her hand: furniture overturned, cupboards and drawers dumped out, not an inch untouched. "I don't even know what they wanted."

With a mixture of pity and anger in his heart, Ret glared at Mr. Coy. "We do. We know what they wanted."

Mr. Coy returned Ret's stare with a look of unpleasant surprise. Then he nodded in conciliatory agreement. "Yes, we do." He pulled the piece of ancient parchment paper out from behind his suit coat. Ret's eyes widened.

"Quick, everyone," Mr. Coy announced, his arm shooting into the air, "to the Batcave!" Nobody moved, choosing instead to stare at him awkwardly. "I've always wanted to say that."

They all climbed in the limo, en route to Coy

Manor, ready for answers to their questions: Pauline, why she'd been robbed by Principal Stone; Ana, how she'd been deceived by Bubba; Paige, how to earn her father's love; Mr. Coy, how to solve his life's ultimate riddle; Ret, how he could possibly be the quintessential element; and Ivan, what his boss would say about tomorrow's front page.

CHAPTER 8

THE STATUTORY STUDATORY

"Bonjour, monsieur!"

Ret's eyes tiredly rolled open at the sound of the soft yet melodious voice of one of Coy Manor's maids. With short, quick steps, she marched to the window and drew the curtains, unveiling the day and flooding the room with the blinding rays of the morning sun.

"Crêpes, monsieur?" the maid said timidly, extending a tray of food towards Ret. A stack of steaming crepes was surrounded by a colorful assortment of fruit fillings, with a sliced baguette on the side and a dollop of whipped cream melting atop a mug of hot cocoa.

"Oui, oui!" Ret replied, employing the little French he knew and suddenly sitting up in his bed with hungry enthusiasm. The maid obligingly set the tray across Ret's lap and then scampered out of the room, passing a gaggle of other maids who were peeking in the doorway. When Ret saw them, they giggled and quickly dispersed.

"Glad to see you're finally awake," Ana remarked as she strolled into the room. Ret made no reply, too enveloped in his flavorful meal. "I take it you're enjoying breakfast."

"Delicious," Ret said quickly between bites.

"A little thin for French toast, if you ask me," Ana joked, "but still good. I see you made some new friends?" She pointed to the now-empty doorway.

"Who, the maids?" Ret asked in disbelief.

"They spent half the morning fighting over who would get to serve you breakfast!" Ana said. "Apparently Paige has told them all about you."

"Well, I'm no Bubba," Ret smirked.

"No," Ana sighed, "but you two *do* look a lot alike."

"How'd we get here anyway?" Ret wondered.

"You'll find out later," Paige answered, suddenly appearing in the doorway. "First, my dad wants everyone to report to his studatory right away."

"What the crepe is a *studatory?*" Ana asked, sampling one of Ret's fillings with her finger.

"It's just a fancy word for the fourth floor's study and laboratory," Paige explained, "although my dad says he named it after himself." They all smiled. "I'll go and get your mom; then we can all go up together."

As soon as they embarked for the studatory, the Coopers felt relieved to have Paige as their guide; otherwise, they most certainly would have gotten lost in the Manor and may not have been found for hours. Ret found it so easy to lose his way, partly because he never really knew where he was going but mostly due to the unending supply of intriguing things to behold.

"My goodness, Paige," Pauline said with wonder in her voice, "how do you know where you're going around here?"

"I have to keep up on it," Paige replied. "Dad likes to rearrange things all the time — take out a hallway here, rearrange an entire floor there. He says it's good for everyone — takes his mind off other things and gives the staff something to do." She paused for a few minutes until they had all reached the next floor by climbing from tail to skull along the fossilized spine of some ancient dinosaur's skeleton. "Except one day I came home from school and spent the rest of the afternoon trying to find my bedroom; turns out, while I was gone, Dad had it moved to the north wing, a couple floors down, and forgot to tell me." She ducked to dodge an oncoming model plane as it whizzed overhead. "He's very specific about where I can and can't go — says it's for my own safety."

"Don't you ever want to just sneak around and see all the cool stuff around here?" Ret asked, staring down a separate corridor where he saw a sea of miscellaneous, metallic objects suspended in midair between a series of large magnets lining the walls.

"Tried it," Paige confessed candidly, "but I got caught. Dad's got eyes everywhere." She pointed to a nearby wall clock, where a tiny lens could be seen in the zero of the number ten. "Besides, most doors require some sort of authentication to unlock them anyway. For example, take the gold-plated door to the studatory." She came to a halt in front of it, then used a jeweled ring from her finger to scratch a word on the door's soft surface. She stepped back to let the Coopers watch her signature disappear as it was absorbed into the door, which promptly opened.

"Sure beats *open sesame,*" Ana whispered as Paige ushered them inside.

So far, Ret had come to find that the only thing to expect in Coy Manor was the unexpected, and the studatory was no different. Every inch of every wall in the round room was filled with every kind of book imaginable: atlases and encyclopedias, brochures and dictionaries, magazines and portfolios, manuals and textbooks, even rolls of scrolls. The floor was transparent glass, and Ret marveled as the Coys' library extended without end above his head and below his feet.

Globes of all colors and sizes roamed the room in their wheeled stands like librarians while long ladders tickled the spines of the books they crossed, stretching out of sight in both directions. It was quiet; it was peaceful. It was a study.

And in the center of the study sat the laboratory. As large as it was, the entire lab was encapsulated by a single bubble – thin enough for a person to pass through but dense enough to prevent any sound from escaping. Inside, Mr. Coy was a scientist hard at work, although, with so many things going on at once all under the same tent, he looked more like the ringleader of a circus. Broths bubbled and venoms veined through a maze of jugs and jars. Flasks and beakers spewed their frothy contents, emitting sparks and gases. A set of soiled slides hung for analysis near a group of microscopes. The surging currents of a pair of electric generators occasionally connected, shooting electricity through the air like lightning. Amid smoke and shrapnel, Mr. Coy lit up the scene with a blowtorch.

"DAD!" Paige yelled, trying to get his attention. "DAD!" Mr. Coy remained undistracted behind his welding mask. "You know, he *still* hasn't apologized for last night," Paige informed Ana as she walked to the outer edge of the lab. She reached inside the bubble, picked up a thick washer from the table, and hurled it in her father's direction. The washer collided with Mr.

Coy's metal mask, knocking him over and many other things with him. Disorder engulfed the lab as chemicals spilled, instruments fell, and solutions exploded. Paige walked back to join the Coopers, who watched the disastrous tumult in shocked silence.

When Mr. Coy at last rose from the wreckage, his knees momentarily gave way at the realization that his guests were present. He turned his back to them just long enough to freshen up. He tucked in halfway the splattered shirt of his tuxedo; then, moistening his hand in whatever substance was oozing down the desk at his side, he slicked back his hair. Turning sharply on his heels, he carefully stepped out of the lab and into the study.

"Welcome to my — *studatory,*" Mr. Coy greeted them as he struck several poses like some kind of muscleman.

"Mr. Coy, you don't look so hot," Ret commented.

"Yes, well, I'm not as young as I used to be," Coy admitted, abandoning his futile flexing.

"No, I mean, you look terrible," Ret reaffirmed. "Did you get any sleep last night?"

"Not a wink, my boy — not a wink!"

Ret believed him. Still outfitted in last night's tux, Mr. Coy's bowtie was dangling from his neck, and large chunks of his hair were sticking out in random directions. His bloodshot eyes drooped in fatigue, and his face had long since seen its five o'clock shadow. Stains and splotches besmirched his suit, whose cuffs looked a bit singed.

"While the rest of you were *snoozing,"* Mr. Coy said with a hint of condescension, "I spent the entire night *perusing* — this!" He slammed a ragged piece of parchment paper on a table near his listeners. Paige picked it up for a closer look.

"In all my years of experience and study in linguistics and translation," Coy continued, *"never* have I encountered such a bewildering bunch of foreign characters. The letters fly the flag of all the world's major languages yet pledge allegiance to none of them."

Paige passed the parchment on to Ana.

"Fortunately," said Coy, "I am hardly a novice when it comes to radiocarbon dating, and my preliminary test results suggest that the artifact is somewhere between five and 500,000 years old."

"Um, Mr. Coy, I'm no scientist," Ana admitted, "but that doesn't sound very — "

" — Exactly!" Coy asserted. "Which is why, after consulting every reference and exhausting every resource, I was stunned by what I saw rising in the smoke of my burned midnight oil." With voice mysteriously subdued, Mr. Coy clawed at the air to portray his search amid metaphorical smoke. A few moments transpired with his listeners on edge to learn of his conclusion.

"What?" Ana asked urgently. "What did you discover?"

"Nothing!" Coy shrieked. "Not a thing!" And, dejectedly, he slumped onto the sofa.

"Sir, if I may ask," Pauline said politely, "where exactly did you get this?" She received the parchment from Ana as it continued to be passed down the line like a baton.

"I stole it from Stone's office," Coy said unabashed.

"You *robbed* our principal?" Paige asked indignantly.

"It was Ret's idea," Coy fibbed.

"It was *not!"* Ret interjected.

"So that's why he invaded *my* house!" Pauline jumped to conclusions. "You knew about this all along, didn't you, Mr. Coy? What are you, some kind of spy?"

Ivan had scarcely set foot in the studatory to deliver refreshments when, upon hearing someone accused of being a spy, he promptly departed, the memory of last night's accusation still fresh in his mind.

"You're not telling us something," Pauline persisted, handing the parchment to Ret so she could plant both of her hands on her hips. "You know more than you're letting on."

"Ma'am, if that's your way of complimenting my superior intellect," Coy said calmly, "then I am flattered indeed."

"Good grief," Pauline complained. "Thank you for your hospitality," she said, facing Paige, "but I feel we have worn out our welcome. Come, Ret and Ana; let's head for home."

"Hold on," Ret petitioned, his eyes glued to the paper now that it was finally his turn to examine it. "You really can't read this, Mr. Coy?"

Mr. Coy stared at Ret in disgust. "Well what a lovely family," he said cheerily. "After Polly knocks 'em to the floor, Boy Wonder kicks 'em while they're down. And how about the girl — what's she do? Spray mace in their eyes?"

"I'm sorry, sir," Ret apologized, "I didn't mean to insult you; it's just — "

"Well that makes *one* of you," Mr. Coy sneered, rolling his eyes at Pauline.

" — It's just that these letters look familiar," Ret explained. Everyone fell silent for a few moments.

"Can you read them?" Paige wondered.

"Yeah," Ret replied, gaining confidence the more he stared at the characters. "It says:

What now is six, must be one;
Earth's imbalance to be undone.
Fill the Oracle, pure elements reunite,
Cure the world; one line has the rite.

"Poetry — yuck!" Ana whined with disdain.

"Did I miss something?" Pauline asked, feeling left out.

"Read it again," Mr. Coy bellowed from the couch. Ret obeyed.

What now is six, must be one;
Earth's imbalance to be undone.
Fill the Oracle, pure elements reunite,
Cure the world; one line has the rite.

"How can you read that?" Paige questioned admiringly.

"I don't know," Ret said, perplexed but pleased. "It's strange; they're not really words, like reading a book or something." He spoke his thoughts slowly to give him time to contemplate. "They're more like — like notes. Yeah, it's like when you read music — how something that's written on paper can be translated into something that's played on strings or blown through reeds. That's the best way I can think to describe it."

"Never mind the description, boy," Coy insisted, rising to his feet in haste. "What does it *mean?* Could it be referring to your scars?"

"Now wait just a minute," Pauline declared with fury in her words. Mr. Coy raised his hand to his face to rub his forehead in frustration, then slunk back on the couch. "What in the world is going on here? Are you all part of this scheme, hmm?" She pierced each person with her fiery gaze. "And what about me, huh? What about your own mother? Do you just expect me to defend myself against armed bandits, breaking into my own home, while the rest of you go gallivanting off to do who knows what?" Ret's heart felt sick; Ana's head hung low. "I am very disappointed," Mrs. Cooper mourned, "*very* disappointed."

"You kids ought to be ashamed of yourselves," Mr. Coy added.

"And *you,*" Pauline turned to rail on the other adult in the room.

Mr. Coy held up his hand to stop his impending chastisement. "Allow me to explain." He reached into his suit. "Ret — catch." He lobbed the sphere towards Ret.

This time when Ret received the sphere from Mr. Coy, he instinctively caught it by clasping both hands around it, so completely that the small object was almost totally covered by his hands and hidden from everyone's view. No sooner was it in his possession than he sensed some force pushing his hands apart. He did not resist as the sphere aligned its scars with the corresponding ones on Ret's palms, as it had done once before, but then gradually began to open for the first time. With a single hinge on its base, the sphere spread apart into six equal wedges, like a peeled and sectioned orange. Ret had another strange sensation, feeling as though each individual wedge was empty. "Weird," he thought as the sphere continued to hover within his palms with astonishing beauty, its transparency causing it to shine and glow.

"Well *that's* new," Coy observed with fascination.

The spectacle was enough to cause Pauline to faint, fortunately falling into the arms of Ana and Paige. Noticing her passing out, Mr. Coy sighed with relief, "Thank goodness."

Ret continued to stare at the unlatched sphere in awe. He again was bathed in clarity as the sensation from his connection with the sphere overcame him. *"Fill the Oracle,"* he involuntarily repeated from the message on the parchment. *"Fill the Oracle."*

"Quite right," Coy interrupted, "and with six pure elements, correct?"

"Yes," Ret agreed, shaken from his trance. "I think this ball is the Oracle, and we need to fill it."

"So where do we find these pure elements?" Ana chimed in.

"You like math, don't you?" Mr. Coy asked. "What we know, plus any and all leads, multiplied by an unknown amount of hours, equals adventure!"

"Awesome!" Ret rejoiced. "When do we leave?"

Meanwhile, the efforts of Ana and Paige to revive Pauline had not been in vain. Though dazed, Mrs. Cooper regained consciousness. As she bounced back, Mr. Coy shuddered and gasped, "Back from the dead." The thought of Mrs. Cooper tagging along seemed unbearable.

"You're not going anywhere, Ret," Pauline overruled, "at least until the end of the school year."

Despite Ret's disappointment, Mr. Coy intervened, "No, no, Ret, this woman is right."

"I am?" Pauline wondered in disbelief.

"Oh, yes; I'll take it from here everyone," Mr. Coy announced. "You've all been very helpful, but I regret to inform you that I am quite full of your help for the time being." He plucked the Oracle out of Ret's hands, causing it to shut, and retrieved the parchment. "Come back in a few months, and I'll tell you all about it."

"That's the first sensible thing I've ever heard you say, Mr. Coy," Pauline told him. He gave her a confused glare, as if he didn't know whether to feel complimented or insulted.

"Speaking of sensible, good mother," Mr. Coy said, "I would highly recommend that you somehow make it very clear to Principal Pebble — "

"It's Stone," Ana corrected.

" — right, Stone," said Coy. "I suggest you make it unmistakably clear to Stone that you are not the owner of the Oracle." He held it out to show it to her. *"This* little doodad is what they were after last night, though I don't know why they came to your house."

"I do," Ret piped up. "Principal Stone asked me a while ago if we had anything that was round and had markings on it, and I told him we did. But I was referring to Jaret's RIB in the attic, so I guess he assumed we had the Oracle. I'm sorry; I didn't know."

"Ah, so there you have it, madam," Coy said in vindicating victory. "No need to apologize for falsely accusing me." Pauline made no attempt to do so anyway. "But, I repeat, if you wish to escape future danger and remove yourself from Stone's hit-list, think of some way to tactfully assure him that you don't have *this.*" Coy waved the Oracle once more and then returned it to his pocket.

"And how do you suggest I do that?" Pauline asked honestly.

Mr. Coy stepped across the studatory and stopped in front of one of the ladders against the wall. "You must ask yourself only one question, missy." He mounted the ladder and started to climb. He stopped and asked, turning to face Pauline, "Have you ever — " Suddenly, the rung he was standing on gave way, and Mr. Coy slid down the ladder and through the glass floor. Though his body disappeared as he flew uncontrollably down the ladder, which faded into the depths of the study's chasm, his voice reverberated off the walls of books, *"Ben Coy?"*

"What did he say?" Pauline wondered.

"Don't worry about it," Paige told her.

❍ ❍ ❍

Despite its lively start, the rest of the holiday recess was rather uneventful for the Coopers. They devoted several days solely to restoring order to their ransacked home, straightening up and repairing things. The cleaning was interrupted frequently by the visits of neighbors and friends throughout the community who came to offer a grieving heart and a helping hand. The Coopers were active citizens who had established a good name for themselves, and their renown and reputation only intensified after Jaret's heroic yet tragic disappearance. Tybee Island was a small community with a big heart.

While Ana was convinced that her mother was exploiting her children by forcing them to reconstruct their home during their vacation, Ret rather enjoyed the physical exertion, as it always helped him to think more clearly. By the end of the holidays, they had both memorized the message from the parchment and had reviewed it countless times, hoping to deduce its meaning. Their scanty and varied interpretations, combined with the unknown implications of the "cure the world" part, permitted Ana's imagination to run wild, while Ret took a more rational approach. They naturally balanced each other that way in most things: she had visions of greatness while he maintained more modest perspectives; she longed for the future while he lived in the present; her nature called for thrills while his thrills came from nature.

So Ret wasn't expecting much from whatever the message meant and its self-proclaimed Oracle entailed. In fact, he presumed that Mr. Coy, being the unpredictable brainchild of innumerable stunts that he was, would reconvene their powwow in a matter of days and either fess up to yet another practical joke (and a very good one, at that) or abandon the ordeal as nothing more than a fairytale's treasure map leading to fool's gold. With such a bleak outlook, Ret was obviously not the type of person to rely on lofty dreams or bombastic fascinations. But that's not to say he never indulged in such things, for he did, although he was much less vocal about them than Ana. In fact, Ret never shared his personal speculations about his past or his future, mostly because no one seemed to ask. But even though nearly every particle of his being anticipated the norm and settled with the mediocre, the precious few and most basic elements of his psyche — the ones that predispose all the rest — hoped for something grander.

❍ ❍ ❍

None of the Coopers was expecting the phone call from Tybee High's office secretary, relaying Principal Stone's desire to meet with Pauline on the first day back to school. Pauline gladly obliged. Ever since the break-in, she seemed a bit paranoid, double-checking locked doors and closed windows, leaving the porch light on all through the night, not sleeping well, even startling at the slightest stray sound — not to mention the stress of figuring out some way to assure Principal Stone of their innocence, while not disclosing Mr. Coy's lack thereof, so that she could finally set her nerves at ease once and for all.

It's hard to imagine anyone hating his job more than Lester Stone did his. In fact, as much as he despised children, he felt he related to them best on Mondays and the first days of resumed classes — days when no one but the bookworm was exactly anxious to get back to school. The first day after the winter recess was no exception. Principal Stone slithered from his car to the administration wing, greeting students with nothing but his usual scowl. Then, on his way inside his office, he coldly passed by his secretary, ignoring her polite "Good morning, Principal Stone" like he had done every day before, and shut the door.

In less than a minute, Principal Stone's door flew open, and he leaned through the doorway to face the adjacent teachers' lounge.

"Quirk!" he barked. Startled, Mr. Quirk spilled his cup of orange juice all over his corduroy jacket and leather pants. "Get in here, now!"

"But, sir," Quirk protested timidly, "my muffins just finished warming up in the — "

"NOW!"

"I take it patience is not one of his new year's resolutions," Quirk muttered as he unhappily reported to Stone's office.

Once inside and with door closed, Stone asked in a strangely unperturbed voice, "What do you notice about my office, Ronald?"

Mr. Quirk surveyed the room and then said, rather displeased, "Well, I see you *still* haven't done anything with those ghastly drapes."

"Look in the chest, Quirk." Without emotion, Stone pointed to the unlocked trunk.

"Well slap me silly," Quirk remarked. "It's empty!"

"And *why* is it empty, Quirk?" Stone asked calmly.

"Don't point any fingers at *me*. *I* didn't touch it. You know very well I couldn't read it anyway."

"Then *where* is it?!" Stone shouted. "Where *is* the prophecy?!"

"Cool your jets, Les," Quirk said with a bit of nervousness. "I'm sure it's around here somewhere." He started to sift through nearby stacks of paper.

"We were so close," Stone continued to rage. "I was sure we finally had it all — you, the boy; and I, the Oracle — until everything fell apart in one night — one blasted night!"

"And what a delightful night it was," Quirk recalled with fondness. "Pity you had to miss the dance, Stone."

"Lye won't have this," Stone worried, completely

ignoring Quirk.

"And *you* can be the one to tell him," Quirk added quickly. "I don't think the old chap is very fond of me." He rummaged through a box in search of the missing parchment. "Knowing him, he probably committed it to memory anyway, whatever it said."

"For once, Quirk, I hope you're right."

"It probably got misplaced that night; seems to be when everything else was thrown into disarray around here — you, turning the Coopers' house upside-down; and little old me, dealing with the bomb scare, the rumored Russian spy, the hubbub surrounding that Coy fellow…'twas quite a night." Quirk moved on to another box. "Say, Stoney, did you ever hear back from Coy?"

"No, *Quirky,*" Principal Stone replied in derision. "Curiously, his contact information is strictly classified, and the school only has on file his daughter's cell phone number and a post office box. My secretary reached the daughter, who would not cooperate, and their P.O. box is full of our letters — believe me, I've checked." He sighed. "The normal, legal way of getting what I want is so inefficient. All I want to do is ask him a few simple questions."

"And by *simple* you mean carefully crafted and intensely pointed. Right, sir?" Quirk expounded, giving him a wink.

"Had I known my search of the Cooper house would prove fruitless," Stone said, "I would have attended the dance, just to get a feel for the one citizen of consequence in this town who I have yet to meet — the elusive Mr. Coy."

Just then, the sweet voice of Principal Stone's secretary sang from the intercom on the telephone: "Lester, Pauline Cooper is here to see you."

"Ah, time for some answers," Stone whispered with satisfaction. "Maybe this time we meet, she'll give me what I want." For several seconds, Mr. Quirk laughed loudly and menacingly, like any evil plotter should.

Stone stared at him with abhorrence and ordered, "Get out."

"Muffin time!" Quirk cheered as he danced out of the office. "Top o' the morning to you, Mrs. Cooper!" He tipped his purple- and yellow-striped bowler hat to Pauline before skipping back into the lounge.

"You must be Pauline," Principal Stone said warmly as he stepped out to greet his guest.

"It's a pleasure to meet you, Principal Stone," Pauline responded, feigning a smile.

"Come right in." Stone filched his secretary's chair while she was away from her desk and rolled it inside his office for Pauline to sit on.

"You wanted to see me, sir?" Pauline played innocent, despite also having an agenda of her own.

"Yes," Stone began. "I heard about the terrible incident that happened at your home — what was it, about two weeks ago now?"

"That's correct," Pauline answered, pleased with the direction the conversation was headed.

"My heart sank at the news," he lied. "Were the criminals ever apprehended?"

"Not yet," answered Pauline, "but they won't be back. They didn't find what they were looking for, and I know we don't have it."

"Oh," said Stone with a hint of pleasant surprise. "Well, you must be relieved. You know what they wanted then?"

"Well, uh…" Pauline stumbled, worrying she had said too much, "not exactly."

"But you just said — "

"The simple fact that they searched my entire house and left empty-handed is proof enough of our innocence." She seemed a bit emotionally unstable.

"I see," Stone replied, mysteriously satisfied with her vagueness, which caused Pauline to feel a bit uneasy. "Well, Mrs. Cooper, given the alarming events of late at my school and in the community (namely, your house), the school board has asked me to reach out to my students and their parents to reassure them that we maintain the most stringent safety and security standards here at Tybee High School. I guarantee that we keep a watchful eye on all of our students, especially yours."

"Well, thank you, Principal Stone," Pauline said appreciatively yet with suspicion.

Just then, the face of Mr. Quirk appeared in the small window in Principal Stone's door. With crumbs of hazelnut muffin stuck to his lips, he gave Stone an encouraging thumbs-up and a supportive smile.

"In fact, Mrs. Cooper," Stone pressed on without abatement despite the distraction on the other side of his door, "I'll be meeting with many other parents this week, assuring them of the same important matter, but I thought you should be the first." Pauline forced a smile of gratitude. "Although, I'm having a difficult time getting a hold of one person in particular — a Mr. Benjamin Coy. Do you know him? I've noticed your children are good friends with his daughter — Paige, is it?"

"Yes," Pauline admitted, though ready to leave. "I've met him."

"Well then, you must be the envy of the whole community, since no one else has been able to so much as shake hands with the most mysterious man on the island."

Pauline said nothing.

"But help me to understand something," Stone continued, leaning forward across his desk. "The day arrived when the town hermit decided to finally show his face, and he attended a high school dance? And as a chaperone, no less?"

"So what?" Pauline asked in return. "Paige is his only daughter, and it was her first formal dance. *I* would've done the same thing."

"And that very same night, at the selfsame venue, my office was broken into, there was a Russian spy in the building, there was a bomb scare, and — "

"A bomb scare?" Pauline questioned in shocked disbelief. "A bomb scare — at the dance?"

"You mean the children didn't tell you?" Principal Stone put forth. "I wonder what else they aren't telling you." Pauline immediately thought of her recent meeting in Coy Manor when it seemed as though everyone was privy to some secret scheme except for her.

"And, if all of that were not enough," Stone added to sweeten his words, "your house was looted — all in the same night, simultaneously. Coincidence, Mrs. Cooper? I think not."

By now, Pauline was thoroughly confused. Apart from the hearsay Mr. Coy had told her, she knew Lester Stone to be an honorable man; his very position as a high school principal confirmed such, and she had no concrete evidence to the contrary. She also knew Ana and Ret loved her as their mother and would never do anything, at least knowingly, to harm her. Her vexation, therefore, centered around the questionable character of Mr. Coy. Principal Stone was right: who *was* this mysterious man, and why had he taken such an interest in Ret? What was his purpose in inconsequential Tybee, and why was he so intensely secretive? Why didn't he answer any of her questions that day in the manor, and why had his first night in public caused such a ruckus? Why was he so quick to blame Stone for breaking into her house when Stone was now reassuring her of their safety? And what exactly was that spherical trinket that Coy possessed and others wanted so desperately that they were willing to violently rob an innocent family?

Suddenly, Pauline didn't know who to place her confidence in anymore, but she could think of many more reasons to trust Principal Stone than Mr. Coy.

"What's he up to? What's he hiding?" Stone asked rhetorically, sensing his pointed questions had thrown Mrs. Cooper into mental dilemma. "I need your help, Pauline. The whole island needs your help. *You* are in a unique position to reveal the secret plans of Mr. Coy and disperse the silent terror that seized every heart when the walls of that ominous manor went up." He knew he was gaining her trust as she stopped breaking eye contact with him. "I suspect he's got something, Pauline — something that doesn't belong to him; something that can harness untold power. He must be stopped, and *you* are the one who can stop him."

Captivated by fear, Pauline then said the very words Stone was hoping to hear: “What must I do?”

Chapter 9

A Whale of a Shadow

In a few months' time, the excitement surrounding the Oracle had faded until it was all but forgotten. Day after day, Ret waited to hear back from Mr. Coy — something, anything — but nothing. The illusion that his future was finally falling into place had turned back into a barren wasteland — quite unlike the world around him, which was blooming with evidence that spring was fast approaching. With budding branches crowding the sky and fresh shoots littering the dirt, Ret found consolation in the harbingers of spring. Birds were back to nest, amphibians returned to mate, and the sun was dancing behind the cottony clouds. All winter long, nature had conserved its energy, which, now that the time was right, it was gradually beginning to release. The natural world's rebirth surged through Ret's being, causing him to feel electrifyingly alive.

But Ret wanted to know why nature had a mind of its own — how the natural world moved and acted according to its own freewill, totally independent of anything manmade. "What is it that prompts a seed to sprout," Ret would wonder, "and how does a root know what to absorb? When does a plant decide the design of its leaf, and why does the rushing wind die? Just what exactly is a fire's flame, and why does the earth ever think to tilt?"

"It just does," Ana would say to his questions. "Just go with it."

And, whether he understood it or not, that is exactly what Ret had to do — *just go with it* — because, despite man's self-proclaimed supremacy over all things natural, there was yet one large swath of nature that had always eluded humanity's control: the elements.

Rain falls. Lightning bolts. Earth quakes. But why? Ret already knew *how* these natural processes happened; now he wished to know *why*.

Because he felt much the same way. Secretly, Ret hated being acted upon, relying on outside people and forces to determine *his* destiny. But he waited — he endured — with all patience and forbearance, trusting in nature's timing, for while he was certain the answers rested in his palms, he also knew the will of nature was out of his hands.

On the other hand, Ana's patience waned thin. "It's time for us to visit Paige," she said as she grabbed Ret and pushed him out the backdoor. "Her father has 'Ben Coy' long enough. We need some answers."

As they drew nearer to the outer fence of the manor, Ret asked, "Should we let Paige know we're here?"

"Way ahead of you, bro," Ana informed. "She unlocked the front gate and is waiting for us in the main entry."

"Wow, you're good," Ret remarked.

"It's called texting," Ana said. "You might want to try it sometime."

Paige welcomed the Coopers through the giant double doors. "Dad's down in the lounge," she told them, knowing the purpose of their visit. "I'm so glad you're here; I hope you can help him." Ret and Ana sensed a hint of nervousness in her voice.

Paige led them into the shadows of one of the many corridors lining the arch of the semicircular entryway. Ret paid little attention to where they were going, so swallowed up was his mind in what new information he hoped Mr. Coy had for them.

They found Mr. Coy in a most unusual setting. The lounge was quite literally a life-size billiards table. With green cloth for carpet, the floor rivaled a football field, its perimeter raised and lined with the traditional strips of rubber cushion. The balls, either striped or solid, were the size of small cars, and one enormous triangle rack hung from the ceiling, waiting for its next use. Ret peered over the edge of the massive corner pocket closest to them but steadied himself upon realizing it was bottomless.

"He's in the cue ball," Paige explained, pointing to the one colorless object on the table. Due to its transparency, the Coopers could see how the cue ball was actually a ball within a ball. Somewhat like an egg, its outer shell enclosed a slightly smaller chamber which had a series of wheels protruding from it. The wheels permitted the inner chamber to move independent of the shell, allowing Mr. Coy to remain upright while the cue ball was in motion.

"Dad," Paige called out to him. "Dad!" There was no answer. "See," Paige said in defeat to Ret and Ana. "He won't even answer me." Apparently oblivious to his daughter, Mr. Coy used the joystick in front of him to aim a red laser at the next ball he wanted to hit. Then he pressed a button, and the cue ball propelled itself, colliding with a striped ball and sending it into a side pocket. Mr. Coy remained emotionless.

"Sir," Ret stepped forward, noticing Paige was at her wit's end. He spoke loudly, unsure if Mr. Coy could hear him. "We're wondering if you've learned anything more about my scars." For several moments, there was silence as Mr. Coy continued to roam around the table. When a turn put him very near his visitors, Ret asked again, "You know — the Oracle?"

"You mean the itch I can't reach," Mr. Coy said at last, though in a very subdued voice.

"Um, sure," Ret replied in confusion. An abnormal somberness had taken hold of Mr. Coy's typically spry demeanor. His customarily quick and vivacious movements had become slow and methodical. His gaze was downcast, his face morose, and his tongue refused to speak the thoughts that seemed to occupy his mind. Only once had Ret seen Mr. Coy in such a mood: when he accidentally insulted his efforts at parenting.

"I went many places," Mr. Coy sighed softly, sounding defeated. "I did many things." Ret had to strain to hear his despondent whispers through the scanty air holes in the cue ball. "But I still cannot reach my meddlesome itch." He whizzed across the table, pocketing another striped ball along the way.

Inwardly, Ret was quite displeased with Mr. Coy. After patiently waiting for three months, they were not any closer to dispelling the mystery surrounding the Oracle. A part of Ret believed he was better off alone, but the possibility that Mr. Coy had some role to play was enough to stick it out as a group, at least for now.

"Mr. Coy," Ret shouted, knowing he could hear him, "I need you to take me to the place where Jaret disappeared." Out of the corner of his eye, Ret saw Ana's jaw drop, but he pretended not to see it. "I'd like to see what's there for myself."

Mr. Coy slowly played his way over to their side of the table again. "I agree," he said in a hushed tone. Ret's heart jumped for joy. "We'll leave first thing Monday morning in the helicopter."

"Thank you, sir," Ret responded, trying to contain his excitement. He turned to rejoin Ana, but before they had exited the lounge, Mr. Coy called out to them.

"Mr. Cooper," he said, "I'm glad you came by today." Ret had never heard more sincere words from Mr. Coy's lips. "For the first time in months, I can finally scratch." And Mr. Coy sent himself sailing into one of the corner pockets, disappearing from sight.

When they were a safe distance away from the manor, Ana turned to Ret and exploded with questions.

"Look," Ret said to cut off her rambling, "all I'm thinking is maybe there are some clues hiding where the ship went down."

"But Ret, the site's been searched a hundred times," Ana reasoned. "Nothing was ever found. What makes you think — "

"Because maybe there's something that only *I* can find — only *I* can understand. Remember the message on the parchment?"

Ana was speechless for the last few minutes of their trek. Ret wondered if he had her support. As they neared the kayak to take them across Tybee Creek, she finally said something: "You *do* realize it'll be like pulling teeth to get Mom to come with us. You know how temperamental she is about the whole thing."

"Then you can just stay home with her," Ret suggested with a smile, knowing Ana would never allow such a thing.

"While *you* spend spring break in the Bahamas? Fat chance!"

"Thought so," Ret remarked happily, for if *he* couldn't convince Pauline of the necessity of the trip, Ana could.

❍ ❍ ❍

Before they knew it, Monday morning had arrived. Fortunately, Ana had been successful in convincing her mother to join them on their adventure, which Pauline did more out of fear for her children than any other motivation.

"Welcome aboard the Coy chopper, ladies and gentlemen," Mr. Coy announced from the cockpit, where he sat next to Ivan. "Please fasten your seatbelts as we will be on our way momentarily." Despite Mr. Coy's infatuation with the intercom, the passengers were willing to endure a little in-flight commentary if it meant keeping the controls in Ivan's care. Ret was pleased to find Mr. Coy in much happier spirits than he had been at their last visit.

Upon arriving at the manor, the Coopers had been escorted to a vast hangar, which they deduced was underground thanks to the several minutes they spent making their descent in an elevator. When the elevator doors at last opened, light spilled into the darkness just long enough to illuminate their path to the helicopter, whose dim cabin light and colored exterior lights did little to penetrate the darkness. A red light on the tail flashed every few seconds, and Ret thought he saw multiple shiny objects catch its reflection deep within the hangar.

The cabin was pleasantly spacious. Two rows of seats ran parallel to one another, allowing passengers to face each other during flight. Mr. Coy was quick to point out the cabin's airtight seal, allowing it to achieve greater altitudes and snuff out the noise of the rotors.

"Should there be a loss in cabin pressure," Mr. Coy continued as head steward, "please hold your breath." Pauline reacted to this directive with a moment of silent consternation.

"Fire up the engines, skipper," Coy instructed Ivan.

"My name ith *not* skeepayrr."

"Roger, Roger."

Annoyed, Ivan set things in motion. The helicopter vibrated as the powerful rotors reached their optimum spinning speed.

"In the event of total engine failure," said Mr. Coy nonchalantly, "please panic quietly so as not to wake other passengers who may be napping. Thank you, and enjoy the flight."

Even though he sensed the craft had lifted off the ground, Ret had little idea where it was headed in the darkness of the hangar. Every few seconds, the chopper's blinking lights informed Ret that they were steadily rising above the hangar's floor. Just when he wondered if they might collide with the ceiling, Ret watched as drops of water began to appear on the cabin's windows.

"Are we outside?" Ana asked, thoroughly confused.

Suddenly, filtered light poured into the hangar as a huge area of the ceiling began to cave upwards, splitting into two large panels, resembling an upside-down funnel. As the panels continued to extend higher, they eventually peeked and revealed blue sky. With millions of gallons of water rushing past the helicopter on all sides, Ret realized that the panels were parting the large lagoon on the manor's grounds.

"Tut-tut, looks like rain," said Mr. Coy. Lightly dusted by the thick mist from the waterfalls surrounding them, the chopper rose through the conduit of the volcano-like throat until it was soaring above Little Tybee Island. Then Ivan set their course southward.

Ret was awestruck by his first known flight. Even if he had flown before he lost his memory, he didn't see how he could forget something so thrilling. In every direction, the mighty Atlantic stretched without end, except to the west, where rows of foamy waves licked the mainland. Never did he feel so small, so helpless.

"To my right is Cape Canaveral," Mr. Coy pointed out, as he had been doing since takeoff. "Known as Cape Kennedy from 1963 to 1973, it is separated from Merritt Island by the Banana River..."

As they made their way down the Florida panhandle, Ivan steered the helicopter in a more south-easterly direction. Though Ret absorbed every minute of the flight and its view, Ana and Paige passed the time by identifying many of the things they had learned in Mr. Quirk's Caribbean Studies — or, rather, World Geography — class.

"...To my left is a terrific view of the Gulf Stream," Mr. Coy observed. "This warm current flows north toward Europe where it joins the North Atlantic Drift..."

"How could anyone see a stream within the ocean?" Pauline murmured incredulously.

"Well, Mother," Ana continued, "the waters of the Gulf Stream look swifter — more unsettled — than the rest of the ocean. Its current *does* move at about five to six miles per hour. At least, that's what Quirk said."

"…But if you think *that's* hard to see, folks" Mr. Coy was heard again, "try spotting the Blake Ridge, the underwater basin we've been flying over since departure. Famous for its large deposits of methane hydrates, which rise through mud volcanoes on the seafloor before being released as natural gas at the surface…"

Soon, the first few islands of the Bahamas came into view.

"…Straight ahead sits Grand Bahama, the fifth largest island in the Bahamas chain," Mr. Coy's nonstop commentary continued. "The Spanish named the island *Gran Bajamar,* meaning 'Great Shallows'…"

"What's that?" Paige interrupted, pointing to a large shadow in the ocean, immediately off the shore of a tiny island to the west.

"Looks like a whale," Ana guessed.

"That's a pretty big whale," Pauline remarked sarcastically.

"Okay," Ana improvised, "maybe it's a pack of whales."

"You mean a *pod?*" Ret butted in. "Let me see." He slid over to their window. As soon as Ret saw what they were looking at, he experienced an acute feeling in his hand. It was not so much a sharp pain as it was a poignant numbness, coming from the symbol of the hook and triangle on his right palm. It was as if there were two magnets under his skin, their like sides facing each other, wanting to connect but annoyingly unable to do so. When Ret looked down to inspect his hand, the sensation fled, only to return when he reaffixed his gaze on the shadow in the water. With Pauline and the girls still pressed up against the window, only Mr. Coy, who peered into the cabin at the commotion, noticed Ret's puzzlement.

"How silly of me, maybe it's a *pod* of whales," Ana corrected herself sneeringly, "and look — it's turning around." Ret looked at her skeptically. "What?" she said, defending herself. "Why else would it have one curled end?" Paige and the Coopers continued to study the image, occasionally offering ideas of what it might be.

Just then, the entire helicopter shook for a moment, as if struck by some sort of tremor. No one had a chance to say anything before the chopper rattled again, this time more violently than the first. When the commotion struck a third time and persisted, Pauline yelled to the cockpit, "Is this thing safe?"

Mr. Coy whispered to Ivan, "Get us out of this, would you?"

"I vould like to, thirr," Ivan replied, "but I am affray-ed all ov zhe eenthtrumentth arre expeeree-encing eenterrfeerrence."

"What?" Coy asked in shock.

"And ve arre lootheeng powerr quite rrapeedly," Ivan added. The helicopter's lights flickered repeatedly, and at times it sounded as if the engine was giving out.

"I think we should turn around," Pauline pled earnestly. Terror-stricken, she clung to whatever she could grab as the helicopter rocked uncontrollably.

"Take us home," Coy instructed.

"Rright avay, thirr," Ivan obeyed.

The helicopter continued to reel with every jolt of turbulence. Soon after Ivan turned around, however, the chaos subsided, and the chopper stabilized.

The return trip to Tybee was deathly quiet, partly because everyone was a bit shaken up by the frightening turbulence but mostly because Mr. Coy didn't say a word. As unpleasant as his commentary had been, Ret and the others found they preferred it over the awkward silence that now engrossed their tour guide. Each of them knew a thing or two about Mr. Coy's unpredictability, but when it turned mute, it was something altogether menacing.

"Is something wrong, Ret?" Pauline broke the silence, noticing how Ret had been caressing his hand for the last several minutes.

"Yeah," Ret said unconvincingly, "I just had this weird feeling in my hand while we were looking at that shadow of the pod of whales — or whatever it was." He continued to massage the scar of the hook and triangle.

"What did it feel like?" Pauline wondered. "Did it hurt? Are you feeling sick? *I'm* feeling a bit of motion sickness myself." She pressed her hand against his forehead as she usually did when her children complained of feeling strange.

"No, I feel fine," he said. "It was just in my hand, under my scar. It felt like — like something was coming together, or at least trying to — under my skin. But it didn't."

Unsure of how to help, Pauline simply patted Ret's knee lovingly. Paige and Ana watched from across the aisle, their moods mellowed by the raucous flight. Ivan's eyes remained alert behind his aviator goggles.

Meanwhile, Mr. Coy was all ears as Ret expounded on the feeling associated with his scar. Though still speechless, he wondered why his helicopter malfunctioned at precisely the same time as when Ret was struck by his sensation — all while flying over that very small island.

Back in the hangar, the tension that had prevailed in the air seemed to disperse as soon as the chopper's skids made contact with the earth. As they exited the craft, Mr. Coy suddenly regained his voice.

"I want to thank each of you for coming, and I apologize for any discomfort you may have experienced," Mr. Coy said sincerely, much to the shock of Paige and the Coopers. "Paige will escort you out." He extended his arm in the direction of the elevator.

"What's gotten into him?" Ana asked as they stepped into the elevator. Paige shrugged. Everyone agreed that Mr. Coy's graciousness was not like him at all.

"I don't know," Pauline remarked, "but it's about time."

Once his daughter and the Coopers were out of earshot, Mr. Coy turned to Ivan and said with exhilaration, "Refuel the bird, and load the diving equipment. We're headed back to that island tonight." Ivan sighed, having just unbuckled his seatbelt. "Look alive, my boy!" Mr. Coy continued. "I think I've solved the mystery of the hook and triangle!"

Chapter 10

Speak of the Devil

"Who was that, Mom?" Ana asked from her seat at the breakfast table as Pauline came in from the porch at the conclusion of her phone call.

"Oh, just Principal Stone, honey," answered Pauline, speaking in a finite tone of voice to discourage any further questions.

"Since when do you and Principal Stone talk on the phone?" Ana said in surprise. "Is Ret in trouble? Am I?"

"No, no," Pauline dismissed. "Everything's fine, which is exactly why I've been checking in with your good principal every now and then: to make sure you and Ret are safe." Ana looked at her mother disbelievingly as she sipped her orange juice. "And you *are*," Pauline reaffirmed. "Now, off you go. Here comes the bus."

But Ana wasn't entirely convinced, and the same could be said of Ret and Paige. Despite Pauline's reassurances, the trio employed extreme caution whenever Stone or Quirk was near. Notwithstanding their trepidation, it seemed to them as though all of Pauline's conversations with Principal Stone were having their intended effect.

Before long, the students of Tybee High found themselves facing the bittersweet reality of final exams at the conclusion of the academic year. Ana and Paige had been studying for weeks in nervous preparation for their first round of high school finals, but Ret found it difficult to hit the books when he would much rather hit the beach. For him, the most challenging thing about school was the windows in the classrooms.

"Quirk's final essay should be a breeze," Ana assessed as they headed to his class on the last day of school.

"Especially since he already told us the prompt," Paige added.

Ana sifted through her notes to read the prompt one more time: *"Choose a topic about the Caribbean that means the most to you personally, and write a three- to five-page essay explaining why.* Piece of cake."

"Yeah, but I doubt Quirk will accept an essay all about Jaret's disappearance," Ret remarked with dissatisfaction, assuming he ought not to choose the topic that truly meant the most to him.

"You never know," said Ana. "If you make it sentimental enough, you might just strike a nerve on Quirk's soft side. After all, word from the teachers' lounge is Quirk has a pink princess lunch pail."

"I'm sure you'll do fine, Ret, just like all the other finals so far," Paige encouraged. "It'll all be over soon. Oh, and guess what? My dad said he wants to celebrate the end of the school year by taking us all on a cruise!"

"Way to go, big P!" Ana cheered. "How'd you score that one, sister?"

"He just came up to me out of the blue, asked when the last day of school was, and told me he wanted to reward us for doing so well in our first year of high school," Paige explained. "Well, actually, he thought it was my last year of *middle* school, but…"

"Who cares?" Ana beamed. "When do we shove off?"

"He wants to leave first thing in the morning, so you'd better come over tonight," Paige said. "He told me he wants to take us back to that island we saw in the helicopter a few months ago."

"Really?" Ret asked with great enthusiasm.

"Yeah," Paige continued. "I told one of the maids about how lame that trip was, so she must have told Dad, so maybe he wants to make it up to us. He ordered the staff to prepare the yacht for the three of us — and your mom; she's invited, too," Paige explained. "You might want to let her know."

"I'll text her right now," Ana said. Taking their seats in Quirk's class, Ret took out pen and paper to start writing his essay on the indigenous tribes of the Lesser Antilles, even though his mind was really focused on the exciting prospects of their impending trip with Mr. Coy.

Somewhere in the bottomless underbelly of Coy Manor sat an extravagant yacht, moored to a dock that stretched into the heart of a placid harbor, surrounded by jagged rocks. Ret reasoned there must have been some kind of inlet to this cavernous bayou, but it was too dark to see much further beyond the ship. The girls excitedly boarded the craft, whose windows and railings shimmered and shined with luxury. Crew members hurried about the decks, buzzing from the galley with their platters of appetizers. Maids bounced in and out of guest cabins, stocking linens and fluffing pillows. Even a string quartet strummed peacefully in the dining room, filling the damp air with elegant ambiance. Never before had three teenagers felt so much like royalty as the evening transpired in deliciousness and entertainment.

"Where's your mom?" Paige asked Ana as they finished off another plate of hors d'oeuvres.

"I don't know," Ana replied. "She wasn't at the house when we got home from school. I texted her a little while ago, and she said she'd meet us here. In the meantime, who's up for another game of shuffleboard?"

The next thing Ret knew, he was aroused from sleep by a sudden jolt. He had dozed off in an armchair in the main deck's stateroom, with Paige and Ana curled up on a nearby couch. As he sat up, he found himself rocking back and forth quite involuntarily. Then he saw the room's chandeliers swaying to the same rhythm. Something like an engine hummed quietly a deck below. Ret looked out the large windows and was shocked by what the approaching dawn revealed: they were at sea.

Before Ret could awaken the girls, a startling, yet somewhat familiar, voice filled the stateroom.

"Shiver me timbers!" Mr. Coy bellowed like a pirate. "Get yer scurvy sea legs into me quarters before I measure ye fer yer chains, ye lousy bilge rats!"

Still drowsy, Ana rose from the couch, hair disheveled and eyes squinted, to see what in the world was going on. Ret continued to stare at Mr. Coy in befuddlement.

Mr. Coy shook his head disapprovingly and sighed. "Meet me in my office," he translated.

"Where?" Ret asked quickly before Mr. Coy left.

"Arrr! 'Where,' says you?" replied Coy the pirate. "Below the poop deck, says I!" He stormed out of the room and said, abandoning his pirate accent, "And hurry up!"

Mr. Coy was right about their sea legs. Perhaps on account of the choppy waves and the misty gales, it was with staggering imbalance that the sleepy trio made their way to the captain's cabin on the upper deck of the yacht. Once inside, they found Mr. Coy standing next to Ivan, who was at his usual post at the controls.

"Allow me to bring you up to speed," Mr. Coy immediately began speaking to them. "This vessel is sailing south, en route to a certain shadow — or, as you previously called it, a pod of whales." Ret's eyes widened with exhilaration. "You see, my loyal first mate, Ivan, and I returned to that tiny little island, which turned out to be the Bahamian island of Bimini, to investigate that shadow, which proved to be so — " Mr. Coy glanced at Ret's hand before finishing, " — so sensational. Come to find out, the shadow was not a pod of whales after all," adding, under his breath, "surprise, surprise."

"Good grief," Ana mumbled, feeling put-upon.

"It is actually a submerged road," said Coy, pausing for dramatic effect, "consisting of several fragments, each arranged from large limestone blocks and laid with impressive uniformity. The largest and most intriguing of these linear features is the half-mile-long road, more particularly the *shape* of its southwest end — ," then pausing to look Ret in the eyes, " — a hook." Mr. Coy's audience glared at him with great intrigue.

"Now that I've got you all *hooked*," Mr. Coy grinned, "consider this. You will recall the turbulence that got your dear mother — bless her heart — all shook up?"

Mr. Coy's mentioning of Pauline jogged Ana's memory. "Mom!" she gasped quietly, retrieving her phone to try to learn her mother's whereabouts.

"Well, on our return trip," Mr. Coy proceeded, "Ivan and I encountered the *same* commotion at the *same* location. Not preferring a crash landing, we instead landed on the fringe of the turbulent quadrant and safely traveled the remaining distance by foot and fin until we arrived at the underwater road. Initially, however, I wondered if my helicopter was problematic, but only in that *one* spot? The logic was absurd. And that was when I realized that the turbulent region was in the western corner of Devil's Triangle."

There were a few seconds of silence before Ret finally asked, "I'm sorry, sir, but what exactly is — "

"Blimey!" Coy barked in outrage. "You mean to tell me you've never heard of Devil's Triangle?" Three blank faces stared back at him. "I say, next year you three really ought to take a World Geography class or something." The three Quirk students in the room rolled their eyes at each other. "Devil's Triangle is, as its name implies, a triangle-shaped region that encompasses much of the Caribbean and Western Atlantic, spanning from Miami to Puerto Rico to Bermuda (which is why some folks call it the 'Bermuda Triangle'). And," he added in a voice of mystery, "it's a place where strange things have been known to happen."

"What sorts of things, Mr. Coy?" Ret questioned with great interest.

"Do you remember when I told you about the methane hydrates that rise from the seafloor in these parts?" Ret nodded. "Well, let's just say any ship, sailing over a sea that's bubbling with those gases, will be a sunken ship faster than you can say Davy Crockett."

"Jaret," Ret whispered inaudibly.

"Don't you mean Davy *Jones?"* Ana suggested, arriving at her mom's voicemail again. "Ugh," she whispered to Ret, "she won't pick up!"

"And," Mr. Coy continued without interruption, "as Ivan can attest, the immense energy surging through the skies above that island will kill the engine and disorient the compass of any plane that tries to fly through it." The faces of Paige and Ana flickered with fear as if sitting around a campfire during the telling of scary ghost stories. "Ships disappearing, planes crashing, entire vessels swallowed by the sea," Coy proceeded. "Yes, some say these waters be haunted, some say they be cursed. Some say it's just terribly rotten luck. But what isn't luck, Mr. Cooper, is now we know exactly where your scar means to take us."

Ret looked at his scar, absorbing Mr. Coy's every word. "Devil's Triangle?"

"Yep," Coy concurred.

"And the hooked road?"

"Double yep," said Coy. "Now, you said you felt a feeling — a strange sensation — when you saw that shadow, is that right?"

"That's right."

"Do you want to know what I think?" Mr. Coy asked. Ret's eager face was answer enough. "I think you felt that sensation because that sunken road is where we're going to find the first of these elements that we're supposed to collect." Then, before Ret could respond, Mr. Coy said, "And do you want to know *why* I think that?" Again, Ret's anxious face answered. "Because," said Coy, "when Ivan and I dove around that road and scrutinized its every crag, we found a larger version of your tiny scar etched in the surface of one of its giant stones."

Ret couldn't believe his ears. He would have figured this was all too good to be true, but it not only sounded good — it felt good, too.

"Now, we'll be dropping anchor soon," said Mr. Coy, "but we'll still be a fair distance away from where we want to be. A craft of this size would never make it through the electromagnetic field surrounding the road, so we'll have to swim to it."

"You expect us to swim — " Ana began to protest, but Mr. Coy interrupted.

"Yes," he said, "in one of these." He parted the closet beside him to reveal some sort of high-tech outfit, hanging upright and gleaming majestically under a spotlight.

"Mr. Coy," Ana asked suspiciously, "are you a superhero?"

"I call it the subsuit," said Coy proudly. "The idea came to me one afternoon while I was doing some work in the Great Barrier Reef. It has all the sophistication of a world-class submarine, yet it remains as practical as scuba gear." Ret wondered how something that looked as simple as a wetsuit with a backpack could yield such results. Then Mr. Coy put his doubts to rest. "But the genius," he said, "rests in *this*." From the suit's facemask, Mr. Coy detached a piece that resembled a doctor's stethoscope. With the device behind his head, he gently pulled the two tips apart and clamped them snugly on his forehead, one on each temple. Instead of culminating in a circular chest piece, the tubing led from the tips to a sort of pronged plug, which Mr. Coy explained should be inserted into its outlet at the top of the backpack.

"And that's going to help us *how?*" Ana questioned, now texting vigorously.

"Just as a stethoscope discloses the pulse of the heart," Mr. Coy taught, "my neuroscope reveals the impulses of the brain. Inside the subsuit's backpack, among other things, is a super-intelligent computer, which sends an electrical current through each of the two tips attached to the forehead, creating a current between them that passes through the brain. This current intercepts the electrical impulses being transmitted among neurons and sends them out of the brain. The neuroscope, which quite literally is a giant exterior axon, carries the impulse to the computer, which interprets and fulfills the message."

Ana stared at Mr. Coy, mouth wide open in confusion, as if he were speaking another language.

Mr. Coy stepped toward the hanging subsuit, close enough so that he could plug the end of the neuroscope into the suit's backpack. "You see, as long as your electrical impulses stay within your brain, your power to do and create is limited to the extent of the human body. But when you withdraw those impulses and insert them into something less restricted and more powerful, then the only limitation is what you can imagine. In essence, the entire globe becomes your brain."

"No way," said Ret, whose jaw had dropped with awe.

"Yes way," Coy replied, well-pleased. "So, Miss Cooper, to answer your question, your subsuit will be nothing *but* help to you. In a few moments, we will deliberately jump ship en route to that submerged, underwater road, and unless *you* are some sort of superhero, my dear, you'll likely need to breathe once or twice before we get there. All your brain can do is tell you what your lungs already know because the brain can't produce oxygen on its own." Suddenly, the subsuit began pumping air through its mouthpiece. "But the subsuit can, even underwater, because it knows a process that the brain doesn't: electrolysis."

"Great," Ana muttered to Paige, "I always wanted to sound like Darth Vader."

"Or say, perhaps, you find yourself being pursued by a hungry predator," Mr. Coy said. "If your first instinct is flight" — without any notice, the room's ceiling fan was ripped from its socket and flew into Mr. Coy's hands where it continued to spin — "then the subsuit will provide you with a way to escape." Paige took a step closer to Ret, using her attempt to avoid the falling sparks from the ceiling as a subtle excuse. "Or, if your first instinct is fight" — a pair of stainless steel spears emerged from the suit's arms, extending just beyond the back of the gloves — "then the subsuit will ensure your victory."

"Nice touch," Ana commented to Ret approvingly. "I dig Wolverine."

"As you can see," Mr. Coy concluded, "the subsuit has the ability to analyze its surroundings down to the minutest molecule and then manipulate them to whatever extent it needs in order to meet your request. Modern science has yet to unlock the full potential of the human brain, so I created my own key to do so." He removed the neuroscope from his head and held it before them. “Maybe someday I’ll show you the host of other uses for this key of keys.” He watched it in silent reverence. “Some people say I’m out of my mind. I say, exactly.”

“Why won’t she answer?” Ana said in hushed frustration.

“Now, the maids will get you outfitted; there’s a subsuit for each of you, including your — ” Mr. Coy stopped abruptly. “Where is your mother?”

“I don’t know,” Ana answered with worry in her voice. “Last night, she texted me and said she’d meet us here, but I haven’t seen her, and now I can’t reach her at all.”

“Get used to it, deary,” Mr. Coy said gruffly. “We be in Devil’s Triangle now.”

❍ ❍ ❍

It was late in the morning the previous day when Pauline received word from Ana of Mr. Coy’s intentions to treat them all to an end-of-the-year voyage. As soon as she received her daughter’s text message, her blood began to boil in panic. She called Principal Stone immediately.

“Coy’s at it again,” she shrieked over the phone. “He says he’s celebrating the end of the year, but I have a feeling he’s just taking them to that dreadful island.” She was panting heavily. “Oh, sir, what should I do? What should I *do?*”

“Meet me at the school,” Principal Stone ordered.

Pauline was there in a flash. She burst into Stone’s office in hysterics.

“Oh, what are we going to do?” she mourned.

“You’re going to keep quiet,” Principal Stone sneered, *“that’s* what you’re going to do.” Pauline went silent and glared at Stone. She was startled when the door shut behind her. “Tie her up, Bubba.” A pair of strong arms gripped Pauline as Bubba emerged from where he had been hiding behind the door.

“Tie me up?” Pauline barked. “What is the meaning of…” — Bubba forced her hands behind her back, his red hair and eyes glowing like fire — “…unhand me, you demon child!”

“Now, now, Mrs. C,” Bubba smirked, “you were rather fond of me once.”

“You’ve been very helpful to us, Mrs. Cooper,” said Principal Stone, “but I’m afraid your services are no longer needed.”

Pauline continued to vocalize her shock and anger.

“Stuff something in her mouth, would you?” Principal Stone added. Bubba obediently wedged a towel between his captive’s jaw. “I’m so sick of listening to her worry about those juvenile kids of hers and pretending I care.” Pauline erupted in a flurry of muffled screams before falling limp at the prick of a tranquilizer.

When Pauline regained consciousness, the first thing she saw was Mr. Quirk's face, hovering a mere inch above her own.

"Welcome aboard!" Mr. Quirk greeted her. Dressed in a flashy tank top and wedgie-prone shorts, Mr. Quirk clearly wasn't trying to hide his farmer's tan. The bridge of his glasses was white from its constant rubbing against the glob of sunscreen smeared on his crooked nose.

"I'm sure you're anxious to recover your miserable children," Quirk taunted a squirming Pauline. "I've been waiting all year for this." A thick patch of chest hair tickled Pauline's face as Mr. Quirk continued to speak to her. "Yes, you will make a fine figurehead, indeed," he cackled.

❍ ❍ ❍

Ret had scarcely zipped up his subsuit when something collided explosively with the yacht, causing it to reel and tremble. When the yacht rebounded, Ret jumped to his feet and rushed on deck.

"What was that?" Ana and Paige wondered, emerging from the cabin where they had put on subsuits of their own. They looked toward the back of the ship where the sound had come from, just in time to see the wind disperse the lingering cloud of smoke.

"We're under attack!" one of the frenzied maids announced as Ret zoomed past her on his way to the stern. After assessing the damage and finding no injuries, Ret's attention turned to identifying their attackers. When he looked behind to see who had fired on them, he saw Principal Stone, Mr. Quirk, and Bubba catching up to them in a speedboat, with Pauline tied to the bow.

Chapter 11

The Road to Sunken Earth

"Batten down the hatches!" Mr. Coy bellowed. "All hands on deck!" Ret burst into the control room, with Paige and Ana close behind. "Prepare for battle!" Coy ordered Ivan.

"Battle?" Ana protested, catching her breath. "In case you haven't noticed, my *mother* is strapped to that —"

"It's more strategic maneuvering than combat," Mr. Coy explained, slightly annoyed. Just then, the yacht shook from another assault from its predator. "Ivan, do you see that restless patch of ocean to the east of us there?"

"Yoo mean zhe bubbleeing vater zat vee have been trry-ing to avoid?" Ivan asked.

"Precisely," replied Coy. "Sail directly into it, and engage hover capabilities. Let's see if Mr. Stone has ever — *Ben Coy.*"

"Are you mad?" Ana put forth indignantly.

"Getting there," Mr. Coy muttered, controlling his patience. "Now, if you three will kindly step outside, I best be changing into my subsuit." He guided them to the door. "I foresee a rescue in the very near future."

It was all Paige and the Coopers could do to stand idly on deck and watch in nervous helplessness. They didn't dare retaliate for fear of harming Pauline who was so strategically affixed to the bow of the speedboat. With every round of enemy fire, the trio was naturally inclined to shield themselves, although it soon became clear that Stone's objective was not to destroy them but instead to knock out the yacht's steering and propulsion systems.

With the yacht now approaching the fringe of the bubbling sea, everyone braced for the unknown. When Ret leaned over the side of the boat for a closer look, he learned what Mr. Coy had meant when he instructed Ivan to engage the craft's hover capabilities. In a flurry of mist, the yacht's entire hull was enclosed by an inflatable skirt. A pair of enormous fans rose above the stern, sending air both *behind* the ship for propulsion as well as *into* the skirt for lift. With a proportionate amount of air escaping through holes in the bottom of the skirt, the yacht was suddenly hovering above the sea. Ret and the girls smiled in amazed relief as they remained afloat despite entering the bubbling waters.

"Don't stop until you are safely on the other side, Ivan," Mr. Coy said as he stepped out of the control room. "Follow me, Ret," he said, throwing one leg over the ship's guardrail. "I'll save the damsel and the redhead. You're in charge of the other two goons." He placed his subsuit's mask over his face and fell overboard, plunging headfirst into the fizzing froth below.

Just as Ret was about to dive in behind Mr. Coy, a startling image flashed before his mind's eye. Like a single frame excised from a film reel, this singular scene caused Ret to shrink with sudden fear. A bubbling sea, a sinking ship, people in distress, billowing flames — was he seeing the past or the near future?

"Mom!" Ana screamed as her mother's squirming body slowly began to disappear under the waves.

While the yacht continued to glide smoothly across the boiling sea, the churning waters were steadily swallowing the speedboat. Realizing their plight, Quirk and Bubba abandoned ship while Principal Stone refused to succumb so quickly. Though futile, he continued to steer the wheel and rev the engine.

"I've got to help them," Ret said bravely.

"Be careful," Paige admonished, grabbing his hand. Ret smiled at Paige, then Ana, and overboard he went.

The visibility underwater was nil. With bubbles bouncing every whichway, it was like wading in a tank filled with jellyfish. As Ret headed in the general direction of the sunken speedboat, he wished he could swim faster. As soon as the thought crossed his mind, a small propeller extended from the outside of each heel of his subsuit like gadgets on a Swiss Army knife. Now cutting through the water like a shark, he arrived at the scene in no time. As the bow of the speedboat was now fully submerged, Ret could discern between the bubbles that Pauline had been liberated. A quick glance upward revealed several pairs of dangling legs. When Ret reached the surface, he found Pauline and Bubba holding on to Mr. Coy for dear life, with Quirk struggling to stay afloat nearby. They all had their attention focused on the doomed speedboat.

"Jump, Stone!" Bubba shouted.

"You're too — young to — die, old man!" Mr. Quirk sputtered, occasionally dipping beneath the waves.

Though obviously distressed, Stone refused their invitations. "I'm not going to die!" Stone asserted. The boat's engine was now smoking from his useless attempts to force himself out of his bind.

"If you don't join us now," Mr. Coy said, "we're *all* going to die. This water is loaded with methane, and any minute now it's going to make contact with your engine and blow this whole place to Timbuktu!"

"I've always wanted to go there," Quirk remarked

as Ret arrived at his side to buoy him up. With haste, Stone turned around and watched in terror as the tremulous ocean waves danced dangerously close to the compartment housing the speedboat's engine. He abandoned ship and swam to the safety of Ret's arm. Lying face-down in the water, Mr. Coy and Ret skimmed across the sea like jet skis, both with each arm linked to their human jetsam.

The rescue party hadn't traveled far, however, when their worst nightmare became a reality as the pervasive methane finally made contact with the speedboat's engine, still running as it sank. First, they saw the scene in front of them light up with the reflection of the inferno; then they heard the deafening explosion that seemed to cause time to stand still for a moment. Still at a dangerously far distance from the end of the bubbling sea where the yacht was waiting for them, they were in a tight race with death by incineration. Ret and Mr. Coy must have made the same wish — namely, to make a quicker getaway — because underneath both of them a kind of sleek surfboard elongated itself from their subsuits' utility belts, greatly reducing their friction and, thus, increasing their speed. Still, Ret began to fret as he watched a wall of fire, both under and above sea level, fast approaching them. Soon, they found themselves rising with the sea as the initial explosion's shockwave caught up to them. With flames licking their feet, Mr. Coy and Ret surfed the wave and rode it safely out of the treacherous sea towards the yacht.

"Are you okay?" Ana asked urgently as the recovery team boarded the yacht, though she was obviously addressing her mother.

"A bit singed," Mr. Coy replied, unaware that Ana was not talking to him, "but fine otherwise."

While everyone else was distracted, Principal Stone quietly tiptoed away from the group, remembering that his rescuers were also his captors.

"Where are you going, Principal Stone?" Ret asked, grabbing him tightly by the arm. All eyes turned to him, many of which glared with anger.

"Lock 'em in the brig!" Coy instructed, once again speaking like a pirate. Ret and the girls used their subsuits to visibly arm themselves as they gladly escorted their prisoners to their cells below deck.

"Impossible!" Coy stated as he helped a weary Pauline to her cabin. "How could Stone have possibly known where we were?"

Pauline's head hung low in shame. "I told them," she confessed softly. Mr. Coy's look of shocked indignation demanded an explanation. "That evil man tricked me," she said in tears. "He lied to me. He used me to get information. I didn't realize it at the time, but I see it now." She'd be a fool not to, Mr. Coy wanted to say as he rolled his eyes. "I'm sorry; I should have trusted you from the beginning, but you're just so — so odd." Mr. Coy wasn't sure if he liked the sound of that but didn't interrupt the sobbing woman. "I'm just a parent who wants to protect her children. I'm sure you know how that goes, Ben."

"Ben?" Mr. Coy mouthed silently in disgust. He was starting to feel a bit uncomfortable.

"It's been so hard for me ever since Jaret disappeared," Pauline continued. "We were so in love. He meant the world to me, just as I'm sure your wife does to you."

"Uh," Mr. Coy stuttered awkwardly, "um, yes."

"Paige speaks very highly of her mother," Pauline said. "I would love to meet her sometime. Maybe when we get back home, we can — "

"I don't think that's possible," Coy said coldly, cutting Pauline off abruptly.

"Why not?" Pauline asked. "Is she sick?"

"No."

"Does she work?"

"No."

"Is she afraid of people?"

"No!" Coy answered emphatically.

"Then, Ben, I don't see any reason why she and I can't — "

"Polly want a cracker?" Coy asked.

"Excuse me?" Pauline asked in confusion as she stepped into her cabin.

"Polly want a cracker?" he asked again.

"No — "

"Then get off my shoulder!" Mr. Coy slammed the door of Pauline's cabin. While she was still standing in shock at Mr. Coy's rudeness, he opened the door just long enough to add, "And stop calling me Ben!"

❍ ❍ ❍

Ret was on his way out of the main deck's fitness room when he found Paige leaning over the side of the yacht, staring out to sea. Laden with sweat from his workout, he said a quick 'hi' and hurried past her, but she called out to him.

"Hey, Ret," she said. He stopped. Paige stepped towards him. "I just wanted to tell you that what you did today was really brave."

Flattered, Ret smiled. "Thanks," was all he could think to say. A gust of salty air blew a strand of Paige's blonde, curly hair in front of her face. As Ret waited for her to move it out of the way, he was taken aback by how striking she looked. Her features may have just seemed more vibrant against the backdrop of black smoke still billowing above the recently-ignited, bubbling sea in the distance, but Ret was somewhat awestruck by the beauty of the girl who was always in Ana's shadow. When Paige made no motion to fix her hair, Ret slowly raised his right hand to push it back behind her ear. Before he could do so, however, he felt a familiar sensation in the palm of his hand.

"What is it?" Paige questioned as Ret took back his hand.

"It's that feeling from the helicopter trip," he explained, "the one that feels like magnets."

"That must mean we're close," Paige concluded with eagerness. They rushed to inform the others.

When everyone had assembled in the captain's quarters, Mr. Coy addressed them with final instructions. "This is as far as my ship can take us," he told them. "We will swim the remaining distance to the underwater road. Each subsuit is equipped with an intercommunications system that will allow us to speak to each other underwater; however, if the powerful electromagnetic field surrounding this region should cause interference, do exactly as I do."

Pauline looked a bit disconcerted as she tried to fit more comfortably in her skintight subsuit.

"Furthermore, if we happen to pass through another wave of methane emissions, please do everything in your power not to think about — and thus conjure up — a flame." Mr. Coy opened the cabin door and stepped onto the deck. "I'll lead the way; Ivan will take up the rear." Then he plunged into the sea, with Ret eagerly following close behind.

It was with a hint of hesitation that Ana and Paige shuffled to the side of the yacht when, like at the top of a waterslide, their turn had arrived. Perhaps due to a trick of the mind, neither one of them had previously realized the prodigious and frightening mystery of the open ocean now that it was time for them to jump into it. The seawater, though clear, still shrouded what might be lurking beneath to greet them.

But the girls' reluctance paled in comparison to the qualms of Pauline. Even though her hair was still a bit damp from her recent swim in the big blue, she was not at all anxious to join the escapade. In the end, however, it was her overarching concern for her children — as well as her lingering misgivings about their guide's mental state — that pushed her over the edge and into the water.

Ret, on the other hand, was thrilled to be back in the water. Now devoid of bubbles, he could fully appreciate the majesty of the underwater world. Painted in every shade of bright green and see-through blue, the Bahamian waters were as clean and clear as glass, full of life and color. Ret marveled at how the submerged world appeared to mimic life on dry land: schools of fish flitted freely like flocks of birds; weeds and grasses swayed peacefully in the waves like trees and bushes in the breeze; crustaceans crawled in the sand like rodents rummaging in the dirt. The sunken world seemed but a continuation of the terrestrial, more alike than different. What impressed Ret most, however, was submarine life's choice to adapt to the circumstances given them: instead of changing their world, they changed themselves.

"The road is up ahead," Mr. Coy's voice was heard through each subsuit's intercom. Now much less than a mile from the shore of the nearby island of Bimini, the ocean bottom had risen steadily until they were swimming in water scarcely deeper than a dozen feet. Even though the water temperature rivaled a warm bath, with some pockets warmer than others, the landscape had changed dramatically, its plants sparser and fish fewer.

"What happened to all the fish?" Ret wondered aloud.

"Maybe they got scared off by a shark!" Ana teased.

"Good grief," Pauline sighed worriedly, looking around just to make sure.

Ret was right: the whole scene had quickly turned dull and boring. The plants, now long and spindly, languidly swayed in pale hues of mostly weak orange and faint purple. The flat seafloor, barren and sand-covered, resembled some kind of underwater desert. Ret wondered if the sky's puffy clouds had swallowed the hot sun, so overshadowed had their path become. He reasoned this would be one of the last places a diver would want to explore.

"This is the hooked portion of the road," Mr. Coy explained, pointing downward. "See how it curves?"

"That's the road?" Ret asked in disbelief. "It looks like just a bunch of rocks."

"Yeah, lame," added Ana.

Ana had a point. Without Mr. Coy's watchful eye, the others would have passed directly over the sunken road, never even noticing it. The pale blocks rose a mere one or two feet from the ground, much less than Ret had anticipated. Covered in sand, the stones would have seemed nothing more than a rough strip of seafloor if they hadn't been the only rocks on the bottom.

"The part I want to show you is at the other end — at the top of the hook's shaft," said Mr. Coy. "Follow me."

Ret's scar throbbed to the point of pain as they swam along the road. The sandstone blocks sat in impressive uniformity, resembling giant loaves of bread with their rounded edges. Though varying in length and width, the cobblestone-like road maintained the same height throughout, despite obvious signs of wear and erosion. As they made their way around the bend and up the shank of the hook-shaped road, Ret could hardly contain himself.

"Here it is," Mr. Coy said, pointing to a spot on the final stone at the top-end of the road. "The symbol." Each in the party took turns examining the larger version of the tiny scar that was on both Ret's hand and the Oracle.

"Now what?" Ana asked.

Ret swam up close to the block a second time. With his right hand, he wiped the rough surface of the rock with his fingers to remove some of the sand and dirt that had accumulated on the symbol. As he did so, he felt something pulling his hand toward the symbol. It was as if there was another magnet behind the symbol on the stone, attracting the ones that were repelling each other under the scar in his palm. Soon, Ret stopped resisting the attraction and placed his hand over the symbol.

Ret waited for a few seconds, but nothing happened. As he slowly removed his hand, however, a stream of particles followed it. The granules of sand were the byproduct of something being etched into the surface of the stone just below the symbol. When it had finished, it was quite clear that the fresh markings were of the same nature as the curious characters on the parchment that Mr. Coy had filched from Principal Stone's office.

"What does it say?" Mr. Coy said urgently, asking the question that was on everyone's lips.

Ret studied the letters briefly and answered: "The road to Sunken Earth."

Even though they were floating, everyone could feel the sudden rumbling that started shaking everything around them. Probably reminded of their ill-fated helicopter ride, Pauline let out a shrill cry as the turbulence intensified. Then the group watched in awe as the entire expanse of the road in front of them began sinking into the ground. The set of stones directly behind the one that Ret was facing sunk into the seafloor, coming to rest when its top was level with where its bottom had just been. Then the next set of stones sunk in the same manner, though sinking even deeper until its tip was flush at the foot of the first sunken stones. With great rapidity, the road continued to sink, one pair of blocks at a time, each plunging further down than its predecessor. When the domino-like ripple had extended out of sight beyond the curve of the hook, the chasm looked somewhat like a descending staircase, though built for a giant. When the sand had finally settled, the startled divers looked down from their vista at the first step into the ominous blackness of the road that appeared to lead into the belly of the earth.

"Didn't see that coming," Ana remarked.

"I've heard of stairway to *heaven*," Mr. Coy said, trying to ease the tension that seemed to grip the group, "but *this* — this is a first, even for me."

Even though Ret was clearly the master key that was continuing to unlock the many latches on the door of this complex mystery, no one bothered to ask him how he felt about the situation or what their next course of action should be. But this was nothing new; he was unfailingly puzzled by his associates' persistence in not seeking out his advice. He hoped their actions were involuntary. It wasn't that Ret thought of himself as some grand source of knowledge; in fact, he somewhat enjoyed being ignored and certainly preferred not to be probed. Though not shy, Ret was an introvert who kept his thoughts and feelings to himself unless asked to share them — and, even then, he did so only partially. To be honest, this whole Oracle business was far outside his comfort zone, and he worried that he would have to vocalize his sentiments more often, even without being asked, rather than keep them caged within the impenetrable, yet safe, confines of his mind.

Ret was the first one to swim beyond the first step. Mr. Coy promptly went next, followed by Paige and Ana side-by-side. Having had quite enough adventure for one day, Pauline was not exactly thrilled to go for a swim into a dark fissure at the bottom of the ocean, but she moved quickly so as not to be at the back of the line, consigning Ivan to bring up the rear.

With each step, the light grew dimmer, the water felt colder, and the pressure became stronger. "In case your ears are buckling under the water pressure," Mr. Coy instructed, "there is a mouthpiece inside the third compartment on the right side of your utility belt. Attach it to the roof of your mouth, and it will automatically regulate the air pressure within your middle ear by injecting air into the throat and up your Eustachian tubes." Everyone gladly obeyed. "The mouthpiece also regulates pressure throughout the entire body, so in the event we reach extreme depths, it should prevent us from being crushed to death."

"Should?" Pauline balked.

"That's why I let Ret go first," said Mr. Coy.

Ret continued to lead the company further along the half-mile road and deeper into the earth. When they began, Ret watched the sides of the gorge turn from sand to clay to rock until he could hardly see a thing.

When he at last reached the bottom of the mammoth staircase, Ret waited for the rest in the group to arrive, though he could hardly see them when they did. Mr. Coy tapped the ring on his finger, providing a faint gleam of light. The wall of rock in front of them stood like an immovable skyscraper. Then, aiming the light at their feet to reveal their next step, they were surprised to find no step at all but instead a bottomless chute. Mr. Coy scooped up a handful of pebbles and dropped them into the hole. Nothing. He shined his ring into the darkness. Nothing.

"What have we got to lose?" Coy asked.

"Lose? Nothing," Ret replied. "Gain? Everything."

"Then after you," said Coy.

Ret dove into the abyss and disappeared in the blackness.

Chapter 12

Sunken Earth

"Okay then," Mr. Coy said cheerily, motioning to the others to follow Ret. "In we go."

"No way, not happening," Pauline asserted.

"No trip down the black hole of death for me, thank you very much," Ana announced.

"I'll pass, too," Paige added politely.

"We haven't come all this way just to turn back now," Mr. Coy petitioned, trying to reason with them.

"You may have gotten us this far, Mr. Coy," said Pauline, "but hole or no hole — "

"What did you call me?"

Ret could hear their bickering through the subsuits' intercom as he continued to wend his way downward — at least, that was the direction he felt he was going, for it was impossible to tell anything about his surroundings. Every now and then, one of his fins or a few of his fingers would brush up against what must have been one of the sides of the vertical channel, helping him to reorient himself as best he could, considering he was upside-down and basically blind. Like descending into the heart of a deep cave, the immediate atmosphere was becoming colder and denser. Shrink-wrapped by the relentless water pressure, Ret was finding it difficult to breathe.

"Come on," Ret said invitingly to the hesitant members of their expedition. "Everything's fine." He was happy to rest as he waited for them to catch up to him, though he had to latch onto the wall to prevent himself from floating upward.

"A light, just a little light," Pauline repeated many times before everyone rejoined Ret. "Hello? I can't see a thing." With trepidation and waning patience in her voice, she was clearly thinking out loud. "I thought you said this suit could conjure up anything I can think of?"

"It can," said Mr. Coy, "*if* the necessary resources are available. Obviously, there is nothing in the vicinity capable of producing light or else this entire cavern would be glowing like neon. And, apparently, your subsuit is unaware of the underwater flare in my possession."

Pauline's face flushed with indignation, though no one could see it on account of the lack of light. "Flare? Well, what are you waiting for? Light it already!"

Even though he was saving his precious commodity for more dire circumstances, Mr. Coy breathed a few of his air bubbles into his hand, forcing them into one large bubble. Working by the light of his ring, whose already-faint glow had now been rendered nearly useless in the murky water, he then inserted the ignition end of the flare into the bubble and lit it.

While the immediate flash of light emitted by the flare shone stupendously, the scene that it illuminated was utterly horrifying. Hanging on the walls all around them were dozens of human skeletons — skulls and bones, entangled in roots and seaweed, dangling like some kind of morbid puppet show. As soon as this gruesome sight registered in the minds of Pauline, Ana, and Paige, they each let out a blood-curdling scream, which startled Mr. Coy enough to lose his grasp on the waterproof flare. They watched the flare sink speedily, casting light upon the corridor's walls immediately around it as it plunged out of sight.

"Still want a light, Polly?" Mr. Coy remarked bitterly.

"Ignorre-ance ith blith," Ivan sighed.

"Or suicide," sneered Pauline.

"My guess is those poor people died while trying to get *out,*" said Coy. "We are trying to get *in*. Big difference."

"And that's supposed to make me feel better?" Pauline questioned.

With their path having been lit (at one point) before them, the party pressed on, though with great hesitancy. Fortunately for Ret, who wanted to keep moving, swimming down this submerged shaft was something like trying to descend an ascending escalator: stopping meant digressing. The low density of their bodies required them to swim constantly and with enough strength to counteract the force being exerted against them by the increasingly denser water. Of course, all they had to do to prevent themselves from floating away was to simply grab hold of the side of the passageway, but that option had recently lost its attractiveness. In fact, an occasional gasp was heard from the lips of one of the girls whenever she grazed the edge of the tunnel, terrified by the grotesque décor she may have touched. It was their imagination that got the better of them, like walking through an unseen spider's web and not knowing the whereabouts of its maker.

In time, however, the passageway began to level out. At the front of the pack, Ret kept his eyes fixed on the path ahead, strained and alert. His heart took courage, therefore, when he noticed small speckles of light in the distance, like faraway stars twinkling in the night sky. Fortunately, the gap between them and this first sign of light was not the expanse of outer space, for soon he was afforded a closer look, which revealed this curious glimmering to be some sort of luminescent glitter mixed throughout the earthen walls. It continued to intensify and increase in concentration with every stroke forward, casting a very filtered — though welcomed — light all around them. Wondering if his eyes were playing tricks on him, it looked like they were now passing through an underwater mine shaft whose belly was bespeckled with fragmented jewels.

"Look!" Ret yelled. "I see the end!" He pointed straight ahead where the end of the road curved upward sharply and light spilled into the water.

"Light at the end of the tunnel, eh?" Ana observed. "How ironic."

Despite their strenuous journey, Ret swam with all his might to the end of the channel. Not once since their launch had fear seized his breast, only hope and a unique sort of happiness — the kind of sustaining anticipation that only comes from the progressive realization of the purpose of one's life. For as long as he could remember (which wasn't very long), Ret had always felt underused and unappreciated — like an untapped oil reserve or a forgotten asteroid — to say nothing of how often he was misunderstood by others. But, for once, he was beginning to feel like things were finally coming together in his life — that, at last, the drill was scratching his surface; that the center of the universe was pulling him back into orbit. At least, that was his hope, for while Ret's five companions had never felt so beside themselves, recent events had awakened such a new hope inside himself.

Like a family of sea otters, the Coopers and the Coys, with their butler Ivan, surfaced in a large pond of water. Quickly finding the nearest edge, they pulled themselves onto the bank and collapsed with fatigue. Happily removing their subsuits and leaving them piled nearby, they found their legs and tried to adjust their eyes to their new environment.

It was a small room, like a foyer leading into something grander. There were no signs of intelligent life, just a patch of grass and adobe walls that came together overhead. From the pond's edge spilled a small stream that flowed with the natural slope of the ground. Despite the room's bareness, there was something about its features that seemed exceptionally bright. Every square inch seemed to shimmer and shine with a pulsating, flickering glow, which, when reflected by the pond's rippling water, caused colorful shadows to dance on the ceiling. The newcomers, however, assumed it was all just the temporary result of having been exposed to sheer blackness for so long.

"I like yoor fanny pack, thir," Ivan complimented Mr. Coy as he prepared for what they might encounter in the near future.

"Utility belt, Ivan," Mr. Coy corrected him, "utility belt. All the great superheroes wear one." He patted it proudly.

"They all wear spandex, too," Ana added.

"Oh, spare us all!" Pauline implored.

Feeling no need to recuperate, Ret had already ventured ahead of them. "Check this out," he called out, his voice echoing off the clay walls. They stammered to his side, catching their balance. Ret had followed the stream until he was standing in front of a large stone door, thick and impassable, whose face bore the symbol of the hook and triangle.

"I feel we should go this way," he suggested to the group.

"Gee, Captain Obvious, I wonder what gave you that idea?" Ana mumbled sarcastically. Besides the conspicuous clue of the symbol etched in the stone's surface, the rock blocked the only apparent way out of the room. It sat directly over the stream, which still managed to flow underneath it without obstruction.

"And how do you feel we should get through?" Mr. Coy asked.

Though he liked being asked his opinion on the matter, Ret could hardly say a word before Pauline read his mind.

"Oh, no," she refused stubbornly, "I am *not* swimming in any more sinkholes today."

Ana sighed. “Really, people?” she said, shocked. “Ret, just use your hand – you know, that wave thingy?”

Ret looked at the scar on his right hand. Never before had it appeared so brilliant. He rotated his hand toward the crude door when instantly the entire thing disintegrated. In a single motion, it was reduced to dust. Everyone was impressed.

“That was easy,” said Coy.

“He must work out,” Ana whispered to Paige, who giggled as they walked across the remains of the barrier and through the passageway.

What they encountered next blew everything they had experienced thus far out of the water – and then some. On the other side of the doorway sat a magnificent civilization, which stretched and sprawled as far as the eye could see. It was grander than anything they had ever seen – the size and magnitude of *their* world’s largest cities, all merged together in one. In the distance, towers rose above towns and villages, hemmed in on every side by thick vegetation. Rivers, great and small, meandered between buildings and around edifices. Where cities stopped, hills of farmland rolled out of sight. It was the metropolis of all metropolises.

This new world’s most striking feature, however, was the enormous mountain directly at its center. Whereas most major cities crowd their downtown districts with skyscrapers, the heart of this megacity was a towering mountain, a giant pyramid of raw earth. Everything else about the city seemed to go out from this central region. In fact, it was so massive that the cloud layer rose scarcely halfway up its slopes, where a thick and threatening group of storm clouds had accumulated, frequently illuminating with strikes of lightning.

"Wait a minute," Ana said. "Aren't we *under* the ocean?" The thought made reason stare. Their journey was proof enough that they were, indeed, under the ocean. But it wasn't until Ana spoke up when they turned their attention to the sky — or the roof, rather. Like a domed sports arena, a light-colored ceiling enclosed the civilization in its entirety. They had, in reality, found a lost city, hidden from the rest of the world, concealed under the Atlantic Ocean.

This helped to explain another oddity. Directly above the mountain, a great waterfall cascaded through the roof. Spewing through a series of small openings in the ceiling, the seawater completely encircled the mountain's peak, enclosing it in a sort of curtain of water. The waterfall gushed mightily, sending water down the mountainside in every direction, feeding the many rivers below.

For several minutes, Ret and the others stood motionless, absorbing the grandeur of the scene, for not only was it a lot to take in for the logical mind but also for the senses. Every particle — each atom — seemed to be electrifyingly alive. The plants were greener; the buildings were more vibrant; even the dirt glowed with a surging pulse of life and energy. Even though there were no new colors, each was much more brilliant and radiant, which combined to give everything an unreal, almost fake appearance. Had it been a photograph, the camera must have had a million megapixels, capable of microscopic resolution. Coupled with the crisp freshness of the warm, humid air, it was enough to overload the senses.

It was no surprise, then, when Ret became aware of a new source of energy, surging through his own body like life-giving blood through veins after vigorous exercise. He felt stronger, more alive; rejuvenated and recharged. The unpleasant sensation under the scar in his hand, once a nearly constant pang of discomfort, had given way to a pulse of empowerment.

"Welcome to Sunken Earth," Mr. Coy said in awe.

"It looks like this place is on steroids or something," Ana commented, helping everyone to shake off the trance caused by the unbelievable sight.

"Let's find out why!" Ret replied with great enthusiasm. He was about to spring from their perch overlooking the city when Pauline interrupted him.

"Yes — *why?*" she said. Everyone turned to find her looking perplexed, with feet firmly planted and arms crossed. "Remind me just why we're here exactly?"

"We're here to find one of the elements, of course," Mr. Coy explained. "Don't you remember the message on the parchment: 'Fill the Oracle, pure elements reunite'?" He retrieved the Oracle from his utility belt and held it in front of Pauline to jog her memory.

"Yes, I remember quite well, thank you," she said. "But *why?* Why do we want to 'fill the Oracle' — why do we want to 'reunite' the elements?" Though she had a history of being obstinate, everyone could tell that Pauline's concern was sincere. Mr. Coy didn't know what to say; in fact, no one knew what to tell her.

After several silent seconds, Ret hunched his shoulders and confessed, "I don't know. I don't know what all of this stuff means, Pauline. I don't know where we are or what we're doing here. I don't know the future or all the reasons for things." Everyone watched Ret, wondering if Pauline's doubts were causing him to falter. "But we don't have to know why. All we need to know is what's right, and then do it, even if it means stepping into the darkness a little." He took a few steps closer to Pauline. "After all, isn't that what Jaret did?" She looked down with a face that was sad but happy. "He didn't know why that ship was burning. He didn't know if anyone was on board. But he did it anyway — because he felt it was the right thing to do." Ret put his hand on Pauline's shoulder. "And he saved me."

"Oh, Ret," she said, embracing him. Together they trotted down the trail ahead of the others. "Now let's go and find this element!" she insisted, her qualms giving way to newfound zeal.

In just a few quick paces, they found themselves engulfed in jungle-like vegetation whose broad foliage and leafy vines left little room for visibility. A thick carpet of low-lying bushes and creeping shrubbery quieted their footsteps while several layers of canopy above shaded them below. Finding the dense growth to be impeding their trek, Mr. Coy advanced to the head of the team and started hacking the herbage with a short, broad sword.

"They didn't call me Cutlass Coy for nothing," he remarked, happy to feel needed.

"Ret, can't you just move stuff out of our way or something?" Ana suggested playfully. Ret thought it was worth a try. Spying a large boulder nearby, he stretched out his hand and moved it according to his will. It rolled in front of Mr. Coy and plowed a trail, felling everything in its path.

"I could get used to this," Ana said triumphantly. Once Mr. Coy had finished chopping the last few branches before the start of Ret's improvised trail, he stopped in shock and dropped the cutlass to his side.

"Now how about you do something about all these mosquitoes, Ret?" Pauline begged desperately.

Now that Ret had simplified their safari to more of a stroll in the park, he and his comrades had much more time to assess their surroundings. It was remarkably quiet for a jungle of its kind; in fact, none of them had so much as seen or heard any signs of life — well, besides the mosquitoes, the universe's only ineradicable organism.

"Haven't you got any bug repellant in that fanny pack of yours?" Pauline asked Mr. Coy.

"This is *not* a fanny pack," Mr. Coy insisted, now a bit annoyed. "We've been through this: it's a utility belt!" Slightly regaining some composure, he continued, "And no, I don't have any bug repellant. When you've been to as many places as I have, your body naturally develops its own repellant."

"Which is why they invented deodorant," Ana joked quietly to Paige.

The team was too enveloped in idle conversation and amazed observation to notice the group of armed guards that was silently closing in on them. From multiple angles, the guards stealthily analyzed their invaders and waited for the opportune moment to seize and capture them.

Without any warning, three large nets fell on Ret and the others like giant birds of prey, knocking them to the ground. Made of very flexible metal, the nets surged with some sort of electricity, making them dangerous to the touch and impossible to sever. Ret could only watch as their assailants emerged from their hiding places and loudly charged toward their catch.

"Cue the natives," Ana sighed.

"Should've seen this coming," Mr. Coy commented.

Ret's initial reaction was to use his powers to free him and the others from their bonds. He easily thought of over a dozen different ways to creatively and resourcefully liberate themselves. But he chose not to do so. Something within himself discouraged such a plan and instead calmed his worried mind. And so, he and the others cooperated when their captors arrived and hauled them away.

"We come in peace," Mr. Coy said gently, trying to converse with the guards. "We are friends."

"Try *amigos,*" Ana advised. "We *are* still in the Caribbean, aren't we?"

It quickly became clear that their attackers did not speak English, employing instead an entirely foreign language of their own. But it wasn't harsh or guttural; rather, it sounded clean and sophisticated. And their appearance could be described in much the same way. They were a neat and comely lot, unlike typical indigenous tribes with their stereotypical loin cloths and shorn heads. With fair skin and bright features, they looked much like Ret and the gang; in fact, they resembled Ret more than they did Ana, Pauline, Ivan, and the Coys. Noticing this, Ret was tempted to speak to them, but he restrained himself, desiring first to learn what they intended to do with their prisoners, for though they seemed civilized, they were certainly dressed as if in preparation for civil unrest. Each of the guards was outfitted in a full-body suit made of thin, stretchy material whose very threads and fibers occasionally transmitted electrical charges from head to toe. While some carried metal staffs with heads of electrically-charged coils, others sported long whips that crackled and contorted like lightning, though each was arrayed with all manner of curious weaponry, including a shiny shield that looked like a mirror. Every time one of the guards stepped on the ground, the dirt immediately around his foot seethed with energy, as if his suit knew how to keep itself charged by robbing the earth of its own energy. A similar thing happened around the wheels of their carriages, which was the best word that Ret could think of to describe the guards' unique mode of transportation. There was no engine, no combustion, not even any kind of hoofed creature; it was just a carriage-like body on wheels, steered by a driver and powered by the energy that it collected through contact with the ground.

"I've got to get me one of these," Mr. Coy vowed, admiring the vehicle's concept and design.

As if acting under strict orders, the guards moved with great haste. Upon emerging from the dense overgrowth of the jungle, the party approached civilization. Ret used the land's great mountain as his sole point of reference, as it was growing larger every moment. The guards hauled their bounty through the streets of town, where Ret was stupefied by what he saw. To say that the city was rundown was a compliment, as Ret and the others had never seen such miserable living conditions. The slums stretched for miles in every direction, including overhead. Like a patchwork quilt sewn from leftover scraps of material, the shacks and shanties covered the land, shoved side-by-side so as to lean against each other for stability. They seemed to sway with the gentle breeze as the guards moved quickly along the dirt road, obviously intent on spending as little time as possible in the ghetto. At first, Ret assumed — and hoped — that these neighborhoods had been abandoned, for he hadn't seen a living soul among them. But a closer look revealed the contrary — indeed, the opposite. Scores of people, like startled insects, retreated to the shadows as the guards cut through town. With alarm on their faces and rags on their backs, they watched in fear until the party passed, only then timidly venturing out.

The mountain loomed ever closer as they neared the end of the slums and approached something entirely different. The carriages climbed a long bridge that spanned a filthy river, on the other side of which stood a colossal wall, almost as thick as it was tall. From the top of the wall rose a series of towers and pillars, each one sending a wide current of electricity to the next, combining to create a sort of force field all around the wall. The convoy passed through an array of gates and barricades before finally gaining access to the other side of the wall.

The scene that lay before them reeked of wealth. Broad boulevards rolled along, edged by leafy trees and ornate streetlights. Quaint shops with their trivial trinkets lined the promenade, while spacious homes with fresh paint and manicured yards dotted the side streets. Free-flowing fountains and crystal-clear waterways curved lazily along banks of lush greenery, where boats and other toys were docked. Children played and friends sipped tea as bountiful amounts of energy lit the indoors and gave life to the goings-on. Ret could almost hear music playing, as if he was strolling merrily in some fantasyland. The guards, whose pace had slowed, were warmly received by everyone, even applauded by some when they noticed the presence of captured prisoners.

The wide base of the mountain filled the background of their view as they passed through the wall and force field at the other end of the glamorous town. Another bridge over another dirty river, and the brigade marched on. Ever since being captured, their path had been a constant incline, some parts steeper than others. Looking over his shoulder, Ret could clearly see how the slums sat quite a ways below suburbia, and yet they were still climbing higher. This third and final ring of structures around the mountain was clearly devoted to industry. The clink and clang of tools and metal filled the air, which billowed with smoke and dust. Powerful machines attacked the mountain on all sides, excavating and digging into it. Dirt-splattered workers scrambled on the ground fulfilling a slew of tasks, as busy as ants but as happy as slaves. A vast network of rivers was lined with ships and barges, transporting their goods to countless destinations. Though Ret and the others had no idea what was going on, this industrial sector was clearly a well-orchestrated operation.

Ret marveled at the tour he had just witnessed. From a distance, this vast, underground civilization looked impressive and majestic — a lost gem, a wonder unknown to the world. Up close, however, it was puzzling, to say the least. Having been transported to the center of the metropolis, Ret felt that there was something unsettling about the whole situation — that a dark shroud clouded his mind.

In a flurry of commands, the guards took their prisoners deep into a heavily-guarded building, which resembled a jail in every particular except for one obvious contrast: currents of electricity replaced the traditional iron bars to keep the incarcerated in their cells. Though dark, Ret could see dozens of dirty hands reaching towards them through the thin gaps between the vertical electrical currents. The sound of heavy chains being shuffled and tugged was muffled by the moans of other inmates. The guards hauled Ret and his five companions into one cell, rolled them out of their nets, and engaged the bolts of energy to lock them behind bars.

"Note to self," Mr. Coy said as they stretched to shake off the soreness of being bound, "this place does not take kindly to visitors." Dark and dank, their quarters were small and isolated. The jail's stone floor felt a bit damp to the touch. A few streaks of light shot through a single, barred window, which looked more like a crude crack in the edifice's thick wall. They huddled together to plan their next move.

"What do we do now?" Pauline asked.

"We eat bread and water and make license plates until we rot, of course," Ana answered.

"What do *you* think, Ret?" Mr. Coy said.

"Ret?" A man's voice emerged from the shadows at the other end of their cell. Ret, Mr. Coy, and Ivan stepped in front of Pauline, Ana, and Paige, shielding them from whatever might come their way. "Ret?" The voice again repeated Ret's name, in a tone that indicated he had heard it before. “Ret Cooper?” The voice sounded deep and young, too soothing to be eerie but too mystic to be at all comforting.

“Yes?” Ret answered bravely. “How do you know my name?”

The voice replied, “Lye said you would come.”

Chapter 13

Jailbreak

"Who is Lye?" Ret asked, thoroughly perplexed. "And who are you?"

"I believe introductions are in order," the concealed speaker announced as he fled the shadows and stepped into the prison's dim light. "My name is Lionel Zarbock." The tension that had gripped Ret and the others melted away immediately upon the emergence of their nonthreatening roommate with his captivating appearance. He was a striking man, perhaps a decade older than Ret, with a countenance truly like lightning. Jet-black hair and dark eyes gave his already-light skin an even brighter glow. He stood tall and firm in his sculpted physique, which was scarred by neither blemish nor wrinkle. Despite his commanding presence, however, there was something inviting about his demeanor. He breathed knowledge and sophistication, resembling the rare kind of individual who people naturally want to believe and follow. Vibrant and attractive, he seemed the epitome of youth, hardly the type of person you'd expect to find in a dingy prison.

"And *you* are…?" Lionel put forth to the group, each of whom was spellbound.

"Sorry," Ret apologized. "This is Mr. Coy; his daughter, Paige; and their butler, Ivan; and this is Pauline and her daughter, Ana." Lionel graciously shook hands with the men, then gently kissed the hand of each woman, greeting them all individually with a warm smile and a welcoming salutation.

"It is truly a pleasure to meet all of you," he said sincerely, "especially *you*, Ret. Lye has told me much about *you*."

"And who is this Lye you speak of?" Mr. Coy asked earnestly. Even though they had only just met, Mr. Coy viewed Lionel with great skepticism, feeling slightly intimidated by his charisma and professionalism. Mr. Coy resolved to try the virtue of Lionel's words at every turn.

"I first met Lye in Vienna, Austria, at the headquarters of the International Atomic Energy Agency, where I serve as one of its principal nuclear physicists."

"So you're not from…*here* — you're not from Sunken Earth?" Mr. Coy pressed urgently.

"No, no," Lionel reaffirmed. "I'm from your world — *our* world — though I've been living here for, gosh, probably close to a year now. You see, Lye approached me and told me that he had found a lost city — an underwater world. At first I didn't believe him — I mean, who could believe such a fairytale? — but he had proof: pictures, artifacts, samples — you name it. And so, being the curious scientist that I am, I was intrigued. I studied his specimens and was dumbfounded; never had I seen anything so miraculous. Shortly thereafter, Lye invited me to return with him to this hidden civilization. He said he needed my help and expertise in studying this new world — in conducting experiments and doing research that he felt could greatly benefit our own, dying world. When I asked if I could bring along some of my colleagues, he vehemently declined, explaining how he wanted to keep it a secret so as to preserve its purity and prevent it from being overrun."

"And you agreed?" asked Coy.

"Well obviously," Lionel replied, causing the others to grin despite Mr. Coy's embarrassment. "I agreed without reservation."

"And how did you get inside?" Mr. Coy questioned, thinking he had caught Lionel in his words, for he remembered how it was only because of Ret's scar that they had reconfigured the submerged stones on the seafloor to become the descending stairway that led them to Sunken Earth.

"Ah, *that* is one of Lye's great, many secrets," Lionel said, stepping towards their cell's tiny, barred window. "You see, just above the peak of that great mountain is a swirling vortex of untold power and energy." He pointed outside, though their view of the peak was blocked by the thick, thunderous storm clouds butted up against the mountainside. "In fact, it houses so much energy that, even though it has destroyed the ceiling immediately above it, it gives off enough upward force to counteract the immense downward pressure being exerted upon it by the billions upon billions of gallons of ocean water that threaten to gush through the roof."

"Except for the water spilling down the mountain," Mr. Coy added, happy to find an inconsistency in Lionel's story.

"Well, right," Lionel consented, "which is fortunate for the people here, considering the seawater that slips through the cracks is their sole source of water."

"Yes, very fortunate for them," Mr. Coy said, acting as if he had something to do with it. Pauline and the girls shot him slightly repulsed looks for his border-line rude behavior toward Lionel. "Anyway, back to how you got in," Mr. Coy reminded Lionel, not willing to let him off the hook so easily.

"But of course," Lionel continued. "As Lye explained to me, we couldn't just pack up and come here whenever we pleased. We had to wait for the exact moment when Mother Nature would reveal this world's door to us. The secret," he said, almost in a whisper, "is a hurricane. You see, the vortex created by the mountain causes the ocean water above it to spin in a clockwise direction, while hurricanes in the northern hemisphere spin in a counterclockwise direction. As soon as we got word of a hurricane forming in the Atlantic that was projected to pass over the vortex, we set sail. It sure wasn't easy to stay hovering above the vortex in the midst of a hurricane, but as soon as the eye of the storm got close enough to passing over the vortex, a truly remarkable thing happened. The opposing forces of the vortex and the hurricane nullified each other, creating a sort of vertical conduit that opened up and sucked us straight down into the belly of the sea, with walls of water on all sides. We passed through the hole in the ceiling and landed on the mountain peak — like a freefall ride at an amusement park."

Everyone was gleefully enthralled by Lionel's story — everyone, except for Mr. Coy.

"Something's fishy about this guy," he mumbled to Ivan. "And how did you survive such a fall, Mr. Zarbock?"

"Fortunately, the terrain at the top of the mountain is extremely pure and refined due to its exposure to such intense energy," Lionel went on. "It was kind of like falling into a container of powdered sugar."

"Oh, how convenient," Mr. Coy grumbled.

"While concealed in the curtain of waterfalls surrounding the peak, Lye instructed me not to come down the mountain until it was dark because he didn't want anyone to see me. When I asked why, he told me how none of the people here has ever been able to summit the great mountain — that each time someone has tried, that person died because he couldn't withstand the intense energy. So no one has ever set foot on the top of the mountain before, and no one knows what it is that gives the mountain its supernatural power. They have lots of theories and legends, of course, but no one knows for certain. So you can imagine the shock everyone felt when, one day, they saw a man emerge from the peak and descend the mountain — alive. Lye had no idea of the feat that he had achieved, but the people revered him — they feared him, and some even worshiped him."

"So why didn't he want you to be known as a survivor of the mountain, too?" Mr. Coy asked.

"Lye said it would defeat the whole purpose of me coming here," said Lionel. "He had asked me to come to explain the countless phenomena of this place — to mingle with the people, learn their language and their culture, taste their food and learn their history. He said the people wouldn't even come close to him for fear of offending him or dying in his very presence. So I did as he told me."

"So, explain this then, buster," Mr. Coy continued his interrogation. "How exactly *did* you and Lye survive the murderous, vaporizing power emitted by the mountain, hmm?"

"Why, sir, I'm insulted," Lionel admitted respectfully. "I have devoted my life to the study of nuclear physics. I can replicate the reactions that take place on the surface of the sun. It should come as no surprise to you that I might have a few tricks up my sleeve to avoid something as elementary as fatal radiation."

"Fair enough," Coy conceded, though perturbed.

"Over the last several months," Lionel carried on, "I've learned volumes about these people and their way of life. Though their genetics vary only slightly from yours and mine, the differences stop there. They dance and sing; they paint and build; they have sports and games, religions and passions, politics and opinions; their history is a mix of fact and myth, while their aspirations are unbounded; they could teach even *our* world's most distinguished thinkers a thing or two — or three." Lionel's face conveyed the appreciation and love that he had developed for the people of Sunken Earth, having spent every waking moment with them for so long. "But the one, overarching thing that everyone depends on and no one can refute is the earth — the dirt, the soil, the very ground they walk on. It is their gold, their elixir, their very livelihood. Because of their earth, they can grow crops without the sun; they can have light in a dark world; they can desalinize seawater and not perish of thirst. Because of their earth, they can power vehicles and sail ships, steer machines and operate equipment; they can weaponize its energy to defend themselves. Because of their earth, they live. Take it away, and they die."

Lionel turned from gazing longingly out the slim window to face his listeners. "But Lye saw it a different way." The joy faded from his voice. "While I was befriending the natives, he was flattering the politicians. He never joined me, but he frequently ordered me to report to him and tell him everything that I was learning and discovering, in great detail. But his intention was never to make peace or to acquire knowledge. His motive was power — and greed." Lionel's brow furrowed more and more in bitterness and disappointment with each statement. "He told me of his success in manipulating the minds of the government officials — how they feared him and would obey his every command. They became his puppets. He eliminated the ones who opposed him and rewarded those who followed orders."

"And I'm guessing you were one of those who opposed him?" Mr. Coy assumed.

"How couldn't I?" Lionel stated, moved with emotion. "Look at what he's done to this beautiful land — to these remarkable people! He's taken control of the mountain and, therefore, everyone's very existence with it. While the rich get richer, the poor get poorer. You've seen the slums and the destitute people who live there. Those people are my friends, as dirty and ill and pathetic as they may seem. We've tried to escape — countless times — but no one can set so much as one foot upon the mountain without Lye finding out about it."

"We know another way," Ret stated, offering the little help he could. "There's the way we came in, the —"

"The underground river on the west side?" Lionel finished Ret's thought. "Yes, we know. Many have tried; none has returned. The pressure is just too great. Besides, no one could ever find the top of that lengthy, vertical tunnel." Ret's hope was dashed to pieces. "But whether they die from nobly trying to escape or from sadly succumbing to disease, the people here do not fear death — some may even envy those who achieve it, with its peace, its rest, its freedom." A solemn gloom fell over Ret and the others to think of circumstances so unpleasant that death would sound appealing. "And so, while Lye and his handpicked few glut themselves," Lionel continued to lament, "the rest of the population function as their pawns and slaves. They get fat while the people they are supposed to serve starve. They drown in pleasure and opulence while the people who support them thirst. And why do they do it? Because they can. Because their bellies are full, their treasuries overflow, and their guards protect them."

Then Lionel looked Ret square in the eye and said, "But just because you *can* do something, doesn't mean you *should*."

It was in that moment when Ret knew he could completely trust and confide in Lionel. Ever since he laid eyes on him, Ret was intensely intrigued by Lionel, and although he made it a habit to never surrender his loyalty to a stranger so quickly before seeing fruits worthy of such loyalty, Ret had seen and heard enough. He felt a connection with Lionel that he had never encountered with anyone else, including his five other comrades there in the prison cell with him. Ret had always dreamed of one day receiving the heavenly gift of a best friend — someone who was similar to him and could identify with what he was experiencing; someone he could turn to for counsel and advice; someone who had his best interests at heart. True, Ret had Ana, but she was a girl, and she didn't have magic scars on her hands, neither were her hair and eyes and skin as bright as the light. But Lionel was another story. For months, he had been living in Sunken Earth and knew its people, who felt and looked more like family to Ret than strangers.

Lionel knew their language and lore, ways and means, history and habits. Lionel even seemed to resemble the people he had come to love. Ret's heart gladdened at the idea of what he could learn from Lionel, of how Lionel could help him, of what part Lionel might play in demystifying Ret's past and unveiling his future.

"Well, nice work blowing that relationship, jailbird," Mr. Coy jabbed at Lionel. "Instead of enjoying tea and crumpets, you're here doing time. How long you in for? Ten? Twenty?" No one smiled at Mr. Coy's immaturity.

"Actually, sir," Lionel said, "I was just on my way out." Everyone looked at Lionel like he was crazy. "My arrest sent the good people of Sunken Earth into a frenzied uproar. During these months of unjust oppression, they've been stockpiling weaponry and amassing great numbers to seize Lye's regime and reestablish peace and justice. Even now, they are prepared to overthrow Lye and take back their rights and liberties. Tonight, on this eve of battle, we storm the bastille and join the ranks."

Lionel's listeners were petrified. As worthy as his goals all seemed, none of them had really expected to risk his or her life by fighting in some civil war. And, besides, they were still incarcerated. Instead of traditional bars of thick metal, they found themselves behind currents of electricity, shooting up from the floor. Too close together to slip between and too powerful to touch, the laser-like currents cackled and buzzed in the damp prison air.

Lionel could sense his newfound friends' consternation. "As I said, the citizens of Sunken Earth have found multiple uses for the energy housed in the earth," he reminded them, stepping next to their cell's electrical door. "But it has one simple antidote." Lionel reached in his pocket and brought out a handful of some white, granular substance. He placed a generous pinch over one of the sockets through which surged an electrical current. Ret watched as the white powder first melted from the immense heat of the current, then absorbed the current, leaving a gap in the cell's door. After a few moments, the white grains had been transformed into silvery metal particles and a yellow-green gas, and the current resumed its blockade.

Ret gazed at Lionel with curious admiration. Holding his hand in front of him, still full of the white substance, he answered the question that was on everyone's mind: "Salt."

"That's impossible!" Mr. Coy gasped. "*Everyone* knows solid salt does not conduct electricity." Ana gave Mr. Coy a strange look, as if disgusted that he would include her in his generalization.

"True, true," Lionel agreed, "but *molten* salt most certainly *does* conduct electricity." Mr. Coy's eyes remained glued on Lionel, awaiting an explanation. "At first, when the salt makes contact with the current, there is no reaction. However, as the salt heats up, it melts, which loosens the ionic bonds between the sodium and chlorine atoms, thus permitting electrical conduction. The positive sodium ions pick up electrons and form sodium metal, which is that soft, silvery metal substance you see there." He pointed to the flecks of metal still surrounding the socket. "The negative chlorine ions oxidize and are given off as the pale, yellowish-green gas that emerged from the reaction." As everyone else listened to Lionel with rapt attention, Mr. Coy crossed his arms and looked away smugly.

"But I must warn you," Lionel cautioned, "sodium metal is — "

" — violently reactive with water," Mr. Coy finished.

Lionel smiled patiently, despite being interrupted. Then, continuing, he said, "And chlorine gas is — "

" — highly toxic," Mr. Coy added again. Everyone glared at Mr. Coy as they would a bothersome child. He smiled broadly.

"And if Lye ever learned what something as abundant as salt can do to his power source — " Lionel paused, waiting for Mr. Coy to complete his sentence.

Mr. Coy thought for a moment and then said, " — then he'd be *assaulted!*"

Nobody laughed.

"Get it? *A-salt-ed,"* Mr. Coy said dejectedly, barely moving his lips. "It was just a joke."

"Right," said Lionel, "then Lye's security forces would be a joke. Fortunately, I didn't tell him *everything* about my research."

Lionel turned to face Pauline, Ana, and Paige. "Now, the three of you will free all the other prisoners," he said, pouring a pile of salt into each of the girls' cupped hands, then turning to face the men, "while we take care of any guards."

"But I — " Pauline started to say.

"Just follow close behind us," Lionel reassured. "We'll clear the way for you. Once the salt absorbs the current, you only have a few seconds before it burns it up and becomes unblocked, so move swiftly. We'll lead everyone to the ground level where a group of friends will be waiting to receive us."

Pauline, recalling her decision to see this thing through, squared her shoulders and rallied with Paige and Ana.

"It's Ivan, right?" Lionel asked, addressing the butler directly.

"Yeth, thir."

"Can you fight?" Lionel wanted to know.

"Like a Boltheveek, thir," Ivan answered respectfully.

Looking a bit confused by Ivan's response, Lionel moved on to Mr. Coy and whispered, "What did he say?"

"He said he doesn't like you," Mr. Coy fibbed, grinning contentedly.

"Right," Lionel said. "Well then, here we go."

One by one, the seven of them stepped across the blockaded sockets of their cell until they were all safely on the other side. As suspenseful as it was to break out of jail, Ret was somewhat disappointed to find that it was probably the most lightly-staffed prison he had ever seen. With relative ease, they snuck up the stairwells and through the hallways, liberating dozens of inmates, whose whispered cheers and hushed applause bolstered everyone's spirits. They rallied around Lionel in grateful appreciation and fell in ranks with Ret and the others, even though neither group really recognized nor verbally communicated with the other.

"Lionel," Ret called out as they reached the ground level, "where are all the guards?"

"Not here," he answered. "They're all out searching the city today, arresting people like you and me so they can bring them here. Lye's orders. That's why we picked today to break out." Ret smiled admiringly at Lionel's brave confidence and resourceful mind.

"Looks like they're back early," Mr. Coy announced nonchalantly, pointing behind them to a large group of guards approaching the backdoor to the prison's main hall, pulling after them a mother who was clutching her small baby. Still on the outside of the door, the guards spotted the large mass of escapees dashing for the front gate. From the electric coils atop their iron staffs, the guards shot bolts of electricity towards the refugees. While those that missed the doorway blew holes in the prison walls, the few strikes that successfully entered the building sent rocks and dust ricocheting in all directions, sending the people cowering for protection.

The sudden flurry of debris, however, jogged Ret's memory and reminded him of his unique ability to manipulate dirt and dust and other earth particles according to his will and pleasure. Just as the guards were about to cross the threshold into the jail, Ret waved his hand and sent the door crashing in on itself, completely blocking the rear entrance.

"Wow, Lye wasn't kidding," Lionel remarked to himself, slightly stunned at witnessing Ret's powers for the first time. "This way!" he ordered, continuing to move to the front gate. "Follow me!"

Ret waited with Mr. Coy and Lionel at the doorway, helping to usher people safely outside the jailhouse.

"Make for the bridge!" Lionel bellowed. "Hurry!"

The prison was situated on a small island,

surrounded by a wide moat. A single, stone bridge provided the only means for crossing the treacherous moat. The liberated captives flew with all haste toward the bridge, and, once the prison had been fully vacated, Mr. Coy and Ivan, followed by Ret and Lionel, picked up the rear.

Shrieks and screams filled the air as hordes of guards spilled onto the scene from the other side of the jail and started firing on the fleeing crowd. Given the distance between them, the guards struggled to strike their moving targets, which continued to successfully cross the bridge and dive into the safety of the forest on the other side.

When Ret had finally crossed, Lionel stopped him at the fringe of the vegetation.

"Destroy the bridge, Ret," he commanded. "Use your powers. Take it down!"

Ret came to a standstill. He knew he could easily topple the earthen bridge, but, for some strange reason, he found Lionel's order unsettling. The more he thought about it, the more confounding it seemed.

"What are you waiting for?" Lionel urged, ducking from the guards' assault. "Take it out before the guards cross it!"

And then Ret heard a woman scream.

He turned around in a flash and saw the source of the distress. The woman, who the guards had just recently brought, sat against the prison wall, helplessly clutching her crying child. Reading Ret's mind, Lionel tried to talk Ret out of saving her.

"It's too dangerous, Ret," he reasoned. "It's not worth the risk."

Ret turned to face Lionel and, with a determined expression, said, "That's not what Jaret would say." Ret leapt from his place of safety and bolted across the bridge.

"So noble," Lionel observed as Ret sped away. The moment Ret set foot on the island, Lionel raised his arm high in the air, held it there for a moment, and then let it fall. Like a colony of bats, hundreds of projectiles emerged from the forest, launched by Lionel's troops who had come to aid the jailbreak. The ashen stones flew through the air before colliding with their targets, the pillars supporting the island's only bridge. Shortly after the rocks made contact with the water, a series of explosions engulfed the bridge. Light and sparks and heat and flames shot in every direction like a fireworks show gone awry, and the bridge came tumbling down.

Mr. Coy, who was only a few steps ahead, stopped dead in his tracks and returned to the moat's edge to see what had occurred.

"What on earth happened here?" Mr. Coy said in outrage.

"Remember how I — I mean, *you* — said sodium metal was violently reactive with water, Coy?" Lionel asked.

"But what about Ret?"

"I'm sure he'll think of something," Lionel said.

As Ret approached the guards, he let his instinct take control. The three guards on his right, he pelted with stones from the river bank; the pair on his left, he buried in earth and then conveniently borrowed one of their glass shields. A squadron was advancing toward him, but Ret turned the hillside into a landslide, which carried them all the way into the river. A single guard stood in front of the terrified woman, hurling bolts of energy in Ret's direction. Still running at full speed and using the glass shield, Ret deflected the guard's every round of fire and then reflected one directly back at him, knocking the guard off his feet. Ret picked up the woman and child and headed back to the bridge.

Having heard the explosion when Lionel caused the bridge to be destroyed, Ret had been thinking about how he would get back across. The guards' assault was relentless, with their missiles of electricity flying like shooting stars. Everyone ceased fire, however, when they saw Ret reach the edge of the island and jump off. But a collective gasp could be heard when they watched Ret, still carrying the woman and child in his arms, rise up on a broken slab of the bridge. By pure mental capacity, Ret caused fragments of the bridge to emerge from the water and hover in the air, one after the other, creating an inclined series of stepping stones. Ret jumped from piece to piece, the one he had just left falling back to the water as it was no longer his concern.

The guards redoubled their attack. Their captain ordered them to abandon trying to hit their elusive human target and instead to focus on obliterating his upcoming steps. Some they fractured, forcing Ret to land on one foot. As he neared the final step, however, the concentrated enemy fire completely destroyed it. Not willing to be outdone, Ret focused all his energy on containing the last, now-ruptured slab. As he launched himself towards his final step, the fragments of the last slab were reunited, just long enough and strong enough to support Ret's weight, before breaking apart into rubble and dust.

Ret collapsed on the other side of the protective vegetation.

"Well done, Ret!" Mr. Coy congratulated. "Well done, indeed!"

"You're a brave man," Lionel said, ruffling Ret's bright, yellow hair. "I'm sure Princess Alana will reward you handsomely."

Chapter 14

Battlefronts

Ret had little idea where he was going. As the rescue party continued to wend its course further and further away from the prison, it was obvious from the chosen route that they were bent on traveling as inconspicuously as possible. Replete with sudden twists and unexpected turns, they passed through secret passageways and plunged into underground tunnels. Though their path hardly seemed the most direct, it certainly was the most unseen.

"This reminds me of your place," Ret remarked to Mr. Coy, who was having considerable difficulty blazing his own trail so as not to be so dependent on Lionel as their guide.

At length, they arrived at another swath of Sunken Earth's endless slums. While a pervasive uneasiness had gripped the escapees all along the way at the prospect of being caught, the tension seemed to vanish upon setting foot in the ghetto, whose very repugnance served as an ample deterrent to the snooping of Lye's uppity guards. The last to arrive, Ret watched in silent joy as those who had once been unjustly incarcerated rejoined their friends and embraced their loved ones. With particular interest, Ret visually followed the woman and child who he had risked his life to save as they found in the crowd their husband and father, who bore several wounds, likely born from his attempt to defend his family.

"*There* you are!" a worried voice called out to Ret from the group of people. No sooner had he heard the familiar voice than he was nearly knocked over when Paige collided with him in a relieved hug. Slightly taken aback, Ret stood motionless for a moment, then slowly reciprocated Paige's embrace. When her mind had finally caught up to her heart, Paige quickly pulled away, embarrassed by her uncharacteristically rash action.

"So you're not dead after all, eh?" Ana asked, squeezing free of the crowd not long after Paige. "We saw you turn back, then heard *crash-boom-bang* and figured you were a goner." Her nonchalant tone was not very befitting of her words.

"Still here," Ret replied cheerfully. Still blushing, Paige smiled.

"And we're all very glad you are," Lionel said loudly. The jubilant crowd hushed and then parted, revealing Lionel's whereabouts. He was walking towards Ret, holding the hand of a fair young woman, and together they slowly approached Ret. Stopping immediately in front of Ret, Lionel grabbed Ret's hand and placed it in the young lady's. "Ret," he said, "meet Princess Alana."

Ret didn't seem to notice that he was the center of attention, for his entire focus was on Alana. She was not afraid to meet Ret and look him in the eye, which confidence only increased his intrigue in her. Although she was neither taller nor thinner than most young women, she was strikingly beautiful, as most princesses are thought to be. Her penetrating, clear-blue eyes blinked above her small nose and red lips, which rested on her fair-skinned face, draped on either side with long, brown hair. Rather than ornate robes and fancy slippers, she wore comely cloth and dusty footwear; instead of a tiara and jewels, there was but a simple flower tucked behind her ear; in place of polish, her fingers bore signs of honest toil. And yet, masked behind the commonness, true royalty, in all its beauty, shined through as plain as day. In a word, Princess Alana was gorgeous.

Joining her other hand to the handshake, the princess shook Ret's hand tenderly. Coming to his senses, Ret blinked several times and took a deep breath.

Alana smiled. "It is well for us to meet," she said a bit awkwardly in her broken English.

Noticing Ret's surprise at hearing his native tongue, Lionel stepped in to clarify. "In exchange for the knowledge they've imparted to *me,*" he said, "I've shared a few things of my own with *them.*" Ret was silently overjoyed.

"We are very glad you have come to help us," Alana said, beaming at Ret.

"Don't hold your breath, sweetheart," Ana sneered to herself, repulsed by the princess' forwardness toward Ret. Paige looked on with worried apprehension.

"Help you?" Mr. Coy asked. "Help you with what?"

"With the war," Alana answered.

"War?" Coy exclaimed in protest.

"Now, now," Lionel intervened. "Don't get your fanny pack in a twist." Mr. Coy shot Lionel an expression of utter loathing. "The war is nothing more than a decoy." Lionel took a few eager steps to a nearby table, where laid a crude sort of map, which, at a glance, resembled three concentric circles. Lionel motioned for the others to gather round. Ret immediately recognized it as a map of Sunken Earth. The great mountain and its industrial district comprised the innermost circle, which was surrounded by the middle circle of suburbia, followed by the outermost circle — by far the largest —

with its innumerable slums. All but the slums were enclosed by wide waterways, which Ret recognized as the two great rivers they had crossed when the guards had escorted them through the slums and then the suburbs en route to the prison. With particular interest, Ret studied the innermost circle, which laid out the location of the government buildings and military strongholds, as well as Lye's personal palace, rising to the highest elevation of any other building throughout the land.

"We are here," Lionel said, pointing to a large clump of slums on the west side of Sunken Earth. "This clan is just a sliver of the dozens that make up the lower level." He waved his hand along the entirety of the outside circle to distinguish the lower level. "Tomorrow, at first light, all members of the lower level will storm each of the entrances into the middle level." Lionel pointed to the several entryways. "With millions of people charging at the gates simultaneously, Lye's security forces will be overwhelmed. Once we seize control of the middle level, we will move on to the upper level."

"And how is this a decoy?" Ret questioned.

"Always a step ahead, aren't you, Ret?" Lionel poked playfully. "While Lye and his minions are preoccupied with our invasion, *you* will be climbing the great mountain."

"Me?" Ret asked incredulously.

"You heard me," Lionel confirmed. "I'll get you safely to the foot of the mountain; then it's all up to you."

"So while we're at ground zero, risking our necks," Mr. Coy said, "Ret will be enjoying a pleasant afternoon of mountaineering. Is that your brilliant plan?"

"As far as *you* are concerned, Mr. Coy," Lionel replied cheerfully, "yes." Apparently, it wasn't one of Lionel's priorities to gain the approval of Mr. Coy. "That mountain is hiding something, I just know it. Why else would Lye guard it so heavily? Why else would he go to such great lengths to protect it?"

"Did you see anything when you descended from the peak?" Ret asked.

"No," Lionel answered. "I didn't know there was anything *to* see. And, besides, Lye told me to stay put." His face indicated his regret. "But, whatever it is, it's what we need in order to win this struggle, to turn the tide, and restore justice to these oppressed people."

"And you're sure about this?" Mr. Coy asked skeptically.

"Definitely," Lionel reaffirmed. "Somewhere within that peak is a substance so pure — so powerful — that it charges the soil, repels the ocean, swirls the vortex. I'm sure of it. And Ret is the only one with the power to acquire it. Ret is the essential element."

The final word from Lionel's lips rang in Ret's ears like the whistle of a freight train. After all that had been said and done since arriving in Sunken Earth, he had nearly forgotten the original purpose of their visit. Slowly, Ret turned and stared at Mr. Coy, hoping that the word *element* had registered in his mind, too. Mr. Coy cordially returned Ret's glance; then, when Ret kept staring at him, Mr. Coy shot him a glare as if to say, "Knock it off!" Rolling his eyes, Ret held up his right hand, with the palm facing Mr. Coy, and pointed to the scar of the hook and triangle. Memory jogged, Mr. Coy's eyes lit up. He instinctively reached in his pocket to check on the Oracle, then returned Ret's helpful stare with a wink and a thumbs-up.

When Ret had finished communicating with Mr. Coy, he was stunned to find a man kneeling at his feet. Finding it a challenge to identify the man whose head was bowed in reverence, Ret looked up to see the woman who he had rescued standing at Princess Alana's side, whispering in her ear.

"You are a brave man," Alana complimented Ret. "Hero," she added, finding the word she was searching for. "You will please join us at our feast." Then Alana kissed Ret lightly on his cheek and excused herself from the group.

"Looks like we've got a live one, Big P," Ana remarked wincingly to an awestruck Paige.

"Well then," Lionel spoke up, breaking the silent puzzlement that had gripped the group from Alana's display of affection. "Shall I show you the preparations for battle?"

Lionel led them down a flight of earthen stairs to a vast network of underground workshops. The place was alive with industry. Piles of ropes and cords sat at the feet of wooden ladders and homemade catapults.

"Besides your traditional weaponry," Lionel yelled above the roar of the bustle, "you'll notice something else." He pointed to the countless mounds of salt, rising in heaps that were too numerous to count. "The secret ingredient in our recipe for victory!" he shouted, smiling with pride.

Ret was intrigued by the desalinization process employed by the peasantry of Sunken Earth, no doubt taught to them by Lionel. The ever-present salt water was heated, producing steam but leaving behind the precious salt.

"We've had to conceal our operation underground," Lionel explained, "or else the large amounts of steam would give us away like Indian smoke signals!"

While a portion of the salt was reserved in solid form, a considerable quantity of it was devoted to creating solid sodium and gaseous chlorine. The sodium pieces were then forged into spheres the size of boulders while the chlorine gas was trapped in hallowed tree trunks or wrapped in patchworks of broad leaves from the forests.

Among all the production was a steady workforce overseeing transport. Being the eve of battle, it was clear that the preparations were on the move. By way of brute strength and rolling wheels, the armory was continuously being emptied as these self-proclaimed soldiers manned their stations.

At one point, cries filled the air as one of the outbound carts tipped over, spilling hundreds of pounds of salt on the ground. After much effort, the crew managed to return the cart to its upright position, and then they began the tedious task of shoveling the salt back aboard the transport. Noticing their need, Ret felt he could lend a helping hand. With one quick flick of his wrist, he lifted the spilled load and returned it to the vehicle. Hearty applause filled the underground chamber as workers swarmed Ret in gratitude. Off to the side, the Coys stood with Ivan and the Cooper women, ignored and forgotten.

For, it seemed, word had gotten around of Ret — his perfectly-timed arrival, his promised assistance, his famous heroics, his special powers. At every turn, Ret was greeted with praise and admiration. Hailed by men and adored by women, even the children clustered around his legs as if in search of his autograph. Some admirers shouted what little English words they knew, but most were content to simply ruffle his hair or touch his scars or look at his eyes.

"What's a celebrity like you doing with a bunch of little people like us?" Ana remarked to Ret when he at last joined them in the modest room that Princess Alana had reserved for her guests.

"What's *that* supposed to mean?" Ret wondered innocently, his smile fading.

"You know exactly what it means, Ret," Ana pressed. "These people love you; you're a superstar. *We* might as well go home and leave you here to live happily ever after with your cheeky princess."

"Now, Ana," Pauline chimed in with disapproval.

"What?" Ana said indignantly. "Don't get mad at me for being the only one brave enough to tell Ret how we all feel." The room fell silent as despondence over-shadowed their faces.

"You *all* feel this way?" Ret asked softly, beyond belief.

"It seems as though we're not needed," Mr. Coy explained.

"Not needed?" Ret repeated, nearly in uproar. "Didn't you see how these people are preparing for their war? They don't stand a chance against Lye. Their only advantage is their sheer numbers. What are they going to do, trample the enemy to death — stampede them into submission?" Ret threw his hands up in hopelessness.

"This isn't war; it's suicide — a massacre!"

"Which is why we want no part in it," Pauline said firmly.

"No part?" Ret said, flabbergasted. "No part? Is that what Jaret would do? Would he just — "

"Don't you dare bring my husband into this, Ret Cooper!" Pauline demanded in all seriousness. Her words, spoken in such a commanding tone, had a profoundly subduing effect on the entire group. Despite his frustration, Ret held his peace.

"As for tomorrow," Pauline continued, though in a much milder manner, "we will return to the place where we entered this land. We should have no problem falling out of the ranks since no one here seems to pay much attention to us anyway, and, thanks to Lionel's 'decoy,' we shouldn't run into any guards on our trek through the wilderness this time." Ret couldn't believe what he was hearing. "There, by the pond at the end of the underwater road, we will wait for you, Ret."

"And what will *I* be doing, according to your plan?" Ret wanted to know, feeling slightly put upon.

"Procuring the element, of course!" Mr. Coy answered. "That's what this lost city is hiding, Ret — the first element. That's why Lionel needs you to scale the mountain — he needs you to acquire the element." It was clear from everyone's agreeable expressions that they had all thought this through a great deal. "Which means you'll be needing this." Mr. Coy retrieved the Oracle from his pocket and tossed it to Ret, who stared at it for several seconds, mulling everything over in his mind.

This was all happening a bit too fast for Ret's liking. They had only just arrived in Sunken Earth, and now it was time to go? There was still so much that Ret wanted to see and do, ask and learn, explore and investigate. Besides obvious occurrences such as the presence of the symbol of his scar, each passing hour continued to reveal more evidences that Ret shared some connection with this newfound land: he resembled the people, their language had a recognizable ring to it, he felt so needed and accepted. Could this be the place of his nativity? Were these people his kinsfolk? Was he finally realizing his destiny?

Ret didn't know. But he *did* know, for the first time, that he was where he belonged. Never had he imagined that a place so foreign could feel so familiar — that amidst such great perplexity, he could find such clarity. This is what the prophecy on the parchment meant by "fill the Oracle"; this is what it meant by "cure the world." Ret was certain of it: he would fill the Oracle with this nation's all-powerful element and, thus, cure this backward civilization of its injustice and tyranny.

"Fine," Ret said at last, with an air of finite resoluteness. "But I'd rather die trying to save others than live trying to save myself."

No one knew quite what to say in reply to that statement. Eventually, Mr. Coy said, "You might feel differently tomorrow, son."

The same solemn bitterness with which Mr. Coy had spoken seemed to suddenly come over Pauline.

Coy finished, "Witnessing death has a way of giving new meaning to life." Then he, with his butler behind him, left the room, followed by Pauline and Ana, who were holding hands.

Now that the others had fled the room, Ret noticed Paige, who had been standing inconspicuously to the side. Without sound and with head down, she approached him. Then, hardly looking up, a few muffled words escaped her lips.

"Good luck tomorrow," she half-whispered. "Please be careful."

"Thanks," Ret said with a bit of displeasure, still feeling abandoned. Paige could sense Ret's discontentment rankling within him. She hoped, by lingering and offering a few kind words, that she could remind Ret of her support, but he stood like a statue, cold and emotionless. With great deliberation, Paige slowly raised her head. Then, with slightly puckered lips, she reached to compensate for Ret's height, but quickly pulled away. Too heartsick to feel embarrassed, she left the room, leaving Ret alone.

❍ ❍ ❍

The evening meal was not a feast by any stretch of the imagination. Clutching hand-carved bowls filled to the brim with some sort of slop, the guests lined the benches of a series of glorified picnic tables, slurping and sipping with great elation. It was obviously a feast to them. Despite his hunger, however, Ret couldn't bring himself to even sample the entrée, which featured chopped leaves and minced bark swimming in a hot broth of salt water. In between the never-ending claps on the back and cheers of praise from jubilant natives, Ret merely stirred his soup, inwardly longing for someone to talk to. When he moved to leave, a man sitting next to him pointed with interest at Ret's untouched soup. Ret happily obliged.

Lonely and pensive, Ret found a rickety sort of balcony away from the noise of the festivities where he could sort out his thoughts. Ever since the guards escorted him and his friends through the levels of Sunken Earth, one question had been weighing heavily on Ret's mind: "Why *are* there levels?" He had never been exposed to such striking distinctions before; in fact, he would have felt right at home in the middle level had his eyes not been opened by what he had just witnessed while passing through the slums. What boggled Ret's mind, however, was not that Lye had instigated such inequality but rather that the middle and upper levels condoned and perpetuated it. In the past, the citizens of Sunken Earth had been fairly equal, having most things in common. Therefore, when Lye showed up and assembled his caste system, it was not possessions that separated the people — it was principles: those who endorsed Lye with their possessions were rewarded by him with the snatched goods of those who held onto their principles. It was a matter of heart.

Such was yet another blow to Ret's rosy worldview. In a profound stupor, his mind staggered in contemplation of the unfathomable inequality of Sunken Earth. The abounding light from the middle level cast a welcome gleam on the walls of the dark slums near him. "How can two things, right next to each other," he wondered, "be so different — so unequal?" He shook his head and sighed, "I'm glad there's nothing like this back home."

Ret's silence was interrupted by the voice of Princess Alana. "Where are your friends?" she asked, stepping onto the teetering balcony.

"Oh, uh," Ret stuttered, "they didn't come — too tired," which was mostly true, except for Ivan who, upon learning what was on the menu, balked at the absence of red meat. "Where's Lionel?"

"He comes and goes a lot," Alana answered. "He has been a great help to my people. I am sure he is very busy preparing for tomorrow. It will be a good day for my people."

"For those who survive," Ret added glumly.

"Lionel says oppression is worse than death," Alana continued. "Lionel says blood is the cost of freedom."

"But it doesn't have to be — it shouldn't," Ret countered. "Are you ready to watch your people die?"

"And die myself," she said nobly.

"You mean you're going to fight, too?"

"Of course," vowed the princess. "If I have the power to declare war, then I also have the duty to fight in it."

"And if you die?"

"Then I die," said Alana, "but I do not plan to die. I plan to live, and see my people thrive, and watch this land blossom in peace and prosperity like it once did." She stood next to Ret and mimicked him in leaning over the side of the balcony, overlooking the city. "In fact, I plan to grow old as their queen, and rule and reign, at the side of a king — a handsome king." With each word, Princess Alana seemed to snuggle deeper into Ret's shoulder. "Just imagine, Ret," she said, picking up Ret's arm and placing it around herself, "tomorrow, we will win our independence, and you and I will be crowned victors, and together — as king and queen — we will turn the page to a new chapter in the history of Sunken Earth."

"Paige?" Ret exclaimed, suddenly springing up and nearly knocking Princess Alana to the ground. "Um,

good luck with that, princess," he said hastily. "See you tomorrow!" Ret awkwardly dashed off. Alana sighed before rejoining the celebration.

Far from the slums, a great distance yet from where the echo of Ret's exclamation had died, a feeble old man slowly climbed a polished set of stairs towards an ornate palace, which sat high above the surrounding buildings along the wide base of the great mountain. Reaching the landing, the winded man pushed open one of the double doors with great delicateness and hobbled inside with the aid of a white, spiraled cane.

"Lord Lye," a weary servant greeted the aged man, "all forces are in place to counter tomorrow's attack by the lower level."

"Excellent," Lye grinned.

Chapter 15

Summiting the Great Mountain

It was a sleepless night. Curled in their shabby cots, the Coys and Coopers lay wide awake, held captive by their conscious nightmares of what the ensuing day might bring. The ground beneath them rattled through the night from the incessant mobilizing of soldiers and ammunition as they migrated from their dens below to their hideouts above. Though aware of each other's restlessness, not a word was spoken, partly because they still felt at odds over recent decisions but mostly due to Ivan's heavy snoring.

"Now you know why his quarters are in the basement," Mr. Coy said in jest of his butler, half-yawning while speaking the first words of the night, which now was approaching dawn.

Not much later, Princess Alana stepped into the room. "Come," she said, parting the tattered sheet that hung in place of a door. "It is time." They followed her into the streets, which were filled with silent commotion. Every man, woman, and child had been summoned to the battlefield to offer whatever help they could render for the cause of freedom.

The citizens of Sunken Earth enjoyed light through interesting means. As with most everything else, the dirt was the key to supplying their light. The energy surging through the soil not only brilliantly reflected the sunshine of the day but also gave off a soft glow in the night. The short shelf life of the energy, however, meant it had to be replaced often, so the fact that the soil in and around the slums had long ago been stripped of its energy — and never replenished — had hitherto been viewed by the lower level as a form of punishment. But on this night it, for once, seemed a great advantage, allowing them to sneak unnoticed through the shadows as they finalized their preparations for war.

And so, while the well-lit middle and upper levels glowed with power, the slums and shanties wallowed in dimness. After usurping the government, Lye had turned the lower level into his personal landfill, making it the dump site of all the overspent earth that was collected and then discarded in the civilization. Like truckloads of dead batteries or burnt-out light bulbs, the waste was carelessly shipped out of Lye's sight, where the peasantry managed to use what little life remained in it to grow and harvest a stunted subsistence. Occasionally, the government was known to spread near-dead dirt throughout the streets of the slums, but only to supply power to their own vehicles when conducting raids and arrests.

"This is where we leave you, Ret," Pauline said. "Do what you need to get the element, and then meet us back where we came in, on the west side." She paused to smile. "And good luck. We love you."

"There you are!" Lionel yelled, rushing up to the group. "I've been looking all over for you. We must hurry; our frontal attack is about to begin!" He turned to hasten away, assuming they would follow him, but when no one moved, he returned to the group.

"We won't be coming," Pauline explained, "only Ret." Ret looked at Lionel in disappointment, slightly embarrassed by the choice of his comrades.

Lionel thought for a moment, processing the information, before saying to the group that was fleeing, "Well, you should be ashamed of yourselves, especially you two." He pointed at the only men in the party: Mr. Coy and Ivan. They looked down in acknowledged humiliation. "Come on, Ret," Lionel said, putting his arm around him. They turned their backs and walked away.

Grabbing Ana and Paige each by the hand, Pauline turned and started the westward trek out of the slums. Mr. Coy and Ivan stood motionless for several moments, looking both ways, unsure of what to do. In the end, they followed after their female counterparts, heads hanging low.

Ret followed Lionel to the inner fringe of the slums, which sat along the wide bank of the first great river, separating the lower level from the middle level. Upon entering the wobbly structures, Ret was stunned to find that they had been completely hollowed out, leaving only a long, high-rising outer shell. The empty shacks had since been filled with all manner of weaponry and ammunition, safely concealed behind the false façade of the slums.

"Don't judge a book by its cover," Lionel remarked, noticing Ret's amazement at the rows and rows of ranks assembled in the carved-out slums, which extended many layers deep. "Now, wait for me by the bridge. I'll come and find you soon after the battle begins."

With each passing minute, additional stealth was needed to remain unnoticed as dawn was now upon them. Ret watched in wonder as the star-like speckles of energy in the earthen, domed ceiling gradually gave way to a general sort of opaqueness as the limited sunlight that filtered through the ocean shone through. Ret wondered if the average inhabitant of Sunken Earth even knew there was an entire ocean — indeed, another world — above them. He marveled at how insignificant this small battle seemed in the grand scheme of things. But, just when he feared he had made a rash decision in not following Pauline and the others, he was reminded how important any struggle is when life and liberty are at stake.

Continuing to gaze at the wondrous ceiling of Sunken Earth, Ret noticed that, despite the fixed amount of natural light, it was that light's reflection in the sparkling soils and shimmering waters that caused the land to appear as illuminated as if it were above ground.

"Psst!" Ret looked around to see who was trying to get his attention. "Ret! Over here!" Princess Alana waved to him from behind a blockade. When Ret had hurried over to her, she pulled him in close so as not to give away their position.

"You look very strong in your armor," she whispered, touching his chest.

"But I'm not wearing any — "

"I know." She leaned in to kiss him.

And she would have if the large swath of slums immediately next to them hadn't exploded.

"We're under attack!" Lionel shouted in surprise. "They were ready for us!" Indeed, they were: from atop the monstrous wall on the other side of the river, a squadron of Lye's soldiers fired a high-powered energy blast directly into the slums.

In one moment, Sunken Earth had gone from calm to chaos. Like a sea of shooting stars, wave after wave of crackling energy bolts soared from the middle level, raining down on the ambushed lower level. The corrugated shanty walls fell and burned like feathers, exposing their beleaguered contents. Lionel and his ranks scurried frantically to regroup as men fell left and right to the fatal electrocutions from enemy fire. Like birds of prey, Lye's servants mercilessly attacked from their posts, on higher ground and behind their impenetrable force field.

Ret knew he had to do something to rescue his associates' ailing attack, but he wasn't entirely sure what he ought to do. He had been outfitted with neither sword nor shield, and even if he was some kind of sharp shooter, the lower level would be completely leveled before he could take out a substantial number of enemies. For some reason, his unique gift — his power over certain elements — never forced itself upon his mind but instead waited patiently until Ret remembered that it was there.

And remember he did.

Without needing to glance at his scar, Ret shut his eyes in an attempt to clear his mind amid so much turmoil. When he opened them, his vision was directed to the countless mounds of salt scattered throughout the leveled slums. He suddenly knew what to do.

With fists clenched, Ret picked up a faraway pile of salt with each hand. He extended his fingers, causing each mound to change form into a sort of sheet. Then, with a quick swish of his hands, the large walls of salt flew into the fray, where Ret held them above the great river.

With the salt absorbing the enemy fire, Lionel and his men enjoyed their first break from the assault. With great haste, they reformed their lines and prepared for an attack of their own. Their hearts took courage while Lye's guards were filled with consternation as they continued to pummel the shields of salt hovering in front of them.

In time, however, the constant stream of energy being funneled into the sheets of salt caused the granules to melt with fervent heat. Now molten, the salt began to dissolve, dropping solid sodium particles into the river below and releasing gaseous chlorine into the air above. Having disbanded the protective barrier, Lye's soldiers celebrated, though their cheers quickly turned to coughs as they inhaled the toxic fumes of chlorine. Meanwhile, the river danced with sparks and explosions as the metal sodium continued to react with the water, the rising smoke of such reactions only adding to the enemy's bamboozlement.

Now Lionel and his men assumed the role of cheering, applauding Ret as they loaded up with ammo.

"Genius, Ret!" Lionel saluted. "Keep it up!"

Like sheets of paper coming hot off the press, Ret raised and leveled mound after mound of salt, shielding his friends from their antagonists. Though most of his concentration was focused on the task at hand, Ret could see Lionel and his men loading their surviving catapults with massive spheres of sodium metal. With dozens poised and ready, Lionel issued the command to commence fire.

Nearly the size of elephants, dozens of colossal balls of sodium hurled through the smoky air, landing just inside the other bank of the river directly at the foot of the bridge's main pylon, which stood underneath and supported the front gate that led into the middle level. Time seemed to stand still as the river's water made contact with the sodium bombs until, all of a sudden, the scene erupted violently like a hidden, exploding geyser. Chunks of stone, large and small, shot like missiles in all directions. Water seemed to spray for miles. The front half of the bridge collapsed in ruin. The entrance to the middle level had been blown to bits, a gaping hole now in its place. The force field blew a fuse, disappearing like dominoes in both directions, and those of Lye's men who had been stationed near the entrance were suddenly launched into orbit.

Far from the battlefield, having reached the vegetated outer edge of Sunken Earth, a party of fleeing visitors spun around in alarm, the explosion of the sodium nuggets reverberating multiple times against the walls of the enclosed land. Pauline and the girls gasped as Mr. Coy worriedly strained to see what had happened.

"I'm sure he's fine," Pauline reassured everyone, though silently panicking herself. She and the girls turned back around and resumed their journey. Paige looked horrified.

Meanwhile, Mr. Coy turned to speak with Ivan. "We've got to go back and help," he whispered passionately, "I feel like a sissy!"

"Yeth," Ivan replied, "I, too, fveel like a — " He then made several painful attempts at saying the word *sissy*.

"Alright, alright," Mr. Coy finally intervened. "Don't hurt yourself."

With Pauline and the girls purposely not looking behind them in an effort to keep themselves from imagining what kind of awful danger Ret might be in, Mr. Coy and Ivan slipped away with no difficulty and headed back to the slums.

Back at the front lines, those who had breached the middle level prepared to advance to the next stage of their coup. As if by a rush of mighty wind, many more of the slums collapsed, uncovering masses of people, ready to storm the middle level. Like a colony of enraged termites, thousands of individuals marched forward and, with the force field down, scrambled into the middle level. Some swam; others laid down boards to span the broken bridge or ladders to climb the wrecked walls; but all were eager to rise to the next level and fight. Hordes of destitute yet determined derelicts flooded the gates, using their sheer numbers to push their way onward.

The blitzing crowds were met head-on by Lye's ground troops. Those at the front of the stampede, who — alive — served as human shields and then — dead — as human barricades, piled up lifelessly as they fell to the barrage of enemy fire. But the troops were wildly outnumbered and eventually overpowered. With weapons as primitive as a good arm and a springy sling, the masses threw and slung their homemade ammunition wherever they could. Small pebbles of sodium rolled their way into front yard fountains and neighborhood streams of the quaint towns of the middle level. Wooden containers of chlorine gas exploded in the streets and boulevards, sending people convulsing and vomiting. Pandemonium swept the suburbs as unprepared residents of the middle level fled for safety within the upper level, mourning shattered stained glass and trampled flower beds along the way.

"Ret!" Lionel called out, running towards him. "Now's our chance to summit the mountain."

"But shouldn't we help them first?" Ret wondered, still standing on the river bank, watching the awful struggle play out before his very eyes.

"They're doing their part," Lionel explained. "Now it is time for us to do ours." Lionel waited for Ret to swallow his words before saying, "Follow me."

Lionel led Ret up and down and all around another winding network of passageways and tunnels. He was moving quickly and without much concern for being discovered, though there wasn't much cause to be concerned since all of Lye's security forces were presently very preoccupied. As such, they encountered little resistance. Ret wondered how Lionel knew so much about the secrets of the middle level. Lionel had to repeatedly wait for Ret to catch up, as Ret was more interested in the progress of the insurrection, frequently looking back.

"Stay focused," Lionel instructed. "The whole purpose of this war is to gain control of the mountain and whatever it might contain. Everyone is counting on *you!*"

Another series of underground paths and hidden trails landed Lionel and Ret in the upper level, where Ret was surprised to find the state of things in nearly as great an uproar as in the middle level. Fleeing the approaching mobs, citizens of the middle level inundated the streets in and around the industrial and government districts, demanding protection and explanation. Though he could not understand what anyone was shouting in their protests and exclamations, Ret could decipher an air of panic and distress.

"What are they saying?" Ret asked Lionel.

Lionel paused for a moment to listen to the tumult.

"They're demanding to see Lye," he translated, "but he's missing!"

"Missing?" Ret asked. "So does that mean — "

"It means *you* need to be extremely careful," Lionel warned. "If I know Lye, he is not one to give up — ever."

Soon, with the terrain changing from pavement to dirt, they arrived at the end of the upper level. Straining his neck and arching his back, Ret's gaze scaled the massive mountainside.

Suddenly, a pair of patrolling guards spotted Ret and Lionel.

"Go on without me," Lionel petitioned as the guards began rushing towards them.

"Let me help you," Ret begged, the guards getting closer.

"No," Lionel insisted. "I can handle them," though Ret wasn't sure, as Lionel looked a bit winded and much wearied from their trek, which had been a nearly constant incline.

"Go!" Lionel urged. "This is *your* task, not mine. Get to the summit!"

"But — "

"I'll be here waiting for you," Lionel promised. "Now go — go!"

With great hesitancy, Ret turned and dashed up the mountainside, taking care not to be followed by the advancing guards. Not only was he nervous without Lionel as his guide but he also was worried that he might possibly lose Lionel, his friend and confidant, to Lye's murderous regime. Still, Ret knew he could trust Lionel, and if he said to go on without him, then Ret was certain Lionel knew what he was doing.

The great mountain was certainly not meant to be climbed. Obviously void of any well-beaten trails, the dirt was extremely refined, almost like sand. With no rocks to rest on or foliage to lean on, Ret struggled to maintain his balance and footing. The mountain seemed to be a living, breathing organism, for quite frequently Ret had to dodge miniature avalanches of earth as the mountain pushed out new soil from within. He soon discovered, however, that it was much easier to use his powers to manipulate the cascading dirt to instead dodge *him*. The trek upwards would have proved impossible had it not been for Ret's powers.

In fact, the earth seemed to obey his command with far greater readiness than any other dirt he had previously experienced. Everything seemed purer — more pulsating — likely because it was so fresh from its source. Ret felt alive like never before, almost giddy — like a toddler in a sandbox. For the first time, Ret was grateful to be alone on the mountain, for no other human could have followed his trail.

As Ret approached the perpetual layer of clouds encircling the midriff of the mountain, he paused from his climb to enjoy the view before it would be enveloped in fog. Immediately upon glancing downward, however, he learned there was nothing to enjoy. War had engulfed the entire nation, with carnage as its only victor. Princess Alana and her band accounted for a tiny fraction of those contending for their rights. While most of the middle level's entrances had been breached, some had not, the cost of which was now lying lifelessly on the ground. The sound of conflict shared the air with the billowing smoke of raging fires. Ret cringed to see the upper level's all-out attack on the middle level, now filled with the fearless fighters of the lower level. Lionel's words rang true in Ret's ears: they were all counting on him now.

Ret pressed forward. With limited visibility, he passed through the cloud coverage, dodging thunderous lightning at times. The mist, which had left him drenched, felt welcomed against the warmth of the energized earth of the mountain. Now above the haze, Ret was afforded a clear view of the remainder of his hike.

Tremendous torrents of ocean water poured through the hole in the ceiling, sending treacherous waterfalls cascading down the mountainside in many directions. The downpours carved deep gorges in the ground before flowing downward to ultimately feed the countless rivers that sprawled throughout Sunken Earth. Wondering how he might get on the other side of these tumultuous waterfalls, Ret was struck with the idea to use the soil to push him through. By simply imagining it, Ret caused a stream of dirt from behind to propel him forward. Bracing himself, the earth struck his back as if from a fire hose and provided enough force to lunge him through the downpour. He collapsed on the inside of the curtains of water, landing in soil that resembled powdered sugar, just as Lionel had described. Being wet, the fine soil stuck to his body, but instead of turning to mud, the dirt particles, which were warm from their electrical charge, turned the water on Ret's body into steam before falling back to the ground, gently as tiny hailstones.

Now that he was standing on the peak of the great mountain, Ret felt a tangible energy in the air like never before. A palpable power surged through every atom of every molecule, giving incredible vibrancy to all things, including Ret. The power was so strong, in fact, that Ret felt a tinge of fear — could he control what he felt? In full view, Ret stared into the heart of the vortex, swirling just a few hundred feet above his head. With awesome majesty, the raw power emanating from the mountain held the mighty ocean in perfect subjection.

Remembering his mission, Ret altered his upward course and decided to trek around the peak. It was on the east side where he discovered a curious-looking building. Though small, it was very attractive and ornate, built of fine materials and crafted with great care. It looked like some sort of house of worship, as if constructed in honor of deity. Much of it had been built into the mountain, and it was clear that the bulk of the brilliantly-white building sat inside the peak.

Ret approached the door, which looked carved by hand and lined with gold. On the large, bronze doorknob was etched the symbol of the hook and triangle. With his right hand, Ret reached to turn the knob, but before he could even touch it, he felt something like a spark, as if he was shocked by the handle. Then he heard the knob unlock, saw it turn itself, and watched as the door slowly swung open on its own.

Ret stepped inside.

Chapter 16

The Guardian

On account of the torrential seawater pouring through the ceiling and rushing down the mountain, Ret couldn't tell if the door creaked as it swung open. He made sure to close it only halfway, partly to let in some light yet shut out some noise but mostly to eliminate any obstructions for a quick getaway if it came to that. With caution, he quietly stepped further into the entryway, which, like a corridor, stretched long and thin with little indication of what was to be found at its end. The walls, bare and cavernous, had been carved out of the mountain, judging by the electricity with which they surged. Ret marveled as the depressions caused by each of his footsteps sprang back, as if he were walking on some sort of living, breathing foam.

At length, Ret arrived at the end of the corridor, the slanted beam of light shining through the front door having been rendered useless many steps ago. Ret halted to analyze his surroundings. He was standing on the edge of a circular room, whose conical layout made it clear that it was located well inside the peak of the mountain. The ceiling rose upward like a cone, the top of which featured a small hole, similar to a skylight, directly under the center of the vortex. In no particular pattern, similar holes and gaps dotted the rounded walls of the room like glassless windows. Besides granting access to humid air and streams of light, these cracks and fissures in the roof and walls were the means by which the spray from the waterfalls accumulated and dripped inside the room, creating small pools of salt water along its circumference.

The obvious focal point sat at the dead center of the room. Each individual ray of light had been purposely configured to shine on it, and the skylight in the rooftop created a sort of brilliant, vertical conduit to enclose it, as would a display case at a museum. Amidst so much concentrated light, Ret could see a small, dark object hovering a few feet in the air. But, whatever it was, it was so little that Ret had to advance closer in order to clearly identify it. When he had done so, he was somewhat thrown off balance when he realized that the object was situated above a seemingly bottomless shaft, whose mouth stretched just a few feet in diameter. With the light from the skylight pouring directly into it, the pit appeared to extend into the earth's core.

When Ret had regained his surefootedness, he returned his attention to the curious object floating in the air, which turned out to be something he had not been expecting.

A dirt clod.

But it was the most extraordinary clod of dirt that Ret had ever beheld. It looked so fresh, so unspoiled; free of sand and silt and certainly any kind of unwanted impurities. Far from clay yet much richer than loam, it was bright and chaste, untainted by rock or any kind of decaying matter. The closest thing that Ret could compare it to was pure manure — "hopefully without the smell," he chuckled to himself. The more he seemed to analyze it, however, the more it seemed to analyze him. He could sense its raw power emanating freely from it, which caused Ret to quite involuntarily feel a bit inferior. How odd, he thought, that such a small thing could exert such a mighty influence.

It would have been an altogether disappointing discovery had it not been for the shape in which the clod was formed. With perfect curvature, it was a rounded wedge, exactly like one sliver of a peeled and sectioned orange. Ret knew, then and there, that he had found the first of the six elements to be housed in the Oracle.

Ret reached inside his pocket to retrieve the Oracle, but when his fingers had scarcely touched it, he was startled by an unknown voice.

"What have you got there?" Ret looked up and around, searching from whence the voice sprang, poised in defense. From across the room, he saw a moving figure disrupting the shadows. Slowly and methodically, the silhouette moved closer to Ret until, stepping into the light, Ret could get a clear look.

He was not a small man, but neither was he intimidating or imposing. Rather, he seemed gentle and easy to be entreated, somewhat like a grandfather. Beyond middle-age, his wrinkled face bore a pleasant smile, which seemed so natural that Ret was sure it had been frequently used over his lifetime. His clean-shaven face matched his balding head for hair, and he seemed to exude an aura of quiet confidence. He was clothed from neck to foot in a simple, unassuming robe whose long, droopy sleeves hung low as he held his hands together in front of his abdomen. As the unnamed man continued his unhurried advance toward the center of the room, Ret hadn't so much as a hint of fear, as there was no reason to be alarmed.

"I see you bear the scars," the man observed, vaguely pointing at Ret's hands. His voice was deep and a bit hoarse, as a grandfather's voice should sound, but it was not unpleasant to listen to. "I've been waiting a long time for one of you to come."

"One of *me?*" Ret asked, wondering if there were more of him in the world.

"One from your line, yes," the man clarified, "the line that bears the scars."

"You mean there are others like me?" Ret questioned with great intrigue. "With scars?"

"Well of course there are," he answered mildly, raising a perplexed eyebrow at Ret's question, as if it pertained to very basic and common information. "Now, go ahead and acquire the element while you still can."

"Acquire the element?" Ret questioned again.

"You know, slip it inside the Oracle — "

"Slip it inside?"

"Slip, cram, shove…just get it inside the sphere!" the old man insisted, on the verge of losing his patience. "How do you not know this, boy? Didn't they teach you what to do?"

"I don't know who you're referring to, sir," Ret confessed, "but no one has told me anything about any of this."

"What?" the man gasped in disbelief. "Did someone hit you over the head or what?"

"Something like that," Ret shrugged in innocent defense. "Your guess is as good as mine."

"Ah," said the man calmly, sensing Ret's sincerity, "I see." He looked down, still bearing his perpetual smile. "Might as well get comfortable then," he sighed, though secretly elated to have someone to talk to. "No sense in standing when we can sit." He waved his hand

and created from the earthen floor a stool for each of them to sit on. Though stunned to have found someone else with power over the earth, Ret gladly took a load off and was all ears.

"I am the Guardian of the earth element," the man began, introducing himself. "Many centuries ago, I was appointed by your First Father to watch and preside over the element of earth."

"My First Father?" Ret questioned, brimming with curiosity.

"How hard did you get hit, son?" the Guardian laughed. "Yes, your First Father. He was the protector of the Oracle. All seven of the other ancient Fathers agreed that, since he was of the most virtuous disposition, he and his line would be defenders of the Oracle through all generations of time, and, should the power prove to corrupt him, the remaining seven would act as a buffer to quell any sort of rebellion."

"So, this Oracle," Ret interrupted, trying to get a handle on things. "What *is* it, exactly? What's its purpose?"

"The Oracle, which you hold in your hand," the Guardian pointed out with awed emphasis, "is as old as the foundations of this earth. It maintains balance among all the elements and, as such, contains untold power. At the time when your line became stewards over it, the Oracle housed the earth's six fundamental elements.

They were pure and undefiled — the sources from which all other elements and compounds on this planet trace their origin. So, quite literally, whoever possesses the Oracle also holds all nature in his control."

"That's a lot of responsibility," Ret remarked.

"A credit to the integrity of your First Father, to be sure," replied the Guardian. "And so, with the Oracle in honest hands, peace reigned on the face of the earth. People were happy, and so was nature. There were no wars or contentions, not even any natural disasters. We lived in harmony with each other and the earth."

"We?" Ret asked. "So you were…"

"Yes, I was alive then," answered the Guardian. "I was one of the eight original ancient Fathers. But those days were never to be repeated, for we had a betrayer among us."

"Lye," Ret predicted.

"Yes," confirmed the Guardian, "another one of the original eight. It was his desire to have been selected as the possessor of the Oracle, but it was the very reason that he wanted it that he couldn't have it. You see, the Oracle — and the scars and elements and such — has a mind and will of its own, as I'm sure you've noticed by now."

Ret nodded in agreement. "Lye may have pledged allegiance to our peaceful ideals — he may have sworn our vows to never use the Oracle for evil — but they were lies, all lies. It was his intention from the beginning to take control and claim the power for himself."

"Sounds familiar," Ret mumbled inaudibly, not wanting to interrupt.

"With his followers, Lye incited an uprising against us," the Guardian explained with remembered disappointment in his gentle eyes. "His revolt was squashed, his gang banished, but his ambition never died. No, the sores from his wounded pride festered; his embarrassing loss only caused his thirst for power to multiply. With his charisma and flattery, he led away many to join his cause, promising them wealth and honor. And since that time, our world has never known peace. No one could escape the havoc that Lye and his forces wrought upon the land — wars and bloodshed, thievery and trickery, secret murders and untraceable terror."

"All for *this,* huh?" Ret surmised, holding up the empty Oracle.

"That is no ordinary trinket you hold there," the Guardian informed with great soberness. "That's no collector's item — no forgotten antique. It is the Oracle — the force that bears all nature up, the object that keeps our world in balance, the source on which our peace depends. For it to fall into evil hands would spell utter ruin."

"Then why not just destroy it?" Ret wondered.

"Preposterous!" the Guardian stated. "The Oracle

cannot be *destroyed* — it is indestructible. But it *can* be emptied, which, fortunately, was something that your First Father understood."

Ret was listening with rapt attention.

"With darkness sweeping over the earth, and the numbers of the faithful dwindling due to either assassination or disillusionment, your First Father determined that it would be better to scatter the elements than to let them fall into wicked hands. In a secret assembly, he met with the six ancient Fathers (who had remained loyal) and explained his intentions to release the six elements and hide them throughout the earth. He knew that physically separating the elements might result in periodic calamites — that even the land itself might pull apart amid such strife and discord — but we all agreed that such risks had to be taken and endured or else evil would prevail. He assigned each of us to guard one of the six elements, and, thus, we became the Guardians of the Elements."

The Guardian's retelling of the past flowed into Ret's mind like pure knowledge.

"Well aware that the release of the elements would unleash awesome power," the Guardian retold, "your First Father decided to sail far into the Great Sea to do the deed, hoping that by so doing he not only could survive it himself but also spare the land of any mayhem that would likely follow. But, somehow, Lye had been informed and headed him off. And so, while he was yet on land, your First Father had no choice but to strike the Oracle with his staff and scatter the elements."

"Did he die?" Ret asked painfully.

"No one knows for certain," the Guardian said. "Since he insisted on dispersing the elements alone so as not to endanger anyone else, no one was with him at the time. The only person even close to the scene was the one who was chasing him: Lye. Ever since then, Lye has always been seen carrying your First Father's white, spirally twisted staff, so everyone immediately assumed that Lye had killed him. But once it became clear that Lye had also gained possession of the Oracle — and that it was empty — we knew that your First Father had successfully scattered the elements. So, content not to give any credit to Lye for the death of your First Father, the legend considers his disappearance as a self sacrifice. No living thing — not even *he* — could have outlived such a cataclysmic event at its epicenter. Elsewhere, the land was thrown into upheaval. The earth shook; rocks broke; mountains were leveled; valleys became hills; cities collapsed; fires raged; the sea was troubled. The whole world was in commotion. The face of the earth became deformed."

"That sounds awful," Ret mourned.

"The worst of it," said the Guardian, "was how it affected the people. Over time, the population, which once lived in harmony and enjoyed a tightly-knit sort of interconnectedness, gradually and literally drifted apart, in every way possible. Granted, civilizations were now divided by newfound seas and rivers and mountain ranges, but the changes in geography also led to drastic changes in anthropology. New languages and customs; differing religions and beliefs; foreign foods and currencies — whereas we had once been many people but one in unity, every tribe and nation was now but one of many, each very different from the next."

"It's not so bad," Ret observed of the present-day world.

"That's because you don't know what it used to be," the Guardian countered. "Lye may not have achieved possession of the Oracle with its contents, but most of his other aspirations have come true, simply by the scattering of the elements. I haven't seen anything beyond this room for a long, long time, but I assume the world has only gotten worse since I came to dwell here."

"I think you'd be surprised," Ret insisted, slightly perturbed by the Guardian's negative outlook.

"You share your First Father's optimism," the Guardian grinned. "The last thing he ever told us was his belief that, at some future date, once the threat of Lye and his followers had died off, a brave soul — one of his own descendents — would rise up to gather the elements and restore peace and equality to our world. He didn't say who that person would be. Nor did he say when it would happen, though we all hoped it would be very soon — but it wasn't." He looked down in defeat. "Fortunately, soon after the scattering of the elements, the members of your family line began to notice six marks slowly growing on their hands — three on each palm — like brandings. With each successive generation, however, they became fainter and obscurer until most people believed they were nothing but ugly birthmarks."

Ret instinctively looked down at his hands.

"But, with those as my only clues," the Guardian carried on, "I was able to find the resting place of my element after decades of searching. Hopefully the others were equally successful." His eyes glistened at the mention of old friends. "Maybe your First Father spoke of you — maybe he didn't. Perhaps it was just an old man's wishful thinking, born of false hope. But one thing remains certain: your First Father's ingenuity, coupled with the six elements' very desire not to be found, continues to keep Lye at bay to this day."

"But how do *you* know Lye is still alive?" Ret asked, wondering how a hermit such as the Guardian could know of Lye's continued existence if he hadn't left his post in the mountain peak of Sunken Earth for so long.

"Because *I'm* still alive!" the Guardian responded. "As long as Lye is on the loose and my element remains uncollected, I cannot die."

"So how is Lye still alive then?" Ret wondered, testing the Guardian's reasoning.

"Well, how should I know?" the Guardian admitted. "Tell you what," he said with a sarcastic tone, "I haven't seen Lye in hundreds of years, but the next time I run into him, I'll ask him."

"Well, you know, he *is* just down the mountain," Ret said casually, knowing he would catch the Guardian off guard. "I could go and ask him real quick…"

"Nictitating nebulae!" the Guardian shrieked. "Are you pulling my leg, boy, because that's a dirty, rotten trick to pull on an old-timer like me…"

"Well, I haven't seen him personally," Ret went on, "but Lionel said — "

"This is outrageous!" the Guardian continued to rant, not listening to Ret. "Right under my nose! Fortunately, because I am the current possessor of the element, I am entitled to its powers, but the moment you return the element to the Oracle, *you* become the bearer and can wield its power in full strength — of course, that also means I will die…"

"Die?" Ret interjected. "You can't die. I have so many things I want to ask you." Ret tried to reassure himself by his own words. "You can stay close to the element — I'll let you hold the Oracle. When we're done here, you can come back with us. I'll show you what the world is like today — how it's not as terrible as you think..."

"No, no," the Guardian replied with a gentle smile, "this is the end for me." Ret's jaw dropped in protest. "The element has given me unnaturally long life. The moment you return it to the Oracle is the moment I go the way of all the earth."

"No!" Ret objected, devastated by the prospect of losing someone who possessed so much knowledge. "You — but you — you can't! I..." The Guardian put up his hand to silence Ret's woes.

"Yes," he spoke softly. "I need a rest."

"But you have so much more to teach me," Ret continued to complain. "I need you to help me to find the — "

"Relax, my boy," the Guardian calmed Ret. "You made it this far without any assistance from the Guardians. That's more than even Lye has been able to do."

Amid so much dialogue, neither Ret nor the Guardian noticed the presence of a third individual who had just entered the structure. Stepping across the threshold through the door that had been left ajar, a frail old man staggered inside. Breathing heavily, it seemed he may collapse at any moment from his arduous journey. Yet, with a thin but sturdy cane to stabilize him, he limped down the corridor, following the voices of the conversing pair at the other end.

The Guardian had just inhaled to speak further when he suddenly stopped and held his breath. Noticing his alarm, Ret fell silent and still. With slight apprehension, they listened to a strange sound — a rhythmic sort of tapping — that grew louder with each passing moment. Soon, the sound of the visitor's cane striking the floor was joined by the shuffling of his aged feet, then the panting of his weary lungs. Having reached the periphery of the circular room, Ret and the Guardian naturally rose to their feet and faced the outlet of the corridor, from whence the noises came.

The mysterious individual advanced just far enough into the light so as to be discerned, and not a step further. Though Ret had no idea who this newcomer was, the Guardian immediately recognized him, thanks to his white, spiraled cane.

Lye wheezed, "Did someone say my name?"

Chapter 17

Lye

"Well, if it isn't Lye himself," the Guardian said loudly, greeting Lye distastefully. "To what do we owe the displeasure?"

"Now, now," Lye replied with a sly grin, "that's no way to talk to an old friend."

"If by 'friend' you mean traitor," the Guardian sneered, "though you *are* looking rather old. The years haven't been so good to you, I see?"

To say Lye was old seemed a gross understatement in Ret's estimation — perhaps even a compliment — for he was truly something ancient. Like a petrified fossil, his cracked and wrinkled skin clung, taut and colorless, to his bones. His bright, white hair from head and long beard contrasted brilliantly against his black, flowing robes. Above his pointed nose and pale lips sat a pair of frightening eyes, the whites of which were sickly yellow while the pupils were milky white, combining to resemble the innards of an inverted egg. He stood like a shriveled prune, hunched and leaning on a white, spirally-twisted — borrowed — cane, clutching it with a timeworn hand whose long, sharp fingernails seemed to warn potential pilferers. Having heard a great deal concerning the might and zeal of someone as menacing and formidable as Lye, Ret was profoundly disappointed by what stood before him: an antiquated relic — his life's season of heyday long-since replaced by his health's cries of mayday. In fact, Lye seemed to age even further with every passing moment, right before Ret's very eyes.

"Easy for *you* to say," Lye scoffed at the Guardian, "loafing these many years in the shadow of your own life-preserving element."

Instead of feeling insulted by Lye's derisive remark, the Guardian was greatly puzzled, for it occurred to him that, without an element of his own, Lye should have died a long time ago. "Just how *are* you still alive?" he asked with great bewilderment.

"Ah," Lye smiled with self-contentment, "now *that* shall remain my little secret."

"Very well," the Guardian stated decisively. "It's now or never," he said, turning to Ret. "You collect the element while I protect you from Lye."

"Really, old chap," Lye said with a surprised laugh, which turned into a cough, "do you really think I have come to contend? Do I look strong enough to put up a fight?"

"I know never to trust you and your lies," said the Guardian.

"To each his own," Lye shrugged, "but I'm sure Ret would like to know how it came to be that he washed ashore on Tybee Island, as a stowaway on Jaret's RIB, now almost two years ago."

Lye's words struck Ret like lightning. All thinking came to a screeching halt; all attention turned to this event from his past. *Never* had Ret expected such a subject to resurface — at such a time as this — from such a source as Lye! For a moment, Ret totally disregarded Lye's incredibility, desperate to hear what he had to say.

Noticing Ret's captivation, Lye continued. "That burning ship — the one that Jaret tried to rescue — that was *my* ship, and you were on board — *with* me. We were friends — partners! — working together…"

"Don't listen to him, Ret!" the Guardian protested. "He can't be trusted!"

Though he believed the Guardian, Ret didn't see how someone as frail as Lye could pose such a dangerous threat. "And what were we working together to do?" Ret asked cautiously.

"Fill the Oracle, of course," Lye said, "Earth's imbalance to be undone — cure the world." Ret recognized Lye's word-for-word quotations from the parchment that Mr. Coy had filched from Principal Stone's office. "I have devoted my life to finding the elements, but I lack the scars — the secrets, the clues — to where the elements are hidden. Your ancestors, though they possessed the scars, had neither the courage nor the desire to help me — until *you* came along. Ret, *you* are a person of faith — a noble, valiant man who rose up and stepped in to fulfill the postponed destiny of your family line."

"A family line whose First Father *you* helped kill!" the Guardian accused.

"To whom I remain loyal to this day," Lye countered. "I have even preserved his staff, which rightfully belongs to you, Ret. My life has been prolonged just long enough to find the rightful heir of your First Father and help him in his quest to procure the elements and, thus, restore peace to a troubled world."

"Lies!" spat the Guardian. "Half-truths!"

"That's where we were going that day — together — on the ship," Lye resumed unabated. "Because of your scars and genius, we had found the location of the first element — *here,* in Sunken Earth! We were wading above the vortex," he said, pointing at the top of the coned room, "waiting for the approaching hurricane to open the passageway, when our ship caught fire; we hadn't anticipated the boiling sea or the release of so much flammable gas. Then, when the fringe of the hurricane fell upon us, you were knocked unconscious and thrown from the ship while I sank and ended up here."

Soon after Lye had commenced in recounting his version of what had happened that fateful day at sea, a list of unspoken questions had begun to form in Ret's mind as Lye glossed over important aspects of the story. But Lye didn't give Ret a chance to speak.

"Even though I had found this lost city, I still needed you in order to procure the earth element — together," Lye said. "With my capability of traveling to and from this land wholly dependent on the prevalence of hurricanes, I enlisted the help of dear friends and associates all over the globe to find you and bring you back to me — and reunite us. And then I learned that the Oracle had been lost in the shipwreck, too. But think of it, Ret — think of it! You *and* the Oracle, found so close together. It was fate — destiny — it was meant to be!"

"Enough," the Guardian intervened.

"And now," Lye carried on, "you, me, *and* the Oracle — all together again, in the presence of the first element! Join me, Ret — *re*join me — and together we will cure the world!"

"I said *enough!*" the Guardian roared. "Ret, collect the element — now!"

"Wait," Ret pled calmly. He stood speechless for a few seconds, taking time to ponder what had just been told him. Stuck in the middle of the verbal tug-of-war that had become this conversation between Lye and the Guardian, Ret was beginning to realize his important position in the grander scheme of things surrounding the Oracle. Just months ago, as the mystery of his scars was beginning to unfold, much of Ret still believed that it was all part of some inconsequential fairytale — a goose chase that would culminate in an imaginary pot of gold at the end of a vanishing rainbow. But now — having discovered a lost city and witnessed innocent people perish; having climbed a perilous mountain and learned the underpinnings of an ancient legend — now, Ret was coming to grips with a fantasy that was actually reality, whose stakes were much, much greater.

But there was yet one question — a grand and glorious key of knowledge — whose answer had thus far eluded Ret. And the question was this: who could he trust? And how would he come to know who he could trust? Ret found himself at a crossroads — at the doorstep of a pivotal decision. Whereas he once disregarded this whole Oracle business as a thing of no real significance, he now understood the gravity of it. Indeed, his decision would determine his destiny — and influence the destiny of countless others. That was something Ret had never contemplated before: the power of choice.

Perhaps this grave responsibility was why none of his other ancestors had chosen to gather the scattered elements — if, in fact, Lye was actually telling the truth. Maybe Mother Nature's divine hand really did guide a shipwrecked Ret and lost-at-sea Oracle to the same shore when they both could have floated virtually anywhere. Could it be that both the Guardian's words and Lye's story were true, despite their stark contradictions?

And so the question remained: who could he trust? At length, Ret decided that he would simply have to ask.

Ret looked boldly into Lye's yellow eyes. "I have some questions," he said.

"By all means," Lye invited.

"So what happened to Jaret?" Ret asked first.

"Well," Lye answered quickly, "I'd rather not go into such depressing things right now…"

"And why," Ret persisted, "would you and I have tried to enter Sunken Earth through the vortex when the scar led *me* to the sunken road?"

"Obviously, you — "

"And Stone and Quirk — your idea of 'dear friends'?"

"I know it may seem like — "

"And why did you — "

"Silence!" Lye yelled defensively, trying to regain control of the conversation. "You clearly don't remember anything of your past, but I assure you," he said, regaining some of his patience, "I assure you, once you rejoin me and we return to working cooperatively — together — everything will begin to make sense."

"I don't think I believe you," Ret concluded.

"You don't have to believe me yet," Lye assured him soothingly. "Have faith. Trust me," he said delicately. "Just collect the element, and hand me the Oracle."

"Never!"

"GIVE ME THE ORACLE!" Lye demanded, lunging towards Ret.

With impeccable timing, the Guardian outstretched both of his arms and commanded two streams of dirt to shoot from opposite sides of the sloped ceiling and pummel Lye in the chest, sending him careening backwards in a flurry of soil.

"Collect the element," the Guardian instructed. "Go, now!"

Ret raced to the pedestal where the small wedge of earth was suspended in midair. He firmly planted his feet on the rim of the bottomless shaft stretching deep into the earth beneath the element. Ret cradled the Oracle in his cupped hands and waited for it to open like it had done before.

Meanwhile, Lye had rebounded. While getting to his feet amid the mound of dirt that had assaulted him, he aimed his staff at one of the room's puddles of sea water and shot a bolt of water directly at Ret's hands. The Oracle was launched from Ret's grasp and into the air. It flew out of Ret's reach, and, instinctively, Ret leapt from his perch along the mouth of the pit to catch the soaring sphere.

Ever mindful of his purpose to protect boy and ball, the Guardian sent a sheet of dirt to Ret's aid, creating a sort of horizontal floor to protectively cover the expanse of the shaft. Ret collapsed on the improvised barrier with Oracle in hand. With great alarm, however, he watched as the Guardian was pelted with a deluge of water from Lye, causing the Guardian to forfeit his concentration on the sturdy, manmade landing for Ret.

Just as the Guardian's floor gave way, Ret reached out and caught hold of the edge of the never-ending hole. Holding himself with one arm, he glanced downward and watched the dirt disappear into oblivion. He lifted himself up and rose to his feet.

Ret was now alive with adrenaline from the excitement of the moment, for Lye had engaged in a full sprint towards him, moving with unanticipated energy and dexterity. It was now clear to Ret that the Guardian, who had called Lye's bluff, was right about their antagonist putting up a false front of elderly fragility. Thankfully, Lye was stopped in his advance by an avalanche of rocks that the Guardian caused to fall in Lye's path.

Without a moment to lose, Ret cradled the Oracle and allowed it to align its marks with the corresponding ones in Ret's palms. Then, levitating above Ret's hands, the Oracle opened, splitting into six individual wedges, all hinged at the base.

Like an agile billy-goat, Lye climbed over the mess of rocks and debris that had thwarted his route to Ret. Not willing to be outdone, the Guardian threw up walls of earth all around Lye, enclosing him in a sort of adobe jail. Lye had scarcely been contained when the bottom of his white cane began to protrude through one of the walls. Suddenly, all the water in the room began flowing into the hollow shaft of the cane, and, in an instant, the Guardian's obstacle was blown to bits from an inner explosion of collected water that reduced the walls to pebbles.

Unsure of what to do next, Ret was relieved when the Oracle began to act with a mind and will of its own. Ret felt it pull him forward as the Oracle slowly gravitated toward the element until it was hovering just below the beautiful clod. Then, with subdued grace, the Oracle started to close in on the element, its wedges coming together again. As the pointed tops of the six sections met once more, Ret watched as the sliver of dirt slid into the wedge that bore the mark of the hook and triangle.

He had collected the first element.

CHAPTER 18

THE RACE TO ESCAPE

For a split second, the world went mute, all sound having been completely extinguished. As if from the center of the earth, an unseen force deep inside the bottomless chasm seemed to inhale like a giant lung, robbing the air of all noise. Then it exhaled with tremendous power, like an electromagnetic pulse, sending forth a rapid shockwave in all directions that nothing could evade. Like an earthquake with its epicenter at the former residence of the element, the awesome tremor rattled Ret's bones, knocking him as well as Lye and the Guardian to the floor. The acquisition of the element had not gone unnoticed.

With the removal of its central core, Sunken Earth, in its entirety, was thrown into violent and irreversible meltdown. Finding itself without support, the swirling vortex gave way to massive deluge, sending an ocean of water crashing down on the mountain. Water poured into the room's center chasm, sending steam in all directions. Under so much stress, the mountain itself was crumbling, now robbed of the strength it once derived from the all-powerful element. Huge pieces of ceiling and wall were falling all around Ret as he scrambled to find the Guardian.

"Sir! Sir!" Ret yelled, finding the place where the Guardian lay, facedown. "Are you okay?" But there was no answer. Ret rolled the lifeless Guardian over until he was face-up, lying on his back. His eyes were closed, yet there was a smile of contentment on his lips, which was proof enough to Ret that his friend, the Guardian, had not been kidding when he explained that the collection of the element would mean his death.

But there was no time to mourn. Large chunks of the peak were fragmenting and rolling down the mountainside. The whole place threatened to disintegrate in a matter of moments. Ret bolted for the corridor that would return him to the door through which he first came. He had nearly reached the hallway when something caught his foot and sent him rolling to the ground.

"Ret," a pathetic voice begged, "don't leave me." Lye, who had tripped Ret with his cane, was lying on the floor, now looking so aged and injured that Ret thought he might die of natural causes even before becoming a casualty of the natural disaster that was underway. "Help me."

It was Ret's merciful nature that caused him to halt his flight. Lye looked so helpless, so pitiable. But when Lye's gaze switched from Ret to Oracle, Ret knew that he must leave Lye to the whims of nature. Realizing that Ret, who was struggling to get to his feet, had no intention of biting his hook, Lye lunged toward him. Ret, noticing some jagged rocks in the room's collapsing roof, waved his hand and sent a barrage of earthen spikes raining down on Lye. With amazing precision, not a single spear struck Lye's body, all instead piercing his robes and pinning him to the ground, rendering him immobile. Impressed, Ret remembered that his control over the earth had greatly multiplied now that he was the rightful possessor of the element.

"Curse you, Ret Cooper!" Lye yelled as Ret dashed down the corridor. "You haven't seen the last of me!" Then all Ret could hear was Lye coughing as he darted through the main door.

Recognizing his need to move with great haste, Ret decided to test the limits of his newfound powers. He formed a flat platform from the dirt at his feet and slid down the mountainside like a snowboarder. The soil obeyed his every command, helping him turn to avoid tumbling debris and creating ramps to send him flying over streams of tempestuous water.

In no time at all, Ret arrived at the place along the foot of the mountain where he had previously left Lionel to begin his climb. But instead of finding and rejoining Lionel, Ret was greeted by a squadron of guards, poised and ready as if they had been anticipating his arrival. Despite the large number of guards, Ret knew he had the power but not the time to take on his ill-willed receiving party. Consequently, he altered the path of his descent, hoping to not only evade the guards but also find Lionel along the way. Wondering what might have happened to Lionel, Ret was thrown into silent panic as he fled the scene like a fugitive, dodging shots of energy beams at every turn.

Ret's route of escape led him to one of the upper level's main waterways. There was still no sign of Lionel, and the guards were gaining on him with their all-terrain vehicles. He was running along the riverbank, hoping to find the next crossing, when he heard a boat headed towards him from upstream. By the sound of it, Ret recognized the craft as one of the speedboats that Lye's soldiers used to patrol the waters. Finding himself in a pickle with the enemy afore and behind him, Ret was a sitting duck.

Imagine his surprise, then, when he saw the likes of Mr. Coy and Ivan, speeding to his rescue aboard the oncoming boat! Ret's heart sighed with cheer as Mr. Coy threw into the air a sturdy rope for Ret to grab. Ret used the earth at his feet to launch him skyward toward the rope, which he caught before plunging into the river. With the ship still in motion, Ret pulled himself onboard, ducking amidst the onslaught of enemy fire from the shore.

"What are you doing here?" Ret asked, gratefully relieved.

"To see if Lye has ever — *Ben Coy* — of course," Mr. Coy said, "and apparently to rescue you! Did you get the element?"

"Procured," Ret said with a satisfied smile.

"Then let's get out of here!" Mr. Coy stated. "Now, drive us straight through!" he instructed Ivan at the controls. "If we slow down to turn around, we'll all be dead men!" Ivan obeyed, maintaining full speed. Glass shattered and the boat reeled as bolt after bolt struck the craft. They had almost escaped unscathed when a stray shot hit Ivan square in the chest. The immense energy from the electric blast surged violently through Ivan's body, igniting his clothes and charring his skin. He instantly went limp and fell overboard.

"NO!" Ret screamed, racing to the side of the boat. "Stop! Stop now! Turn around!"

"Are you mad?" Mr. Coy replied, rushing to take command of the speeding boat. "We can't! Do you want to die, too?" Mr. Coy maintained control of the wheel despite Ret's attempts to turn it around. "One hit from those bolts means certain death, Ret."

“We have to go back,” Ret urged with all of his emotion. “He could still be alive. We have to at least check!” His voice trembled with doubt as he spoke, for he had not seen Ivan resurface since falling into the river.

Mr. Coy made no response. Ret marched in front of him and stared Mr. Coy boldly in the face.

“How can you be so heartless?” Ret asked. “You’re just going to leave him? How can you do this?”

“I’ve learned to not get attached,” was all Mr. Coy said, straight-faced.

“Not get attached?” Ret balked. “You talk as if Ivan was your pet — a favorite toy. He was your *friend* — your right-hand man. Now turn around!”

“Learn to let go,” Mr. Coy said without emotion.

“Learn to — ” Ret started to repeat, then voluntarily stopped, astronomically amazed at Mr. Coy’s ambivalence. “You know, Mr. Coy, you’ve got problems — serious problems. Everyone else sees it but you. Not only do you pretend like your own daughter doesn’t exist but now this? I mean, what’s going through your — ”

Ret’s speech was stopped midsentence as Mr. Coy grabbed him with both hands by the shirt and lifted him off the ground, pinning Ret up against the side of the boat.

“You have *no* idea what I’ve been through, kid — *no* idea,” he breathed through his teeth, obviously controlling a storm of emotion brewing within himself. "Learn to let go." He dropped Ret to his feet and returned to the wheel.

Ret took a deep, finite breath, evidence of his willingness to let the conversation die. As he turned to walk away, he noticed a wet streak on Mr. Coy's cheek, the glistening remnants of a tear.

Mr. Coy maneuvered the boat until they arrived at the banks closest to the slums where Princess Alana and her people once resided. The shanties had been reduced to smithereens, now covered in a thick layer of ash and soot and dirt and dust. The ground, which rose in disorganized yet frequent lumps, had now been transformed into an outdoor morgue.

"The quickest path is back the way we came," Mr. Coy directed. "The girls are waiting for us there. Hurry!" They set off en route to the westside entrance, but they hadn't gone far when Ret heard someone call for him.

"Ret," the hoarse voice said. Recognizing the voice, Ret feared the worst, which was exactly what he found. Princess Alana lay nearby, obviously wounded and approaching death.

"We did it, Ret," Alana cheered softly when Ret arrived at her side. "We won our independence. We are free."

Ret hadn't the heart to inform her of the imminent destruction that was enveloping her entire civilization.

"It wasn't until you arrived that my people first began to believe that we could succeed," she continued. "I will die as their queen, but you will live as their king, Ret."

For the first time, it occurred to Ret that, by taking the element out of this land, *he* had ensured its destruction.

"Thank you, Ret," Alana said graciously. "Thank you."

As the life of the princess slipped into shadow, Ret looked to his side to find Mr. Coy looking at him with a watchful eye. His words echoed in Ret's mind: "Learn to let go." Ret's tears moistened Alana's tattered dress as he laid down her head, closed her eyelids, and stood up to rejoin Mr. Coy.

Back at the place where they had entered Sunken Earth, the girls were rife with anxiety, having watched the events unfold from their bird's-eye ledge. They paced back and forth, not speaking much, trying to convince themselves that their fears would not be reality. With the environment around them quickly falling apart, they wondered at what point they would save themselves and depart without the boys. It was with part happiness and part apprehension, therefore, when they saw the vegetation before them begin to rustle, evidence of someone approaching. Their hearts seemed to stop as they waited for whoever was nearing to show themselves.

"Oh, thank goodness!" Pauline shouted as soon as she saw Ret and Mr. Coy. "Thank goodness you're safe!" The girls rushed to their sides and embraced them.

"Where's Ivan?" Paige asked after hugging Ret.

Ret looked at Mr. Coy; the girls did the same, anticipating grave news.

"He fell," said Coy. Then, stepping between them, he walked away to fetch the subsuits. The girls' heads dropped in sorrow, and Paige's weeping was muffled in Ret's shoulder.

As everyone else filed into the foyer toward the mouth of the submerged road's underwater shaft, Ret decided to take one final look at Sunken Earth before joining them. He turned around and winced at the sight. The great mountain, which once stood staunchly, was now half its original size and crumbling rapidly under the gushing flood of water that was pulverizing it continuously and mercilessly. Originating at the hole in the ceiling, massive fissures extended in all directions across the dome, evidence that the roof was succumbing under the gargantuan weight of the ocean above. Through these gaping cracks came torrents of sea water, inundating the land below. Through tear-filled eyes, Ret could only watch as helpless herds of the remaining people tried with futility to escape the tsunami-like waves, which wiped out villages and washed over buildings without leaving so much as a trace. Like a garden hose held over an anthill, Sunken Earth was drowning and would soon be nothing more than a memory.

Ret wanted to extend his hands and contain the destruction. He longed for power over water to command the floods to abate. He shuddered to witness something that *he* had caused. *He* was the one who had collected — stolen — the element. No one forced him to do it; he willingly chose to do so. And, as a result, *he* had ended a great civilization and caused countless innocent deaths. It was *his* fault that the Guardian was dead; it was because of *him* that Ivan had been killed; it was due to *his* mission that Alana hadn't survived. Ret wondered if the end result of the Oracle would be worth the price that had been paid by Sunken Earth. He thought it a strange thing that, in order to cure the world, he might have to destroy it.

"Thus ends Sunken Earth," a familiar voice rang in Ret's ears as a wet arm was laid on his shoulder.

"Lionel!" Ret said in surprise, embracing him. "I'm so glad you're alive!"

"Me, too," Lionel agreed, hinting at the arduous task it must have been to survive what he had been through. "I waited for you at the foot of the mountain until I saw the peak explode, which I assumed meant that you had succeeded," he explained. "It soon became too dangerous for me to wait for you, so I started heading here, where I hoped I would find all of you."

"Why are you all wet?" Ret wondered.

"I took the river. I figured it was the safest and most direct route," Lionel said. "Did you get what you needed?"

"Yeah," said Ret in defeated triumph, holding out the Oracle, "but Ivan and Alana died, and the Guardian — "

"Then you succeeded, Ret," said Lionel consolingly, "and that's all that matters."

"But look what I've done," Ret mourned, pointing at the tragic scene before them. "Look what I've caused."

"Sunken Earth has fulfilled its purpose," Lionel taught. "You have relieved them of their duty; you have set them free."

Ret hadn't thought of it that way before. He could picture the contentment that had swaddled the Guardian even in death. The parting words of Princess Alana — "We are free" — came to his remembrance.

"Thanks, Lionel," Ret said sincerely, somewhat comforted. He reciprocated Lionel's arm clasp. "I'm glad to have your help."

"Likewise, my friend. Likewise."

Just then, a deep cracking noise filled the air and echoed against the collapsing walls as an enormous portion of the ceiling broke off near where they were standing at the westside entrance. The fragment shook the earth when it collided into the ground, and more ocean came pouring in, helping to raise the ever-increasing water line.

"Time to go!" Mr. Coy announced.

The party of six rushed inside the foyer and quickly got outfitted in their subsuits.

"What's this?" Lionel asked, holding Ivan's subsuit up against his body.

"You're a smart guy," Mr. Coy responded. "I'm sure you'll figure it out."

One by one, they jumped into the pool and swam back the way they came. Ret was the last one to do so. He looked back once more at the land he had grown to love. The ceiling was nearly gone now, and rough water was licking the elevated ledge that led into the foyer. Ret's thoughts turned to Lye, wondering how he would escape after having told Ret so confidently that they would meet again. Wanting to ensure Lye's demise, Ret waved his hand and expedited the impending collapse that would soon greet this room of Sunken Earth.

"You coming, Ret?" Lionel asked from the water, having returned to check on Ret.

"Right behind you."

Just as the walls came crashing down to seal their

route of escape, Ret jumped in the water and followed after Lionel.

Chapter 19

Return to Tybee

It proved to be a much easier task to float up the underwater shaft toward the submerged road than it had been to swim down it. In fact, besides the help from such natural exertions as gravity and density, there seemed to be an additional force slurping them upwards, similar to the pumping of a plunger. With ever-increasing speed, the party ascended out of the vertical tunnel, retraced their steps — though this time upwards — along the submerged road, and reentered open water safely. Or so they thought, for they instantly realized the source of the great suction they had felt just moments earlier while in the vertical shaft.

"Look!" Mr. Coy announced alarmingly over the subsuits' intercom. "The seafloor is caving in!" All eyes searched frantically to assess their dangerous circumstances. Immediately around them, everything seemed to lean eastwardly — an underwater wind tilting kelp and slanting seagrass; an unnatural current sending shells rolling backwards and fish swimming sideways; a strange force sucking sand like a vacuum and causing the entire floor to slide.

Looking back the way they came, they saw the underwater road begin to buckle as if it was alive. Then, in a matter of seconds, it refolded itself from the inside out, as if each individual stone was connected to the next on a string, like the recoiling of a giant yo-yo.

Ret was awestruck as he stared into the vast expanse of sea surrounding them. What was going on? The entire ocean, which had previously been clean and clear, now looked murky and clouded — befuddled by a colloidal mixture of disturbed sand and debris. This once tranquil island, with its playful beaches and calm currents, was transforming into a spiraling sinkhole of chaos, as if someone had pulled the plug of this gigantic bathtub called the Atlantic Ocean. Had the removal of the element really caused all of this?

"Everyone," Mr. Coy instructed, as they all tried to swim against the increasingly strong current with little success, "we need to get to the yacht. Think *fast!*"

Ret and Mr. Coy, who had previously needed a quick getaway while wearing their subsuits, immediately thought to employ the small propellers located within the suits' heels. The women followed suit. Curiously, however, nothing seemed to change about Lionel, and yet he swam like a fish, keeping pace with everyone else as they sped towards the yacht.

Entering deeper waters, the group watched as the cracking and crumbling of the vanishing seafloor chased them ruthlessly. They felt the pull of the sinking earth tugging and dragging them down. Though they had won the race to the yacht, they were still far from safety.

"Fire up the engines, Ivan," Mr. Coy ordered as they collapsed on deck, "engage the — "

He stopped himself, recognizing his blunder. The mention of Ivan's name caused everyone to freeze, then slowly turn and gaze at he who uttered it. Mr. Coy avoided their stares, lowered his head, and paced away to the control room — in silence, and alone.

The yacht creaked and groaned as the still waters around it were almost instantly transformed into raging rapids. Quite literally, the hundreds of thousands of square miles of Atlantic seafloor, which fell under the boundaries of Devil's Triangle and doubled as the ceiling of Sunken Earth, had given way, resulting in a truly cataclysmic — even apocalyptic — event. As far as the eye could see, the ocean was steadily sinking, unavoidably dragging everything with it. Schools of fish were flung from their classrooms; flukes of whales waved goodbye before plunging; even entire islands wallowed in the maelstrom before being swallowed in the massive sinkhole.

Now chugging up the side of the pit, the yacht engaged its hover capabilities, sending the inflatable skirt around the hull and a wall of mist into the air. Then, with a great lunge, the ship employed its emergency propulsion engines, launching itself up and out of the widening crater. Mr. Coy continued to use all of the yacht's power until his instruments confirmed they had sailed safely beyond the periphery of Devil's Triangle.

With their safe escape assured, Mr. Coy relinquished the ship's controls and returned to the main deck to join the others, all removing their subsuits.

"Dad," Paige said in a relieved voice, giving her father a hug. "What happened back there?"

Mr. Coy looked at Ret. "I think that element is extremely more powerful than any of us had expected."

"Where's Lionel?" Ret asked, grateful to change the subject. They all exchanged blank stares.

"I saw him get on the yacht," Pauline said, offering what little information she knew.

"I don't like this," said Mr. Coy with an air of suspicion. "Hurry, let's find the bloke." Mr. Coy quickly scurried off, looking in every place and in all directions, while the others followed behind.

"I've never liked this Lionel character," Coy grumpily mumbled to himself repeatedly as the group searched the upper decks and middle sections. "Now he's snooping around my beautiful yacht!"

As they were making their way to the lower levels, Mr. Coy literally ran into a member of the crew.

"Sir," the crewmember said earnestly, addressing Mr. Coy, "the prisoners escaped. Come and see!" Temporarily delaying their search for Lionel, they rushed away with the crewman.

"What happened here?" Mr. Coy asked upon arriving at the vault. The crewman directed their attention to the metal bars behind which the trio had been kept. The entire console surrounding and including the cell's lock had been melted away.

"And *how* could they do a thing like that?" Pauline said indignantly, upset that her captors had gotten away. She continued to interrogate the crewman like a detective. "Did you loan them a blowtorch or something?"

"No, ma'am," the respectful crewman replied. "There ain't nothin' on this ship that coulda done somethin' like *that*. We found this here key, lying on the floor, but it don't go to nothin' on *this* ship."

Mr. Coy took the key from the crewman's hand. It was large and rusted, like something from a medieval era. After examining it, Mr. Coy slipped it into his pocket without saying a word.

"Those sneaky little crooks," Pauline frowned.

"We think they done it at night," the crewman continued, "even stole one of our lifeboats."

"They *were* a fiery lot," Pauline sighed as Ret examined the melted ore, "I'll give 'em that."

The search for Lionel continued but soon ended when Ret entered one of the cabins on the lower level. On the bed, he found a subsuit lying neatly, next to a handwritten note:

Dear Ret,

Sorry for leaving so soon; I've been gone a long time and needed to get back. Thanks for saving me down there – I owe you one. I'll be in touch soon.

Your friend,
Lionel Zarbock

P.S. Tell Coy thanks for letting me use this suit. I couldn't quite figure out the science behind it – very…Coy.

Ret's heart sank. Why did Lionel leave so soon? Was he not interested in what happened at the mountain's summit? Did he not know of the long list of questions he wanted to ask? How could he go without at least saying goodbye?

Leaving the note for the others to read, Ret trudged to the end of the yacht's stern and sat wearily on a large wooden crate. With heavy eyes, he followed the ship's wake back to the scene of destruction, which now, so far in the distance, seemed but a small whirlpool. The setting sun warmed his right side and cast a crimson reflection across the surface of the sea. It reminded Ret of the blood that had been spilt, largely at his hand.

"What have I done?" he said softly to himself, burying his face in his hands. "Ivan, the Guardian, Princess Alana and all her people, even Lye — all dead. And for what?" he asked, taking the Oracle from his pocket. *"This?* How can *this* be worth so much pain — so much loss?" He rolled the sphere from one hand to the other, then back and forth several times. It seemed such a small thing; it all felt so trivial. But, at the same time, the Oracle was breathtaking, awe-inspiring, and intriguing. And now it housed the first element of six: the earth element. Catching the rays of the waning sun, the soil shined with purity. Ret studied the pure element, noticing its true beauty and full majesty.

"So that's it, huh?" Ana remarked as she and Paige approached Ret from behind. "We did all that for a piece of poop?" The girls inspected the element for the first time while Ret smiled at Ana's playful humor. He knew her intent was to lighten his spirits. She had a knack for sensing other people's moods.

"It's tragic about all those people," Paige observed in a somber tone, sitting down and scooting close to Ret on the crate. "My heart aches for what happened back there." Ret was pleased to hear someone else express his similar sorrows. Paige's words helped ease his burden and soothe his extreme pain. "We were worried *you* might not make it," she said, resting her head on Ret's shoulder.

"A part of me wishes I hadn't," Ret admitted. "Why did *I* survive when no one else did?"

"Well," Ana said loudly, trying to shake Ret from his woes, "what's done is done. There's no turning back now. You did everything you could, right?" She sat down at Ret's other side and supportively put her arm around his back.

"Yeah, I guess you're right," Ret concluded, adding Ana's encouraging words to what Alana and Lionel had already told him.

He held out the Oracle for all to see, with the earth element sparkling in the setting sun. "One element down," said Ret, "five to go." There, at the rear of the yacht, the three of them sat, talking and reminiscing — together — all the way back home.

Made in the USA
Middletown, DE
06 January 2019